CHARLOTTE

JS Anthony

1

Charlotte sat on the wagon seat, her back straight, her chin held high, her hands folded tightly in her lap. She looked neither right or left, or even ahead. Her eyes seemed to see nothing, her gaze turned inward. Her thoughts were gathered deep inside where no harm could come to them.

There was little to see anyway. The prairie grass extended away to the horizon in every direction, an endless faintly green and golden sea. If she concentrated, she might notice the wind sweeping through in shifting patterns, stirring the grass in waves. She might also notice the swarms of insects that rose and fell silently or the hawks soaring overhead. She chose not to notice any of these things. If she concentrated on anything, it was that small core at the center of her being, the person who she was, the truth that she would not let go of no matter what. This was the vow she'd made to herself. This was the vow she'd keep.

She felt the sun, that couldn't be helped. She'd refused to put on a bonnet, though one had been offered to her. She knew the gesture represented one of so few kindnesses, and that she should at least have been gracious in that regard. But where in the name of heaven, she wanted to ask someone, did graciousness belong in this world as she now knew it. The sun was in fact welcome, warming her skin, easing the hurt that still lived in her battered face, hopefully turning away the bruises, suffusing her cheek with rose-colored hues rather than awful black and blue.

Charlotte could also hear without having to listen. The hawk that had been circling above cried out on its broad downward arc. The wind vibrated against the arched canvas, making a humming sound in the struts. The horses' harnesses jangled and the horses themselves blew and snorted as they walked along in the heat.

Beside her, Charlotte's father remained silent as well, his thoughts also turned inward. He held the reins between the fingers of both hands and flipped them now and then, though there was no reason. Only one pace could be had, and that was ploddingly slow. Only one direction could be followed, and that was south.

Charlotte's father, Samuel, was a solid man, well-built and strong, with firm hands and a still handsome but unsmiling face. He radiated authority even doing nothing, having no intentions of any sort toward anyone. It was just how he was, the way he carried himself, who he knew himself to be. So much since the beginning of his life had gone into the creation of his bearing, his calm, his confidence. No one feared him, not exactly. But they would not cross him either, or doubt his word. Charlotte had his same bearing but without the authority that had been bequeathed to him, and her actions as a result had caused him to despair.

They'd traveled for three days. Charlotte did not know where they were going, though her father did. As the sun rose higher in the sky, the landscape changed. The prairie began to undulate. Gentle rolling hills appeared with forest off in the distance. To the west, a line of quaking aspens signaled the presence of a river.

Charlotte grew alert, sensing the shift. As she watched, a track appeared, at first just a faint line in the prairie. As the weary horses drew closer, the track enlarged into a dusty byway running from east to west, a broad expanse packed down hard by the iron wheels of untold numbers of wagons, the hooves of mules, oxen, horses and trampling herds of livestock.

Her father turned the team of horses onto the track heading west. Before the river, he guided the wagon into shelter underneath a large spreading elm. He pulled in the reins and the horses came to a halt, their heads drooping. Still Samuel sat on the

4

wagon seat, not moving. He sighed once heavily, wondering why life had to be so difficult, but that was all.

"Where are we?" Charlotte said. She was numb and at the same time burning inside.

"At the river."

"I can see that."

"This is the trail west."

"West to where?"

Her father sighed again. Never did he imagine he would be doing such a thing, but it was required. The forces at work, the situation as it had come to be, dictated that this solution was the only one. There was no other. This most dire of cases defied any easy answer, left choices and options by the wayside. He didn't believe that his wisdom had failed him. He was certain he'd succeeded with a plan where before there had been no plan, no hope. He'd spent some very dark days and nights in preparations.

"West to the desert."

"And what's out there?"

"Your uncle."

"Tobias?"

"Yes."

"I thought he was banished."

"He was."

"Then am I being banished too?"

"Not exactly."

Charlotte had had enough. "Are you going to give this to me one sentence at a time and take the rest of the day doing it, or are you finally going to tell me what you have in mind?"

Samuel shook his head. "Don't be impertinent. I'm your father."

"I'm not afraid of you, you know."

"I hope I never raised you so that you would be," he said more gently. "I hope I gave you everything I had in the way of affection and I know, you know as well, that I never raised a hand to you or kept anything from you."

"It's not easy growing up having your father be the First Elder."

5

"I understand that."

"Other people are afraid of you."

"I'm sorry if that's true. I can only be the person I'm required to be."

Charlotte clenched her hands together even more tightly. "But we're not getting anywhere. Tell me what you have to tell me and be done with it."

"You're too bold. You've always been too bold."

"And look where it's got me. But I will say again, and I don't care whether you believe me or not, it wasn't my fault."

"Conner Mathis was a fine man. An upright citizen, a pillar of the community. He was of the lineage of a Witness."

"I don't mean to upset you right here at what seems like an important moment, but you weren't married to him, you didn't have to cook his meals and share his bed. From where a woman stands, and it could have been anyone, not just me, he was not a pillar of anything. He was not a good man."

Samuel got down from the wagon, his troubles showing in the exhausted contours of his face. "Daughter," he said. "I don't know what to do with you."

Charlotte fought back her tears. "Actually, it seems that you do know. You're still not telling me everything."

"Step down from the wagon." His voice had become that of the First Elder. Charlotte gathered her skirts and stepped down. He set his hands on her shoulders.

"My wild, ungovernable child. Look at you." There were tears in his eyes as well, despite the tone of his voice. "Your hair. Your beautiful face. How did this happen?" But it was only a question to the universe, not to her.

Charlotte cast her gaze down. She did not want to make her father cry.

"Tobias and those with him are out in the desert for contemplation's sake, it's true, but also to take measure of the country, lay down new beginnings for the time when we'll need them. This is where you are to go. This is where you will live. And Charlotte…?"

6

"Yes?"

"There'll be another husband waiting for you. Tobias chose this one. He believes he's more capable in this regard than I, even if he hardly remembers you. Do you want to know the name?"

"No."

"I'm sorry if you so strongly feel the terrible burden of being my child, but it's how you came into the world and you can't put that aside. There's responsibility to it that may not always be wanted but also, if you'd stop ever for just one moment to consider, rare privilege."

Charlotte could recite this argument word for word. She'd heard it a thousand times before. "It doesn't sound like you're coming with me."

"I am not."

"What if I get killed or kidnapped? Where is this wonderful plan of yours then?"

Her father spoke with enforced patience. "They were going to put you on trial. When they had found you guilty, they were going to hang you. It wouldn't have mattered that you were my child. The tribunal would speak and their word would be law. They'd already commissioned the gallows."

"Those men always hated me." She knew the people on the tribunal and despised all of them, along with the three fearful women who had held her down and cut off her hair as punishment even before the facts were established. They could have waited at least that long, because there were facts. But her crime made them shudder.

"I doubt that's true, but we're getting sidetracked." Samuel gripped her shoulders more tightly. "You won't be going alone, so for once, listen to me. You are not to move from this spot. You are to stay camped here, not a mile away, or fifty yards, or down by the river. *Right here*. Do you understand?"

"Yes."

"In a matter of days, a wagon train will come by. The man leading it is Ellis Gray. He has a great deal of experience and I trust him."

"Experience in what? Widows by their own hand?"

"Please, we can't speak of that anymore. Let me finish. You'll be under his protection until you reach Fort Randall. There you will wait again until Tobias comes for you. I doubt you've felt any reason to take an interest in the wagon as of yet, but it holds all you'll need for the journey and more, I made sure of that." He had done the cooking, tended to all the chores while Charlotte stared into the distance, still stunned and barely able to breathe.

"My clothes?"

"Everything. Food, cooking utensils, bedding, your linens and flatware, anything else of a personal nature that I could discover and pack up. An amount of silver coin is hidden under the floorboards, be careful with it. There are documents pertaining to your membership in the Family. I've given you almost all the guns. I'm leaving you the team and the mare."

"You're leaving the horses, but you're also leaving me."

"They were going to hang you. Your fate would be a lesson to the others." Samuel closed his eyes, thinking about how close they'd come.

Charlotte wouldn't be there to watch him grow old. Maybe she would never see him again. He'd done an acceptable job of raising her under the circumstances, which were at all times difficult, though he never complained.

"You've put a great deal of faith in me that I'll be able to do this," she said.

"I've told you, there was no other choice. I had to get you away from there. If I ride hard, I'll be back among them with time yet to try and smooth the turbulent waters. Yes, I have faith in you. You were old enough to remember the Second Migration, what we did to survive. And Lord knows I would fear for anyone who came up against you."

"Father."

"Well I would. But now, immediately, we must say goodbye." Samuel pulled his child to him and held her hard. Then he let her go. "You will be in my thoughts every minute of every day."

Swiftly, he untied the second horse from behind the wagon and mounted.

"You are always my daughter," he said, his voice breaking. He turned his horse away and galloped off. Charlotte stood and watched until the small spot that had been him became indistinguishable from the prairie grass. She was numb again. Her mouth was dry from tangled up nerves and fear, her heart beating wildly. She waited to cry but no tears came.

2

Except for the wind stirring the leaves of the elm, there was no sound. Charlotte stayed rooted in one place, for how long she couldn't tell. Shock didn't begin to convey her state of mind anymore. When you've shot and killed your husband, she thought, it's surely something more than shock and whatever it is, it won't be leaving for a while. Gradually she became aware of the silence and her place in it. She was alone, one person in a vast landscape under a huge cloudless sky. With time, she began to hear again. The horses stamped and blew. The three of them were now under her care. She could stand here all day hoping her father would come back or she could do something about the horses.

She undid the harnesses and turned the team loose to graze. The grass here by the river was rich and green. They shook their coats and seemed to relax, glad to be free of the traces. She knew she had to get in the wagon before she unhitched the mare, though getting in the wagon was the last thing she wanted to do.

Charlotte gently nudged the mare aside, climbed up on the back and stuck her head in beneath the taut white canopy. Her eyes grew wide, her mouth dropped open. Samuel was the most orderly of men. Everything in his daily existence had a place and a reason for being. The inside of the wagon looked like a tornado had gone through. Charlotte realized then how quickly he had moved, how much of the time allotted he had spent on this endeavor, how frightened and sad he must have been. She would sort it all out, the clothes from the pots and pans, the blankets from the sacks of food, the folded up tent canvas from the amazing clutter of overturned books, hairbrushes, boots, a velvet coat she hadn't worn in years.

Keep going, she told herself. Don't think about this now. What she wanted most were the pickets, which she found with only a minimum amount of digging, and the guns within easy reach, carefully placed together on one side. Thank you, she said silently. If it had to be like this, thank you.

After checking that the rifle was loaded, she leaned it barrel down under the front seat of the wagon. She untied the mare and picketed her so that she could graze, but not far. Later she would lead them all down to the river and let them drink.

In this way, in the great silence, Charlotte kept herself busy, in motion with tasks to perform. She did remember the Second Migration, when the Family had been run out of town because they were suspect, different, carried odd beliefs about which there were too many rumors to put down. Though she had never seen a reason to put the rumors down. The Family's beliefs *were* odd and she was always in the middle of the conversation, her father being who he was, the First Elder, the fountainhead of those beliefs. It was then, on that long journey, being in charge of her father's wagon, that she had learned to manage, cope, improvise, find ways to make do with what they had.

As the afternoon faded, she found herself exhausted. If she let go for even one fraction of a second, she knew she would break down, but the energy needed to hold on was becoming unbearable. Eat, she told herself. It was an answer, gave her something else to do.

She cleared a circle, outlined it with rocks, laid a fire with the wood she'd gathered and settled in for a meal of bacon and corncakes, sitting in the grass with her tin plate and fork, trying not to fall apart into a thousand pieces. At dusk, she took the horses down to the river and filled a bucket of water for herself. Swallows swooped overhead, seining insects from the air. The river was unlovely, broad and slow, easy to ford, she supposed, but not promising for fish.

A question arose: keep the fire going or let it die? Charlotte chose to let it die. She picketed the horses closer in, washed up with water from the bucket, then cleaned the tin plate and put it aside. She prayed the wolves wouldn't come because she had no defense. If it was an entire pack, she would never be able to shoot them all.

11

The night sky was filled with billions of stars. She'd seen these same stars so often from farther north, where the Family lived out in the nowhere, where her father would lie again alone in his narrow bed in his sturdy house. Holding that thought dear, she made up her own bed among the gnarled roots of the elm, using the mare's saddle as a pillow with the old coat folded over it. Wrapped up in a blanket, her hand on one of the Colt revolvers, with the rifle beside her, she turned, hid her face in the soft velvet and cried until there were no tears left.

3

Charlotte woke with the sun. The horses were still there, the Colt, the rifle, the wagon. No one had stolen anything from her in the night and the wolves hadn't come. Unfortunately, she was still in the same place, alone, an unrepentant criminal facing a decidedly unpleasant future, stopped in other people's tracks in the middle of God knows where. Getting up required more exertion that she'd expected. She knew from experience however that structure aided living on the trail, routines repeated over and over, staying with whatever could possibly be familiar, in this way keeping down the anxiety, the inevitable fear.

Breakfast was familiar because she made it so, bacon and corn cakes. The horses were released from their pickets and hobbled so that they could wander farther afield without running off. The interior of the wagon loomed, a mountain of a task and every step of it tied to her father's face, his hands, his well-meaning though sometimes misplaced goodness. But it needed to be done if any of the contents were to be of use to her, and certainly he had had her well being in mind with every item that he so hastily chose.

Charlotte spent the morning stacking and rearranging, bringing order to the chaos. Despite the obvious implications of her predicament, she smiled without meaning to at the objects she found. There was coffee and she didn't drink coffee, but could it be offered as a trade to those for whom it was a precious and scarce commodity? A boot hook, but none of the boots requiring it. Drawers, camisoles, shifts, petticoats, now she pitied him. He was not the kind to be voluntarily rummaging through women's undergarments. All her dresses and skirts, every shawl she owned, her hand mirror and lilac soap. She stopped, one hand over her mouth, not knowing whether to laugh or cry. Here were her bone and tortoiseshell hair clips, obviously swept in a pile off the dresser in what had been the bedroom of her married life. These for the thick tresses of auburn hair which now stuck out from her head in

13

minute, grievously butchered lengths immune to the aid of any hair clip ever devised.

There were lotions, medicinal herbs, a saw, a shovel, an extra wheel and axle, lengths of rope and chain, wagon grease, flints, a hatchet and hunting knife, a mallet and wooden pins, dried apples, six tins of oysters, a single piece of sheet music out of the thousands that were the Family's most prized and strictly guarded possessions, the translations of which only her father could undertake. She sat down in the wagon bed and held the parchment to her heart, her eyes welling up with tears. He could only have been thinking one thing when he'd included it, that he loved her beyond all reason, she was his only child, and here was the last protection left that he had to offer her.

How could she have done this to him? In her mind, it was not even a question. She could repeat that night, play it over and over again and it would still come out exactly the same. Conner Mathis was a big man with a loud voice and the smallest, weakest, most pathetic and cowardly person inside that she had ever known. He was a false front, a broad-shouldered square-jawed prop with nothing behind it. That he had taken in all of the Elders, even the First Elder, who was supposed to be the wisest and most discerning of them all, made her want to be sick.

You should have been the one married to Conner, she wanted to tell all of them, then you'd know. Having acquired the first Elder's daughter, the prize, as his wife, he pressed his bullying advantage relentlessly enough during the day, but when it came to the nights, he succeeded in nothing but alienating his bride with his boastful, angry, hurtful incompetence. Finally, she said no. It was as if he had never considered defiance, as if he had possibly never heard the word no before from a woman or anyone. She said it again, quite clearly. Shouted it, even. When he grabbed her, meaning to exert his will, she sank her teeth into his hand, leaving him screaming, and escaped. Cornered in the kitchen with nowhere to go, still she taunted him. His fist came at her face hard, bone cracking against bone, knocking her to the floor. The shotgun stood against the back door for the coyotes that were stealing the chickens. She lunged at it. Then he was on top of her, his knees digging into her legs, his hands on her throat. I hate you, she said as her head jerked back, his thumbs pressing hard. The look in his eyes said he hated her more. Gasping for air, she wrenched the shotgun up between them and pulled the trigger.

It didn't have to be that way, she'd thought since. He made it that way, all or nothing, you or me and violence to settle the equation. His was a disgusting, warped view of the world that had only him and his needs at its center. Why couldn't you see it? she wanted to shout at them. Why didn't you know what was behind that lying smile?

Flushed, her head throbbing, Charlotte put down the piece of sheet music and climbed shakily out from the back of the wagon. There were oats for the horses. Samuel placed great value on the care of his animals. This would steady her, allow her to breathe again. She filled the feedbag, attached it and led the mare over to the wagon. Returning from under the shade of the elm to retrieve the team, she stopped dead in her tracks.

There in the middle of the wide dusty road was an even more frightening sight, one she had never once allowed herself to imagine or she would have bolted at a breakneck pace screaming back to the Family and a hanging which would likely be a better ending than this one. The member of the tribes sat his horse easily, casually almost, leaning on one knee that was bent and resting on the saddle horn. He wore buckskin pants, moccasins, silver at his ears and wrists, a bow slung across his lean torso, a knife at his waist, a rifle in his lap. His shining black hair flew off in odd directions as if it had met somewhere with a dull knife. His skin glowed warmly, his face was open and smooth-planed, his eyes troubled. His horse was a big dappled gray, sleek and muscled.

God help me, Charlotte thought. Watching him closely, never turning away, she stepped backward until her heel hit the saddle on the ground. Slowly she reached down and picked up the Colt. Though he clearly saw what she was doing, he didn't seem to be concerned. She walked toward him, stopped when she felt the distance was right, took an open stance and raised the Colt with both hands till it was aimed at him, though her hands weren't steady. She didn't intend to have any more souls on her conscience, but she had to at least make a show of defending herself.

"Throw down your weapons," she said loudly, momentarily freeing one hand to execute a motion that would likely not be correctly interpreted in any kind of sign language. Still he made no move, and it didn't appear as if he would any time soon.

"I'm not afraid to shoot." This time she would take aim and try to hit an extremity. But what if she shot the horse? It was a beautiful animal. She'd feel terrible about that. She didn't suppose she could ask him to get off the horse first. Should she count to ten? What if he had no idea what she was doing? That wouldn't be fair either. Just when she felt she was running out of options, he spoke.

"How many times do you think I've held a gun against a woman?" he said.

She was completely taken aback, not understanding at all. "Why do you speak English?" Perfect English, she noted. How could that be?

"Why do *you* speak English?"

Oh no, she wasn't getting into this kind of conversation. "How many times have you held a gun against a woman? I don't know. Ten? A hundred?"

"None. How many times have you held a gun against a man?"

"I'm not answering that," she said, thinking she could have lied but that would just be compounding the sins. The Colt was getting very heavy.

"Is that because it's none and you don't think that's a good answer or it's some and you don't think that's a good answer?"

He spoke way too much English actually and Charlotte was tired of the whole thing. "Are you going to shoot me or not?"

"I'm not interested in shooting anyone."

She sighed. "Then I'm putting down this gun. It's too heavy and it makes my arms ache." She was fairly sure he was going to kill her one horrible way or another when he got around to it and she would die where her father had left her. She hoped someone from the wagon train would at least take the time to bury her and care for the horses. On further consideration, she realized he would take the horses. That would be what made this whole encounter worth his while. He still hadn't moved.

"What happened to you?" he said.

Charlotte's hand went to her face. The one thing she'd avoided in the wagon was the hand mirror. Not being constantly reminded, she'd managed to forget for a fraction of a second what she looked like, the hair chopped off like a dog's, the black eye and purple cheek, the swollen jaw. Then the fierce determination of that night rose in her again. She knew it showed in her eyes. It didn't matter who he was or what he thought. He'd asked the question, he'd get the answer.

"I won."

"And someone lost." She nodded. "A man?" She nodded again. "So is it that you're alive and he's not?"

"Yes."

"But if you'd lost, he'd be alive and you wouldn't."

She stared at him. "Not everyone has understood that. In fact, no one."

"Are you in mourning?"

She frowned, puzzled. "No. Is that what this looks like? Mourning?"

"For my people, yes. In grief, they cut off their hair."

"That part was punishment. For disobeying my husband."

"Your husband's the one you killed?"

"Yes, and for that I was going to be hanged."

"I see," he said. She couldn't imagine what it was he thought he saw. "But one more thing I don't understand. I've watched you all morning and you're sitting, you're not traveling."

Oh, God, what had she been doing this morning? She didn't even want to think. She started to mention how rude that was, but stopped herself. Under the circumstances, such an observation seemed ridiculous.

"I'm supposed to stay here until the wagon train comes."

17

"What wagon train?"

"The one belonging to Ellis Gray." He seemed unsettled by that information, which was even more confusing.

"Why?"

"It's long and complicated." What could he possibly care?

"No, I mean it," he said. "Why?"

She considered that this whole conversation was getting very strange. "Because my father left me here and Ellis Gray is going to see me to the next awful place in my life which is out in the desert somewhere. It was either that or get hanged. What does it matter to you anyway?"

"It doesn't. I've been scouting this country and there's nothing out there right now. You'll be safe for a day or two at least." Before she had time to react, he abruptly sat up, laid the reins over and turned his horse down the road toward the river. Then he changed his mind and led his horse back around in a circle to where she stood. Fear gripped her again.

"What is that gun?" he said. Now nothing made any sense.

"A new kind of Colt. It's my father's. It's the only thing he allows himself to spend money on. Guns."

"Do you mind if I see it?" What difference did anything make at this point? If he was going to shoot her with her own gun, she didn't have enough energy left to object. If he was going to steal it, here, take it, it's yours.

She handed up the gun. He tested the weight, opened the chamber, clicked it shut, held out the gun and sighted down its length.

"Go ahead if you want," she said. He sighted again carefully, waited, then fired a shot that blew a branch off a tree across the road. He leaned down and gave her back the gun.

"It's a good gun," he said. "There's a dead squirrel out there if you feel like finding it." He turned again and was gone.

4

Charlotte roasted the squirrel with onions and turnips for dinner. It wasn't the first one she'd ever cooked. Even in times of plenty, the Family had always lived simply. It was one of the Twenty-Seven Rules and her father enforced them strictly. He said the discipline kept them from temptation, from losing sight of their purpose, of why they were put on this earth. It also prepared them for the hardships he'd known were coming. That was his role, to see the future and guide them safely through it.

But for the rest, Charlotte was completely unnerved. She felt certain in every way that her visitor was long gone, headed off in some distant direction, back to whatever life he led. Still, eyes crept up and down her back, followed her hands at the fire, the water she washed her face with, the boots she took off, the blankets she wrapped herself in when evening fell. It was strange. On one hand, she had the sensation of being watched at every moment. On the other hand, she'd never felt more alone. She chose to believe him, that there weren't wolves or marauders nearby. She unwrapped the blankets, dragged the saddle out from under the elm tree, lay down again out in the open and spent a good part of the night watching the stars revolve across the heavens. When at last she slept, her dreams were shattered by blood, pain, the shotgun going off and she woke up screaming. It occurred to her that maybe she was in fact in mourning, not ever for Conner Mathis but for herself, the person she had been and could never be again.

Charlotte served up more bacon and corncakes for breakfast. Already the repetition of this meal was making her weary, though gruel had been a staple at one point in their lives and corncakes were a major improvement over gruel. She rearranged the interior of the wagon again. On the Second Migration, the wagons were filled to the top and the Family slept at night in tents. She could see Samuel going back over all the details of that other journey, trying to remember. But now, without furniture or a cookstove to contend with, she had the luxury of constructing a bed inside. She placed an extra wagon board across the crates of books and piled on all her blankets and quilts. Though of no use now when she was required to be her own sentry, she could foresee a time when she'd be glad to have it.

The day passed slowly. She hauled jugs of water from the river. Another cloud of swallows dipped and swirled over the river's surface in military precision, veering quickly left and right. She brushed the horses till they nickered softly and shivered with pleasure. That plus the oats and grass to roll in meant that if they believed in heaven, this was it. A mourning dove called over and over again from the woods. The grasses gave rise to flocks of noisy sparrows and all at once an invasion of brilliant blue dragonflies.

Charlotte dozed in the sun, walked in circles, sang every song she knew, tried to read a book and failed. Her restless attention wouldn't keep to the printed words on the page. Alarmed by the dozing, she vowed to stay more alert, on guard against who knew what. If a person of the tribes could show up out of nowhere, then anything could happen, and might at any minute.

Sundown came. She'd brushed the horses again simply for something to do and was afraid they'd feel so pampered they'd never be willing to work again. She replaced the corncakes with beans and was glad for the change. Cooked over a banked down fire with bacon grease and peppers, the beans provided if nothing else a meaningful way to pass the time. And they were delicious if she did say so herself.

The pattern of the stars had inched forward across the sky. The sliver of moon set, leaving darkness. Charlotte lay in her blankets, the velvet coat against her cheek. Either bats or nighthawks flitted overhead, she couldn't tell which. When she woke screaming, a large bird obviously disturbed from its rest flapped out of the highest branches of the elm tree. As the faintest light crept across the sky, she fell gratefully into a deep, dreamless sleep.

Surely, Charlotte thought on waking, this would be the day. She made herself breakfast and sat staring into the fire. No use trying to form a vision of the future, she would just have to let events occur as they would. She only hoped she had the courage to face whatever they might prove to be. Finally, she stood up, turned in a watchful circle, eyes narrowed, and decided that she would take a chance on truly being alone and wash herself in the cold buckets of river water.

The sun rose. The day progressed. Anxious, she scanned the eastern horizon for movement, a shimmer in the heat, a telltale cloud of dust. The track remained empty for as far as she could see. She got out her sketchpad and drew the wagon, the elm, the horses, the aspens down by the river, the wildflowers, the sparrows, a dragonfly. At noon she shaded her eyes and peered into the distance for the hundredth time. Nothing. She picked long strands of grass and wove them into necklaces, braided tiny wildflowers into bracelets, then threw all of it away.

At some point in the middle of the afternoon, she collapsed into a panic. They weren't coming. She was aware of how many disasters could befall a wagon train. If she had to get to Fort Randall, wherever that was, by herself, then she would do just that. Somehow. The track was obvious. It headed in only one direction. In that case, her first challenge would be getting across the river. She stood on the bank and threw stones out into the slow current, trying to gauge the depth. The stones sank immediately and told her nothing. She would take the mare in first as a test. Then she'd come back for the wagon. Turning the mare around in midstream would be the problem. She closed her eyes. The truth was, she couldn't do this by herself. It was impossible. Every avenue she chose seemed to lead to the same conclusion. The only way she could survive was to turn around and head back to the Family, the irony being that then she was absolutely guaranteed not to survive at all. Calm down, she told herself. It's not that bad yet. Wait one more day.

On the afternoon of the fourth day she saw a mirage that turned into dust rising up not from a wagon train but from the hooves of one lone horse and rider.

5

Ellis Gray came on at a gallop. He reined in when he saw her and slowed his horse to a walk, then stopped and swung down from the saddle. He removed his hat and pounded the dust off against his leg. Charlotte stood back, wary. He had a weathered face and watchful steel blue eyes. He stood for just a minute taking in the sight of her. Again, she'd forgotten what she looked like. Her hand went self-consciously to her face as if by doing so she could hide the damage.

"Ellis Gray," he said.

"Charlotte," she said. "But I suppose you knew that. Who else would be out here alone in the middle of nowhere?"

His handshake was firm but so was hers.

"We're a day late," he said. "Some things happened."

"I understand about travel by wagons." She wondered if he was aware of that history, or cared.

"I need to ask about yours. What's in there? Any furniture?"

"No. Just personal belongings and supplies."

"Is it all right if I check anyway?"

"Yes."

He pulled aside the white canopy and quickly surveyed the interior. "No cookstove. That's a help." He kept his eyes on her. "You seem like a straightforward woman so I'm going to be honest with you. This idea of taking on an additional wagon didn't fare so well, even with your father promising enough supplies to feed them from here to hell and back, which is where I'd like some of them to go. He let me know it'd be hard to hide your situation and I see now that's true. The only thing good is that there're so many damn fools among the company they couldn't get farther than their own front door without me and the smarter ones realize that."

Charlotte bit her lip. Her eyes had filled despite her best efforts. "I wasn't told anything. For it to cause this kind of trouble, I couldn't bear it, I don't want to…"

23

"Never mind about that. They're not worth it. Fording the river's the important thing. They're coming up close behind me so it's in our best interest to get you across first."

Charlotte hastened to harness the horses and Ellis Gray stepped in to help. "The river's broad and shallow, but murky. You have to feel your way across the bottom so you don't get stuck. We can talk later about anything you want. But right now I've got to ask a lot from you and I need you to be okay with that. Are you?"

Charlotte nodded. Her hands were shaking. She hoped he hadn't noticed. "I am," she said.

"Then I'll go ahead and take your mare with me. You follow with the wagon and keep to exactly where I go. Do you know your horses?"

"I do." She realized fear was about to take away her speech.

Ellis Gray swung back up onto his horse and took the mare's lead. "Just don't lose your grip," he said.

Too late for that.

Ellis Gray walked his horse down the bank and into the river trailing the mare. The water rose quickly to his boots but no farther. Charlotte took a deep breath and slapped the reins. Thankfully, the team didn't balk. The wagon rocked heading down the bank, the horses needed more urging, then the water flowed underneath them, the river opening up on either side. Each step seemed precarious but Ellis Gray's horse waded on, the mare followed without protest and the team horses nosed in behind, leaning forward against the current swirling around their knees and the softer bottom that dragged at the wagon's wheels. When Ellis reached the distant bank, which seemed like an hour's journey to her, he tied up the two horses and waded back in to bring the team and the wagon onto dry land.

"Keep going. Up through that wide cut and into the clearing." She nodded. The last time she'd driven a wagon alone she was fifteen. Fortunately, she remembered the experience in vivid detail.

Ellis mounted and rode up to her again when she reached the clearing. "Stay here," he said. "A rider'll come by, he might stop to talk but I doubt it. That's Miller Dawson, our pilot. He'll be moving on ahead to scout out a place to camp for the night. We've got a herd of cattle, not much of them'll make it to the end, but we need to accommodate them while they're with us and that requires space.

"I'm going back to the other side to bring everybody across. It'll take some time. As soon as they've regrouped, they'll start off again. Wait for me."

Charlotte nodded. She wasn't actually hearing what he said anymore and he didn't wait to find out if she understood. Instead, he turned his horse back to the river.

She positioned the wagon farther off the track, turned to the side. She didn't want to be staring into each new face, especially if all of them were going to be full of disapproval. That was something she hadn't counted on. She climbed down from the wagon seat and loosened the traces so the horses could graze.

She heard galloping hooves. As she watched, Miller Dawson rode by without a glance in her direction. Faintly in the distance came the sound of the wagon train, growing louder as it approached the river, the still air punctuated by whistles and shouts, creaking harnesses, the grinding of wood on wood as the caravan lumbered along.

She surveyed the scene from her hidden vantage point beside the wagon. The horse and oxen teams drew to a halt. Slowly the riverbank filled with men, hands on their hips, studying the crossing. Ellis stood in front of them, talking. When it seemed they all understood, the reins jangled, the whips cracked and the procession moved forward again, slowly down the bank into the river, following Ellis in his second journey across the current with the cattle streaming out behind them, eyes wide, bellowing.

Charlotte grew more nervous as they approached the near bank. She climbed to the wagon seat and leaned back into the deep shade. It seemed to take forever, but finally the first wagon jolted up the cut and went by, then another, then another, some accompanied by men walking alongside and dogs panting in the heat. A few of the men turned in her direction but she sat far enough back to be unavailable for inspection. At one point, a group of women walked by on the far side of the wagons. She could see their sunbonnets and skirts but that was all.

Lastly the herd of cattle filed past, issuing loud complaints and stirring up even more dust. Men on horseback and foot attended them, those on foot prodding the animals with long sticks.

Ellis Gray appeared.

"Let me get the horses back in harness," she said.

"I'll do that," he said. "Then move over and I'll take the reins."

He hitched up the horses, tied his own fine-looking bay at the back alongside the mare and climbed up into the seat. Charlotte took her place beside him as she had beside her father. Even though Ellis Gray wasn't nearly as old, she felt that somehow in the handoff he and her father had become the same person.

The wagon jolted along the track. "I'm staying a ways back," he said. "Otherwise the dust's intolerable behind all that cattle." They rode in silence. Then he spoke again. "Let me tell you some things, just so you know. We came out of Missouri, but half of them are from back in Illinois. There's nineteen wagons, fifty-seven men, eight women and twenty-nine children. Next week or so there'll be another one born which means we'll stop for at least a day or if it's Sunday we'll stop for two. There's lots of people related to each other somehow and that means not everyone gets along, not to mention the old woman who's taken ill five times now and one hothead in particular who thinks he has a better way to do everything.

"With you, there's just general mistrust of a woman alone. When they see you, and I'm being honest one more time, they'll have even more questions to which there won't be any answers. You can do what you want about the rest of it, but the one thing you can't do is let on as to your real situation, and that's serious."

Ellis Gray held his silence for a minute, the reins in his hands. "Your father posted a letter laying all this out, must have cost a fortune having a rider get it to me. One of his biggest concerns was that word would get out and the law would be looking for you."

26

Charlotte's jaw dropped. This was something that had never crossed her mind either.

"Not some small town sheriff, it'd be out of their jurisdiction, not their problem. But maybe a federal marshal, that's where the possibility would be. So don't give anybody the chance to be figuring something out."

"I won't," she said, her voice barely audible. Regarding herself as a fugitive was even a further shock than what she'd had already. She'd wanted to believe that this whole large expanse of empty country would swallow her up, that she could start over, different if not better, and never have to dwell on the past again. Apparently she was wrong.

Charlotte had a thought come to her that she didn't need. "Samuel's paying you, isn't he?"

"Yes, he is. That's the way it's done.'

"Is it a lot?"

"That too. But I give what I've got no matter what, and looking at you, there's not many who wouldn't want to do the same. I don't believe you deserve where you've ended up."

"And I'm not even there yet." She bowed her head, humiliated. "But thank you, I appreciate it."

6

The wagons had already reeled off into their broad circle. Ellis Gray eased Charlotte's wagon into the space at the back left open for it. The cattle were herded out to pasture, the horses turned to grazing within the wagon enclosure. He'd assured them that the local tribes would steal the horses out from under anybody, but would leave the cattle every time.

"No water today," Ellis said, "but we'll be on a creek by tomorrow. Do you always haul your own firewood?"

Charlotte was building herself a fire from wood in the wagon. "I was near a good supply back there. Might as well keep some."

"There's a council meeting tonight, which is a polite way of saying yet one more mule-like shouting match. There's a woman that cooks for the men on meeting nights. But after dinner, folk usually gather to socialize or have music or whatever eases their minds after a long day. I can bring you into it, obviously they're aware that you're here. Or I can leave you be, say you're tired or shy."

"Say I'm tired or shy, whichever."

"Another thing, I'll be sleeping here." Charlotte started up in alarm. "On the ground," he said. "Like I always do."

"I wake up screaming sometimes," she said.

"So do I. You just have to talk yourself out of it."

What was *that* about? "Sometime tell me how you accomplish that exactly."

She'd brought river rocks too and laid a grill across them.

"You're resourceful," he said.

"I came up that way. I'll contribute to the food. I know that's required."

"I told you, there's already money being paid, enough to cover far more than your share."

"I'll contribute anyway."

"Do what you want," he said. "The meeting usually ends up around dark."

Charlotte ate her dinner sitting on the ground. The people in the wagons to either side of her pitched their tents then went off. All she'd seen were men. They glanced at her then quickly away and she never met their eyes at all.

As dusk fell, there was shouting, a heated argument, then later laughter and a violin started up. On the Second Migration, she'd been in the middle of that laughter, the favored child. Now she had no complaints about being on the outside, the farther away the better, wishing she couldn't hear them at all.

The first stars appeared. Night faded from blue to black and the heavens opened up. The small fire was company and she kept it going. She acknowledged that she felt in some odd way more lonely here among people than she had out in the emptiness with only the mourning doves. She missed Samuel with a burning pain so deep it frightened her. She forgot to tell Ellis Gray that she also cried at night, even if it was into a velvet coat that muffled the sound, but no one should pay it any mind.

Then he was back, carrying his saddle and bedroll.

"You're still up."

"I had four days to sleep. Did your meeting go well?"

"No, but it never does."

"Was any of it about me?" She couldn't help asking.

"Some, not much. They more had on their minds why we had a whole herd of cattle with us that only belonged to one family and was that family paying their fair share of the traveling for everyone having to put up with the cattle. This particular discussion dates exactly from the day we started out. There's a bigger headache though. The hothead has heard tales of a cutoff that takes weeks from the journey and he believes we should start thinking about that cutoff."

"And there isn't one?"

"No there is, just not a safe one. But I've done this trip enough times to know that there's always someone willing to try it out and those who are dumb enough to follow. Doesn't end well, ever."

He eased down beside his saddle. He seemed weary. The violin was still playing.

Two coyotes howled back and forth across an echoing distance, giving her the chills. Another tent went up nearby, but quietly. A small boy's voice could be heard. Ellis had hand rolled a cigarette and the coal end of it glowed, the tobacco scent pungent in the still air. Charlotte wrapped her arms around her knees.

"My father says tobacco will kill you," she said.

"Maybe that's true," he said. "I'll keep hoping."

Who *was* this man?

"We'll be up early," he said. "The sentinel's rifle goes off while it's still dark."

She was up and brushing off her skirts, ready to lie down on her soft bed of books. "I'm fine with that," she said.

"I imagine you are."

7

Charlotte woke to screaming in the night, but it wasn't hers. She sat bolt upright in bed. The peculiar rhythm of the screaming was familiar. Then she knew, it was a woman in labor. She lay listening to the anguished chorus, the rise and fall, the vehement teeth-clenched godawful sounds that only a woman trying to give birth could produce. The sounds escalated to fill the night with no promise of an end.

Something occurred to Charlotte. She put aside the covers and climbed out of the wagon. It was so dark she almost stepped on Ellis Gray. He had to put a hand on her leg to prevent that from happening.

"Oh Lord," she said. "Sorry." She leaned down beside him, barely able to see his face. "What do you know about her?"

"She's strong, walked most of the way here. Should be okay. Doubt there'll be anybody getting sleep."

"There's no water."

"Those women have their ways."

"I have water. Will you take it to them? Please?"

He got up slowly, took two jugs of water away and came back. "They're grateful as much as put out women can be. It's not easy leaving the home you know to follow a headstrong husband somewhere you might not've ever wanted to go."

"I understand."

"I can't listen to this anymore," Ellis said. "Can you manage by yourself?"

"I have so far."

He picked up his saddle and left her in the darkness. His bedroll and saddlebags were still on the ground. She wondered just briefly whose guns were better, but she didn't dare look through his belongings and was appalled that she'd even thought such a thing. Chastened, she climbed back into the wagon, wrapped a blanket around her head and eventually drifted off into a troubled sleep.

In the morning there was no screaming and she had no way of discovering what had happened. Out in the bushes, she saw two women holding up their skirts to shield a third performing her morning ablutions. None of them noticed Charlotte and she quickly backed away, finding another bush behind which to shield herself. There was no one she could ask.

Charlotte was making breakfast when Ellis Gray returned. She didn't question where he'd been or if he'd slept.

"The baby?" she said anxiously.

"A girl. Her husband's not pleased but at least he's still got a wife, which is more than he deserves."

While Ellis Gray made his way through the wagons, hearing complaints about water as if it was his fault the Lord had been so stupid as to forget to put a creek here, Charlotte set up her tin oven and baked six loaves of molasses bread. It didn't take long before she recognized the error of her ways. She hadn't foreseen the reach of the inviting aroma. First, she noticed creeping in the grass beyond the wagon, then hands coming around the edges, noses, eyes, and suddenly she was confronted with three less than clean children. The small girl's apron bled red with berry stains down the entire front. The two boys' bare feet were black as coal. Their eyes lit on her, making what kind of judgment she couldn't even begin to guess. Before her hand could fly defensively to her face, their eyes shifted entirely to the cooling loaves of bread.

"I don't know what to do," she said. "I made these loaves to give to your mothers. I'd let you eat some but maybe I shouldn't." Children perplexed her. Family matters in general perplexed her.

Another figure presented itself from around the corner of the wagon. How could this have been such a bad idea? The girl was possibly eleven or twelve, barefoot like the others, with wild hair and freckles across the bridge of her nose. She wore a gingham dress that didn't fit with torn petticoats showing underneath and a necklace of braided wildflowers.

"I think you should let them have some," she said.

"And who are you?" Charlotte asked, her voice not entirely gentle.

"Ada. And who are you?" Ada's voice was not entirely gentle either.

"That's for me to know and you to find out. Are you in charge?"

"Of these I surely am. They're my brothers and sister."

"Oh," Charlotte said.

"What do you put in that bread to make it smell that way?" Ada asked, and it was almost a challenge.

"Molasses."

"What happened to your hair?"

"It got cut off. What happened to yours?"

Ada smiled triumphantly. "Nothing," she said.

"Then we're even."

"I don't think so. But you should give them some bread. It's not fair when it smells so good to have it just sit there."

"Are you hungry?"

"Not always," Ada said and Charlotte realized that without thinking, the girl had taken her question to be meant in the larger sense.

"What about the other children?"

"I'll go get them."

Oh no. "Wait," Charlotte said. "Let's not do that." She thought a moment. "Can I trust you?" The others shifted their gaze impatiently back and forth from Charlotte and their sister to the bread.

"No."

Charlotte stared the girl down. "Somehow I believe you. Which one of these," she said, gesturing toward the descending scale of dirty feet and curly heads, "can I trust?"

Ada grabbed the older boy by his collar. He stumbled forward but didn't seem to mind being roughly handled. "This one."

"Does he have a name? No, wait. I refuse to ask you. I'm going to ask him."

"That's fine by me."

Charlotte turned to the boy. He remained completely calm, unfazed by any of this. "What's your name?" Charlotte said and felt that finally she'd found someone she could be gentle with.

"Brewster," he said.

"And is that really your sister?" Instead of a wicked mouthy witch impersonating a twelve-year-old.

Brewster nodded. "Ever since I can remember."

"What should I do with the bread, Brewster?"

"How we do it in our family with anything good we get is use some, save some, give some away."

"I'm sorry," Charlotte said. "You two can't possibly be related."

In the end, she gave Brewster all the bread to do with as he saw fit.

"I told you," Ada said.

<>

Charlotte put the tin oven away and vowed never to use it again. In the afternoon, she sat in the shade and read. She wanted to go into the circle and check on the horses but that meant exposing herself to other people's eyes. Restless, she went in search of more firewood, though the brush was thinning out.

As the sun began its descent of the sky, leaving long shadows, Ellis Gray reappeared. She'd almost stopped thinking about him, stopped thinking about anything at all.

"Molasses bread," he said and she made a small sound.

"I think it was a mistake," she said.

"I hear it was a kindness, not a mistake."

"The child, Ada? I'm done for. She's smart and she'll be telling what she saw."

Ellis Gray studied her. "Ada? If that's the wild one with all the hair, I don't think she talks to anyone at all. But I came to tell you one of the farmers shot a deer."

"That's a good thing, isn't it? Fresh meat?"

"It's a lucky thing. Mostly, being farmers and shopkeepers and such, they're more likely to shoot their own foot off. But with the birthing and the buck, there'll be a celebration of sorts and that

34

doesn't normally happen. It's the same question again, if you want to be there."

"I don't."

"Just tell me and I won't ask anymore. You've seen how this works. It ends up being a community, has to."

So he was aware. "I couldn't take curious questions, let alone angry ones," she said. "Thank you but I'm better off staying to myself."

As the light was beginning to fade, Charlotte watched a shadow figure coming down along the circle of wagons, headed slowly, painfully in her direction. She stood up, wondering what this was. Then she was hastening forward, protectively holding out her arms.

"What are you doing?" she said, almost frantic. The woman wore a plain dress that rode far up over her midsection and was carrying a newborn child. Each step seemed more difficult than the last, but she kept coming. When she reached Charlotte she stopped.

"I'm fine," she said. "Just a little breathless. It's better to get up and walk around than just lie there."

"I'm not so sure," Charlotte said, wondering what she could possibly provide in the way of assistance. "I don't have anywhere to sit."

"If I sat I'd never get up," the woman said. She was tall and her face was young but worn. "I'm Fiona. I wanted to show you my baby." She unwrapped the bundle in her arms just enough to expose a tiny pink child with a bow mouth and eyes shut tight. "And I wanted to thank you in person for the water. Bad planning on my part, giving birth still one day away from the creek. I suppose I could have managed somehow without those jugs, but I'm so glad I didn't have to." Her tired eyes were warm with emotion. There was suddenly so much in Charlotte's heart that she didn't know what to say. "You did the right thing maybe without even knowing it," Fiona continued wearily, "choosing Brewster to parcel out the bread. It's funny, for a child, he's the only one who could possibly have done it fair. So thank you for that, too. It was delicious."

Brewster had given a piece to the mother who'd just had a child? Charlotte was completely lost. She only wished this woman would sit down somewhere before she fell down with an infant in her arms. Then unexpectedly, Fiona reached up and touched Charlotte's battered face. Tears were in her eyes.

"I'll take you back to your wagon," Charlotte said hastily. "You're exhausted, and no wonder."

"I'll take her back," her husband said. Charlotte looked up into his eyes and might as well have been looking at Conner Mathis again. She recognized him without any doubt in her mind as the hothead Ellis Gray had spoken about. She stepped back as if she'd been burned. It was what he had expected her to do, step very far back. Maybe Ada didn't talk, but this one likely couldn't wait to spread the word.

8

The sentinel's rifle did go off early. Charlotte rose from her bed. She sat among the covers for a moment, disoriented. She thought they would rest one more day. Was she confused? Didn't Ellis Gray say that was the plan, to rest the mother and new baby?

She climbed out of the wagon. No dawn was breaking. The stars still hung in the sky. Not wanting to step on anybody, she softly called out Ellis Gray's name. There was no answer. She waited till her eyes found their way through the dark. His saddle was gone along with all of his belongings.

If they were moving, having breakfast would matter. She'd laughed then cried when she discovered while making the molasses bread that her father had pressed eggs and a jar of butter deep within the protective confines of the flour sack. How he thought she was supposed to find them, she couldn't even fathom. Then she realized that her father had tried to anticipate every move she would make. She wondered if the pain in her heart would ever go away.

Quickly she dressed and built a small fire in the dark. She made enough pancakes and stewed apples to last the day. As the sun inched over the horizon and the sky began to lighten, she made a decision. She'd found the sunbonnet, white and ridiculously large with broad wings that completely cut off sight to either side. She felt more like a cloistered religious in it than a prairie woman. Last night she'd been determined to wear it, never wanting to see that hate in anyone's eyes again. This morning she threw it back in the wagon. To hell with the husband. To hell with all of them. Well, almost all of them.

Fueled by her newfound determination, she entered the circle of wagons and moved among the horses till she found her own. Men and boys performed the same chore all around her. Some stared in the faint light. Others glanced up and thought nothing.

At least no one came over and shook a fist in her face or spit on her, as she'd feared might happen.

Charlotte fed the horses their oats, backed the team into the traces and tethered the mare. She could smell the offerings from other cooking fires and even a hint of the deep rich scent of venison still perfuming the air from last night's feast. All around her were the sounds of a camp breaking up and preparing to move on. She climbed onto the wagon seat, as ready as anyone, but after that she had no idea what to do.

Ellis Gray rode up at the last minute. She'd begun to see that this was how it would be with him, blank spaces of time, an appearance only when most needed. She felt he winced every time he saw her. He glanced at the ready wagon.

"You don't exactly need looking after."

"So the day of birth was the day of rest?" she said.

"They voted. Have to keep moving to get where they're going. If they hit snow in the mountains, nobody has a prayer."

"No, I know. Just seems…"

"Hard. And it is. They're about ready to file out and it'll be in the same order as always. You come in at the back. Ahead of the cattle, not behind. Unless you want to be up front with me."

"At the back."

"I appreciate women who know their own mind even if I don't agree," he said. Then he rode off again.

Charlotte watched the wagons pull out of the circle, one coming from the left, then the right, the pattern repeated till the circle transformed into a caravan stretching out along the road. The last wagon before hers was driven by a youth with his hair sticking up in every direction from the sleep that still showed in his face. He seemed so dazed and preoccupied that she didn't think he even saw her.

The morning went by in a humid haze, the sunlight dim behind high clouds. The cattle stank. Dust hung in the air. A pack of wolves arrayed themselves along a ridge watching the cattle and the dogs intently. Turkey vultures soared overhead on broad dark wings. The land flattened out again into endless prairie. Charlotte

38

worked at keeping her mind on the reins, the horses, the ruts in the worn track.

I can do this, she thought, growing more confident with every boring hour. Chances were that she could get to Fort Randall somehow on her own if she had to, if her relations with the wagon train went completely wrong. Then an interesting question came to mind. But really, why would she want to do that? She hadn't seen Tobias in many years, though she remembered him somewhat fondly as a quiet and unassuming uncle with a big wife. When the big wife took up with the blacksmith in town, Tobias, bowed by the humiliation and the scandal, had tried to leave the Family. Since that wasn't actually ever possible, Samuel had sent him instead to the desert, seemingly, Charlotte thought now, with some purpose in mind.

The question remained. What attraction could the desert and an even more isolated outpost of the Family possibly hold for her? Others would benefit. Ellis Gray was being paid a handsome sum as her benefactor. The wagon train would receive a worthy compensation for her unwanted inclusion. And she, lucky person, would get to be a wife again, wed to a man about whom she knew absolutely nothing. Did she need that? She imagined her father falling off his chair gasping at this train of thought, then running out the door after her. But here she was enviably out of reach.

The wagon train halted at the noon hour. The stop would be brief, rest for the horses, not the people. The rhythm of the journey was coming back to Charlotte, the pace of the days and nights, the different priorities involved in such a life, finding the privacy of a bush from time to time being one of those. She fit into the structure of it, the slow plodding forward motion, the land barely changing, the sense of time standing still. If she did not fit into the community, so be it. She didn't need them. She only needed Ellis Gray.

A space was left again for her at the bottom of the circle. At least they continued to recognize her existence, though whether that was a good thing, she couldn't tell. She talked to the horses and stroked their necks before sitting down in the grass to eat her lunch. She wished she could visit Fiona and see the new baby again, but with that husband lurking anywhere nearby she didn't dare.

A presence announced itself by her side. Charlotte was aware of dusty boots, trousers, a holstered gun, a stranger. She jumped to her feet, still swallowing a bite of pancake.

"Didn't mean to startle you," he said. The rest of him was young, fresh-faced, with unkempt cowlicked hair and an easy smile. He was the first person she'd met who didn't seem to have any idea of what her appearance implied. "Miller Dawson," he said and held out his hand. She shook it, but couldn't help being amazed. He was likely very close to her in age.

"Charlotte," she said. "But you're the pilot? I heard about you. You're barely out of your teens."

"Not yet," he said and smiled again. "Least I don't think so."

Charlotte took in the vastness all around her, the horizon visible in every direction. "How are you so familiar with this land being as young as you are? Doesn't that take years and years?"

"I grew up here. Know it like my own face."

"Grew up where? There's nobody here."

"Used to be tribes just like there used to be buffalo. I've got to go. I heard about you, too. I just wanted to, I don't know, I just wanted to pay my respects."

"Thank you," Charlotte said. "That's very sweet. Come back some time. I want to know more."

"There's nothing interesting," he said. "But I will if I can." He had his hat in his hand, and now he hesitated. "If you were ever to make that molasses bread again, I don't think anybody'd mind."

Charlotte shook her head. It was only six loaves. Had Brewster really managed to give everyone in the company a piece?

When Miller Dawson was gone, she was still thinking, what do the tribes have to do with anything?

<>

Midway through a glacially slow afternoon, Charlotte received another guest. Ada stood in the dust beside the track. If Charlotte could believe her eyes, the purpose of the girl's flailing upraised

40

arms was to flag her down. Oh, no you don't. She kept going. Ada walked alongside.

"Let me up," the child said.

"Why on earth would I do that?"

"Because I never get to ride."

"You have parents. Go talk to them about your problems."

"You have to stop," Ada said. "I can't climb up when the wheel's moving."

"I'm not stopping because I don't want you to climb up."

"If you don't stop, I'll get in at the back."

"That's something you are not going to do."

"I would, though."

Charlotte had had enough. She reined in the horses. Before she could tell the girl a thing or two, Ada was up and seated beside her.

"I'm happy now," she said.

"Guess what," Charlotte said. "I'm not." But she slapped the reins anyway and started the wagon in motion again. The last thing she wanted was to be surrounded by cattle.

"I never get to be alone," Ada said.

Now there was going to be conversation. "Of course not. You've got so many people in that family they're tripping over each other. That's just your life. Get used to it."

"How many people are in your family?"

"None."

"You're an orphan?"

Charlotte closed her eyes. This was going to be a long ride. "I'm not an orphan. I have a father. It's me and him." And all those other people, that whole embracing, constricting, demanding, unnerving group that I live with. Lived with. "But I don't want to talk about that."

"Then what do you want to talk about?"

"I don't want to talk about anything, especially with a twelve-year-old."

"How did you know how old I am?"

"Because I was twelve once."

41

"And were you a problem?"

Charlotte's eyebrows went up. "Is that what people say about you?"

"Yes, even though I work really hard."

"Being the oldest isn't easy." So many things weren't easy.

Charlotte could feel the girl staring at her. Then there were gentle fingers on her face. Why were people suddenly touching her?

"Stop that," she said and took the girl's hand away.

"How did you get like that?" Charlotte was half tempted to tell her, as a warning, but just in time Ellis Gray's stern words came back to her.

"I got trampled by wild horses," she said, "and my cheek got broken and there was so much blood in my hair that they had to cut it off and they sewed a hundred stitches into my scalp and…"

"If you don't want to tell me, that's fine," Ada said, "but don't treat me like a child."

"Unfortunately, in case you hadn't noticed, you are a child."

"Just don't treat me like one."

"Okay, I won't. So what do you want to talk about?"

"Ask me questions, any ones, and I'll answer them."

"Questions?" Charlotte said. "I don't have any."

"Think about it."

Charlotte furrowed her brow but what passed through her mind was that talking to a twelve-year-old was exhausting. "What do you know about Indians?"

"Nothing," Ada said. She would never tell what she knew about Indians.

"You're useless."

"Ask me something else."

"Do you think Miller Dawson's nice to look at?"

"That's a stupid question. Something else."

"You have no opinion on Miller Dawson?"

"I'm too young."

"Oh no, lady," Charlotte said. "You can't have it both ways, too old and too young. And just for your information, he is nice to look at. Keep your eye on him for when you grow up."

"If you're going to ask silly questions about people like that, then pick somebody your own age."

"He is my own age."

"Somebody like Captain Gray."

Charlotte fought the impulse to pull on the reins. "Do you know how close I am to throwing you off that seat? Captain Gray is at least halfway to my father's age. Which means about a hundred years older than me." Or maybe ten. Fifteen at the outside. But still.

"When they think no one hears them, they talk about him."

"Who talks about him? Where in Jesus' name are you going with this?"

"Don't swear."

"I'll swear if I want to."

"The women."

"What women?"

"There's only so many. All of them. And they look like they're far away when they're doing it."

"You are such a strange child. So you spy on them? But I'll tell you what. That's sad to me because Ellis Gray is as likely to be the answer to their problems as a prairie chicken is likely to come walking up and lay itself down in the fire and say here, please roast me for dinner."

"You don't understand."

"That's so true. I don't. Help me out."

"He's got a tragedy. That's what they talk about. How they want to go over and hold his head against their heart. Did I say that right?"

"Stop right there. You can't be listening to that kind of thing ever again. But what tragedy?"

Ada sighed, her thin shoulders moving up and down in her ill-fitting dress. She pushed the wild hair back from her face and

Charlotte, watching her, saw how terribly young she actually was, especially for all the burdens placed on her.

"He was a soldier," Ada said.

"He was?"

"And he had a wife."

"He did?"

"And she was an Indian."

"*What?*"

"And she went back to her people and the soldiers killed all of them, even the women and children. But not him. He wasn't there. He didn't know about it. Then he found out about it."

"That's so horrible it can't even be true."

"Ask him," Ada said.

"No I'm not going to ask him. I don't talk to anybody about anything."

"See?" Ada said. "You're just like me."

9

Miller Dawson and Ellis Gray proved their worth by getting the strung out caravan past the wolves and far enough through the bleached-out day to reach a camping place with the two essentials, grass for the animals and water from a spring-fed creek. The women bent to the task of washing what they could and refilling their jugs and canvas bags. Charlotte hoped Ada would think to dip her brothers' coal black feet in the current, possibly with the addition of soap. But with all those mouths to feed, dirty feet were probably not high on the list of concerns.

Charlotte worked her way through the evening chores, which from now on would include brushing down the team horses and the mare regardless of who saw her. The smell of smoke rose from newly lit cooking fires surrounding the camp. She made her own fire and got out the pot of beans. The man approaching with his saddle would be Ellis Gray, who showed up when he wanted to and never when she considered that he should.

He threw the saddle and bedroll down on the ground. "Mind if I join you?"

"How can I mind?" she said. "You're supposed to be protecting me."

Something occurred that she hadn't anticipated. Ellis Gray laughed.

"I can do that without being here, you know."

"Really? That makes me feel so much safer."

"Have you received a threat from any corner? If not, then I'm doing my job."

"No threats," she said, and smiled. Then she hesitated. "But have you come up against anyone out searching for a fugitive?" She realized that fear had been weighing on her. He realized it too.

"I regret I told you that."

"You had to. It's the truth."

"But I'm not sure at all of the possibility, so let's not think about it."

"You can not think about it," she said. "Have you eaten?"

She had no idea where he went and what he did all day.

"No, but I'll fix my own."

"No you won't," she said. "I made enough, it's what I do. No meeting tonight?"

"Can't be a meeting every night or some of them would end up killing each other." He sat back against the wagon wheel with his legs stretched out.

"I met the hothead," she said.

"You did?"

She handed him a plate. "He's Fiona's husband, isn't he? I feel for her but I also feel for you."

"Takes all kinds."

"I guess. I met Miller Dawson today. He's the first person who didn't even seem to see what I looked like."

"He's that way," Ellis said. Charlotte listened as the violin began to play. "So how well do you know this uncle?"

"I haven't seen him in years, but he was part of my growing up."

"And you trust him?"

Trust him, she thought. "I don't know if that's the right word. I suppose he's as reliable as anybody. Everything he and I are part of is all mixed up and crazy anyway, so what does it matter?"

Ellis ate quickly. "I'm grateful for the food," he said and handed her back the empty plate. "I liked your father. He's an honest man. I just don't want to be delivering you into some other kind of hell whether I'm being paid for it or not."

"You met my father? When?"

"Your people stopped at Fort Leland that year they went traveling. I was the lieutenant stationed there."

"Maybe you met me then? I was fifteen."

"Could have, I suppose."

And now here they were. How strange.

Ellis Gray rolled a cigarette and struck a match, the flame casting shadows on his face. Charlotte watched him closely. Though she wanted badly to ask about the things Ada had told her, she knew he wasn't approachable in that way. Maybe she was as bold as her father said, but not with this. Give it time, she cautioned herself.

"How are you faring back here?" he asked.

"It's dusty and a little lonely but I don't mind. Lonely's better than a whole lot of other things."

"I'll be staying close the next day or two."

"Because of the wolf pack?"

He hesitated. "No, not exactly. Come to the front tomorrow if you want. I'll take the reins."

"That'd mean putting myself out there."

"Making molasses bread put you out there already."

Why was Brewster wasting his time as a child? He should be running for governor or something.

<>

In the night the wolves howled, the sound eerie and unsettling, echoing out over the prairie. In the morning, clouds covered the sky. Ellis Gray was gone when Charlotte woke to the sentinel's rifle blast, but he returned before the wagons started to move. She'd made pancakes again with dried apples in them. She offered him one.

"Thanks," he said, gulping down the pancake in two bites. "You've got a knack for cooking. What do you think, front or back?"

She was tired of the dust and tired of being afraid of people's opinions. "Front," she said.

"Then let's get going." He tied his horse next to the mare and swung up onto the seat from one side while she climbed up the wheel on the other side. He slapped the reins, guiding the team along the outside of the circle and Charlotte immediately wished for the sunbonnet. It felt as if all the eyes in the company were on her.

"You could've let me sit over there," she said.

"I told you before, don't worry what they think. And I hope you made up some explanation."

"I told Ada I got trampled by a herd of wild horses and there was so much blood in my hair they had to cut it off. She didn't believe me."

"I wonder why." The wagons had filed in behind them and another day of achingly slow travel lay ahead.

"She's a different kind of child," Charlotte said.

"They get like that out on the trail. It's a whole other way of life. Some find when there's a chance to live normal again, they can't. Turns out they don't like walls anymore, or rules." Then Ellis changed the subject entirely. "How is it that this wagon doesn't creak?"

"We have good craftsmen. Everyone's required to have a skill since we live so much on our own."

"No offense, but I considered them an unusual bunch."

"They'd have to be with what they believe in."

"And you don't?"

"I was raised in it but if you can believe and not believe at the same time, that's where I am."

Charlotte waited, taking in the fresh air and the scenery, the gray green prairie grass, the dusty track. She was uncomfortable talking about the Family.

"I heard you were a soldier," she said, changing the subject herself. "But I can't see you as one. Is that rude?"

"No it's not rude. I can't see myself as one either."

"But you were."

"Seven years, three forts. And for most of that time, I believed."

No, she couldn't go any further. A man's sorrows were his own.

"Rain's coming," he said. "Not much but I hope you don't mind getting wet."

"I've been wet before."

The rain started as a fine mist and turned into a spray kicked up by the wind. Charlotte wrapped her shawl around her. She could

48

taste the water on her face. When the spray became a sudden driving downpour, Charlotte climbed unceremoniously over Ellis Gray and pulled down the flaps covering the wagon's openings. She couldn't see the expression on his face. She climbed back into her seat again in the same manner. It was clear the downpour was just a squall that would quickly blow itself out. There wouldn't even be time for the track to muddy up.

"I know they talk," Ellis said. "The women. That's where you were headed."

"I don't mean to interfere in what's personal."

"It's not interfering. I'll tell you. I had a wife. She was from the tribes, I guess you know that, but she was gentle and kind and beautiful, the best thing that ever happened to me. When she died, and knowing how she died, something in me broke right in half. It was my own people. Some out of the company I rode with. Others mostly volunteer soldiers who'd lost their minds. I can't ever travel far enough out here to get away from it."

"I'm so sorry," Charlotte said.

"It leaves a hole in you forever," he said.

"It would have to. I imagine that shooting a man and taking his life is going to leave that same hole in me."

Ellis Gray was silent for a long time, squinting into the rain. Charlotte put her shawl over her head. Water dripped off her eyelashes and her nose.

"You and I shouldn't talk about these things," he said. "Despite the difference in our ages…"

"Which is a hundred years."

"Which is not a hundred years…I think we both have too much of an understanding about the dark places."

"I wish that neither of us did."

"Wishing won't do it."

The sky began to lighten as the squall passed overhead and the rain let up.

"How many times have you made this trip?" Charlotte said, wanting to move on to any other topic.

"This one's the third." Or would have been, he thought.

49

"Have you always got all the way to California?"

"Not California. It's Oregon Territory."

"Oregon? There's no gold that way, is there?"

"No, there's land, so much of it, good for settling down on. That's why all these folks are headed there."

Charlotte grew thoughtful. "What's Oregon Territory like?"

"Lots of rain, makes it as green as anything you've ever seen. Dark rich soil that'll support whatever a person might want to be growing, from cows to cabbage and back again. And there's the ocean if you choose that farther distance."

"Sounds like it might appeal to you one day."

"Maybe. I can't get that far in the future, though. There're other things coming before land-owning."

Charlotte turned inward, imagining the greenest hills, black furrows ready for planting, a fine-built house, cows and cabbage. How she would accomplish such a thing on her own, she didn't know. It was just an idea. She made the mistake of voicing the idea out loud.

"Maybe I should go to Oregon Territory," she mused quietly.

Ellis Gray almost forgot where he was, at the head of a wagon train, and stopped himself at the last minute from pulling on the reins. "Now we're back on what we talked about before," he said. "I *asked* if you were clear about Fort Randall and I thought you said *yes. Didn't you?*"

She was stunned. He was angry. "Why are you yelling?" she said. "I guess I just don't want somebody telling me what I have to do with my life. Even if it is my father." And the Family.

"Goddammit," he said. He watched the horizon, scowling, and she saw the muscle twitching in his jaw. "I thought I had this worked out and now I don't have it worked out at all. You and I have to sit down and get some things straight. Not now. Miller's due to go out soon…" As he spoke, Miller Dawson drew his horse up alongside the wagon and smiled, touching the brim of his cowhand hat. Charlotte couldn't help smiling back at him. "….and I need to go with him."

Charlotte stared at him, wide-eyed. "What, you're leaving me alone at the head of the wagon train? They'll kill me."

"Get Ada up here with you."

"She's a child. What good is she going to do?"

"Just stay steady on the track, it's broad and clear here. I trust you. There's only one way you can go."

"When will you be back?" she said. She was almost frantic now. He was already down and on his horse.

"Before the noon break."

"What about the wolves?" What if they attacked? Would they do that? And he'd said none of the men were very good shots.

"The wolves aren't the problem," he said. The next thing she knew, he was riding off in the distance, raising up a cloud of dust, with Miller Dawson at his side.

Charlotte couldn't understand what had suddenly come between them. What had she said that was wrong? Why had he been shouting at her?

10

The next day brought with it the promise of heat. Charlotte was alone once more at the back of the wagon train, but this time she felt banished. She knew this was the fate of those who fell behind for whatever reason, and the reasons were legion, an illness, a birth, a lame horse, a broken axle, it could be anything. When the wagon caught up again, it was unceremoniously consigned to the back. Charlotte felt she occupied this position not because of any emergency but solely for who she was. The misfits in front of her, someone's various male relatives, had likely earned their place the same way, by being rowdy and stupid, or maybe just poor and unable to contribute anything.

Ellis Gray had returned to lead her wagon out before the circle formed for the noon break. He was still scowling. He said nothing, then disappeared again. In the evening, she washed discreetly in the stream they'd camped by and hung her drawers out to dry. She cooked beans with chilies and hard sausage, enough for two, then ate by herself. She knew Ellis Gray slept beside her wagon. She'd been ripped from sleep by the urge to scream, somehow kept the scream from rising in her throat, then, fully awake, looked out to see him in the faint moonlight, dead to the world, his head resting on his saddle. He was gone before the sun rose.

She made biscuits for breakfast and saved enough for the day. She brushed the horses and fed them oats. When the sentinel called out for movement and the wagons began to lumber forward, she sighed and took the reins. Loneliness was nothing, she finally told herself, compared to a hanging. Her life lay in front of her now, somewhere. And obviously Ellis Gray had character deficiencies, interior quarrels, discontents of his own.

Charlotte was saved from the trail's monotony, as she'd felt she was going to be, by the appearance of Ada standing at the side of the track and waiting for her. This time, she stopped the wagon voluntarily, providing no obstacle to the girl climbing up and joining her on the seat.

"You've got a different dress on," Charlotte said.

"You don't," Ada observed.

"True, but I did wash my drawers, which I'll bet you didn't. What happened to your apron?"

"So many things. What is that smell?"

"What smell?"

Ada closed her eyes and sniffed the air. "The good one."

"You don't think you're referring to biscuits, do you?"

"Could be, but I won't ask for one."

"Why, because you're so stubborn? Reach down. They should be right back there in a tin."

Charlotte couldn't help but notice that Ada climbed over her in the same way that she'd climbed over Ellis Gray, which gave her pause. Familiarity, perhaps misplaced. Then Ada suddenly leaned too far and tumbled into the wagon. Charlotte knew that now she was in for it.

"What is this sheet music?" Ada called out. It had taken two seconds for the girl to start finding things.

"Don't know."

"Do you play?" Ada said loudly.

"No. Do you?"

"I wanted to but it's hard without a piano."

"That would be true."

"What are all these books for?"

"To sleep on," Charlotte said.

Ada climbed back out of the wagon holding two biscuits. "Have you read them all?"

"Lots. Not all. Do you read?"

Ada was indignant. "Of course I read."

"Good. Then I'll pick out the ones you need most and give them to you. Books are as important as anything. But two biscuits? Really?"

"One's for Brewster, if that's okay with you."

"I didn't see that coming. Sorry. I thought it was for you."

"Brewster never gets enough to eat. He shouldn't give so much to the younger ones."

This life was too hard, Charlotte thought, and they were made for better. She hoped the green lush hills and rich growing land were more than figments of someone's imagination, a dubious paradise just seen on one of its better days.

Ada inhaled the biscuit she'd kept for herself. "When you get to whatever place you're supposed to be you ought to open a shop. Do you think there's such a thing? A biscuit and bread shop?"

Charlotte laughed. "Not where farmers' wives can cook just fine on their own. Maybe in a town, though. Or a mining camp." She heard what she was saying.

"Where are you bound?" Ada asked. "With us to Oregon?" Charlotte shook her head. She'd found the only twelve-year-old practicing to be an attorney.

"To Fort Randall."

"Where's that?"

"I'm not sure. Before the mountains, that's all I know."

"What's in Fort Randall?"

"You're a child. You don't have to know these things."

"Why? Is it only for adults? Is it bad and children can't hear about it?"

"No," Charlotte said. That's all she needed, for that rumor to start spreading. "My uncle's waiting for me in Fort Randall. And then I'll go to live with him in the desert." Charlotte almost choked over the words.

"You don't seem happy about it," Ada said.

"Enough. We're not discussing this anymore."

"Okay. I've got something else."

"I can hardly wait."

"Why were you and Captain Gray shouting at each other?"

Charlotte imagined the word passing from one wagon to the next till people knew who didn't even want to know.

"You realize that there is something called privacy. Even in a damned wagon train."

"Don't swear," Ada said.

54

"Please try and remember the conversations we've already had. I'll swear when I want to. And no one was shouting at anyone. Well, not exactly."

Ada folded her arms. "Your face looks better anyway. There's some yellow and less of that awful dark purple."

"Thank you for that report."

"But why are you alone? Why aren't you married?"

Charlotte yanked back on the reins and the team halted. "Okay. That's it. If you don't get off, I'll throw you off. You know I've threatened that before."

Ada's brown eyes were flecked with green, her face deceivingly heart-shaped, her hair so incredibly wild. "I want to stay," she said, her voice gone small.

Charlotte waited till she regained her composure. She didn't want anything bad to ever happen to this child. "You can stay, but you can't say a word. Not for a very long time. Not a word."

"I can do that. You'd be surprised."

Charlotte was grateful for the silence, but also to have someone sitting next to her. It occurred to her that, strange as it might be, she'd seen Ellis Gray as her one and only friend. As the morning passed, the sun rose blistering hot, bearing down on the hard-packed dirt of the track, the whispering grass. The land rolled by in shimmering waves broken only by the faint line of cottonwoods where a stream broke through. The heat made Charlotte weary. If she sat on this seat any longer, she was in danger of nodding off. Without any preamble, she handed the reins over to Ada, whose expression was the very same one Charlotte had worn when Ellis Gray put responsibility for the front wagon on her shoulders and then abandoned her.

"Do you know how to hold them?" Ada shook her head yes. "Have you ever driven a wagon by yourself?" Ada shook her head no. Charlotte smiled. Now she had a mute child, no smart remarks, no questions.

"I'm just going to walk for a bit. So I don't fall asleep and have another accident. Like the one I had before," she added. "But I'll be right here beside you." With that, she jumped down from the

55

wagon while it was still moving, nimbly pulling her skirts out of the way at the last minute, leaving Ada in possible terror, but that was none of her concern.

Stretching her legs felt good. Walking felt good. Living with her father, she'd been busy every minute of the day, working in the fields, doing endless chores, galloping the mare across the hills. She acknowledged that the current state of inactivity was dulling her mind, making her crazy. How did these women, or even the women of the Family, manage such a journey? How did they cope with the myriad demands made on their time by children, by husbands, all the never-ending challenges? How did they deal with the fright, the anxiety?

Charlotte turned her face to the sun. She would be tan as a berry soon. Ada already was. That was a hopeful thought. The bruises would be camouflaged as well as faded. Some day they would be gone completely, her cheekbone and jaw mended, the blood and explosions ceasing to visit her in the night. Ellis Gray was right, though. The hole inside would be there forever.

Lost in thought, Charlotte became aware of frantic arm-waving to her right. She turned to see Ada pointing up ahead.

"Good grief. You can talk if it's something important. And I know you were just proving a point anyway. What is all that?"

Though the wagons kept moving, it seemed the entire contingent of women had gathered at the side of the road. Charlotte raised a questioning eyebrow at Ada.

"Probably a grave. Usually that's what it is."

"Rein in the horses."

"They won't hurt you." Charlotte glanced up, wondering again about this child. And those women would hurt her. Charlotte knew that instinctively. She would wait till they'd had their fill and moved on.

"What you don't know, little girl." When the women dispersed, Charlotte signaled Ada to move the horses on again. As they drew abreast of the marker, Ada halted the horses herself and jumped down.

"What is it?"

"You were right," Charlotte said. She bent down to read the inscription crudely carved into the slab of wood leaning over a small pile of rocks. Ada was beside her.

"Benjamin John Parker. Born and died in the same year. What must that be like, to hardly get to be here?" As Charlotte watched, Ada took off her wildflower necklace and hung it from one corner of the piece of wood. "Rest in peace, little one," she said, and Charlotte's eyes stung.

"Are you still going to ride with me?" Charlotte asked.

"I can't. I've been away too long already."

"Do you have the biscuit for Brewster?"

Ada patted her dress. "It's in my pocket."

"Don't worry, I really do like you. I just can't let you know, that's all." Ada grinned. Charlotte had a thought. "Wait. How many of you are there?"

"If you mean children, five altogether with the baby."

Charlotte climbed up onto the seat and reached back into the wagon for the tin. She held it out to Ada. "Here. Take all of them. But today it's for your family. Tell Brewster not to go parceling them out one crumb at a time. I'll make more tomorrow that he can divide up any way he wants."

Ada grinned again then walked quickly off holding the precious cargo in both her hands.

11

In the afternoon, Charlotte made peace with the dust, the heat, the stench of the cattle, the loneliness, the absence of Ellis Gray. Who was, she reminded herself again, being paid to escort her to Fort Randall. What kind of escort was it who never laid eyes on you? She could be back here dead, asleep and fallen off the wagon, run over, cracked her head, took a seizure, whatever it was, and he'd be the last person to know.

She decided to think more about Miller Dawson. She'd caught glimpses of two older girls who she bet had none of Ada's reticence when discussing this young man. His smile was enough by itself. But if they cared to dig further, she sensed that there was a whole other person behind the smile.

Then, she considered as the wagon rocked along behind the weary team, there was the question of practical, care-worn but completely sane women swooning over Ellis Gray. Get to know him, she wanted to tell them. Realize that you'll never see him. That his heart's broken. That he's torn up inside. And crazy maybe.

Done with those musings, Charlotte turned her attention to food. Baking seemed to provide her only relationship with the thankfully closed world of the wagon train. The trouble was the lack of a kitchen. A tin oven could only produce so many goods. Not to mention a finite amount of supplies. The country they were riding through hadn't turned dry yet, but there was no hint of tangled brush in this monochrome landscape, no possibility of wild berries to be foraged, which she was longing for.

She was contemplating ginger cake when she noticed Ada not running but flying in her direction down the long line of the wagons. Ada might be a child, and exasperating, but this time, she definitely had something urgent on her mind.

"Good Lord, what is it?" Charlotte said.

Ada was hanging onto the side of the wagon, panting. "Indians."

Charlotte froze. "Where?"

"They're gone now, but they were way up front on the ridge."

"How many?"

"Eleven, on horses."

"What did they look like?"

"They looked..." Ada searched for the right word. "...sad."

"Sad? How odd. What made you say that?"

Ada considered this for a moment. "Some of them were old."

"Did they have war paint and rifles and lances?"

"No war paint or lances. They wore blankets."

Charlotte frowned. None of that made any sense. "Is everyone frightened?"

"They are. This is our first time and bad things can happen. You don't know."

Charlotte stared at the girl. "And you do?"

Ada shivered. "I listen when I shouldn't. But there's something else."

"I'm afraid for you to say."

"Captain Gray rode out to talk to them."

Charlotte closed her eyes. She felt as if a ball of lead had just been dropped into the pit of her stomach. "And what then?"

"They all went over the ridge together. But he's coming back. He told me to tell you that."

"I appreciate your letting me know."

"I wish you'd seen them."

"If I had," Charlotte said, "I'd likely have fainted dead away."

<>

As the wagons moved forward again, the paralysis gripping the company became palpable. Charlotte understood their fears. When a journey was perilous enough to begin with, every obstacle loomed large as the final threat. Would they still get to Oregon Territory or was their awful end to come at the hands of a hundred members of the tribes waiting behind those few? Would Ellis Gray, their captain, return or might he not? Did he mean to protect them at all costs, or, she could see the hothead suggesting, was he somehow linked with the Indians, he'd had that wife after all, and plotting against them?

Charlotte realized that she feared this mindset as much as she feared members of the tribes. As she watched, men on horseback with guns took up positions along the margins of the caravan, but not, she noticed, at the very back. She would have to take care of herself. To that end, she halted the horses just long enough to find the Colt and the rifle and place them next to her. She couldn't dwell on the likelihood of having to use them.

After what seemed like endless tense hours, the afternoon finally closed and the wagons halted for the day. There had been no attack. No one was dead, not even the old woman with the vapors. With his sure grasp of the landscape, the young pilot had brought them home again to grass and water. Charlotte was certain, however, that there would be no violin music tonight. Instead, all concerned would sit grim-faced by their fires and armies of sentries would be posted around the clock.

Charlotte bent over her small fire, intent on adding fried onions to last night's beans even though she might not be able to get them down. She saw the rider coming and waited, seeking relief of her terrible anxiety, praying it was Ellis Gray. Instead she found herself made even more anxious by the sweet but troubled face of Miller Dawson.

"Would it be all right if I joined you for a bit?" he said.

"If you do, you have to eat."

He tied up his horse, a tentative smile competing with what seemed to be serious worries of his own. "I'd welcome that," he said. "I wouldn't ever pass up the offer of a meal."

He sat down and she handed him a plate. "And while you're eating I'm sorry to be impolite, but I have questions that need to be answered pretty quickly."

Miller nodded and swallowed. "That's why I'm here."

"Then the first one is…" she started to say, then halted. "I've got another one before that. Miller, do you notice that my hair's all

60

chopped off?" She had a hard time believing a person like him existed.

He appeared, with his innocent, guileless face, to be seeing her hair for the first time.

"Looks nice that way."

Charlotte would have laughed if she didn't feel so sick. "My real question is where's Ellis?"

"In the council meeting, that's what I came to tell you, and it's not going so good."

Charlotte bowed her head with relief. "Thank God. He's not dead then, or gone forever or anything."

"No, ma'am. He's right here."

"Miller, you can't call me ma'am. We're the same damn age." He looked at her. "Never mind," she said. "But you have to tell me and you've got to understand how afraid I am of the answer. Who are they? Why did he go with them?"

Miller put his fork down and waited, choosing his words. "That's her family. His wife's."

Charlotte sat stunned. She didn't know why she hadn't thought of this, hadn't seen it coming.

"They've been following us since early yesterday," he said. "Just letting Ellis know they were here."

"Why?"

"It's what the grandfather wants. He's the last of the old ones to stand up for his people. They were given land and now the land's being taken away from them, being sold, because in someone's eyes it was too much land. They were gonna raise cattle, but that would make them rich, and in someone's eyes they shouldn't be rich. And then the valley happened."

"What does this have to do with Ellis? How can he be of any use to them?"

Miller worked at the answer until it came to him in the right way. "The grandfather intends on going to Washington City and talking to the white people's old ones."

"He can do that?"

"He's done it before. He wears the peace medal they gave him the first time." Miller put his fork down again, trying to sort out his thoughts. "He doesn't blame Ellis, but he does hold him accountable, since it was soldiers that did it. Doesn't matter how it happened, whose fault it was in the end. He wants Ellis to come with him to Washington, make the argument for him. It won't work, Ellis told him that, but sometimes the old ones don't want to listen."

"What does this mean for the wagon train?" Charlotte asked, watching Miller wade through the quagmire that the conversation had become, but appreciating his seriousness and care with the difficulties.

"Means finding a new captain."

"What does it mean for me?"

"I think they're dwelling on that right now."

Charlotte suddenly had a thought, one she didn't want. "When do they want Ellis to leave?"

Miller slowly stopped eating and every trace of a smile was gone. "Tomorrow," he said.

"Tomorrow?" She pressed her forehead against her knees. Her life was over again and it hadn't even gotten done being over the first time. Now apparently what she had left would be the ashes. Then it occurred to her that Miller wasn't untouched.

"This affects you just as much, doesn't it?"

"Yes…" he started to say ma'am, but stopped just in time. "…it does. Sometimes, though, things turn out not so bad as you thought they might."

"Sometimes they turn out worse."

"Maybe." Charlotte watched him. He was innocent, but there was something else.

"Who was your family that you could grow up out here where there's nothing?"

"Them," he said simply. "Those on the ridge."

"How?" Her heart went out to him.

"I don't know. I was too young to remember anything but being part of the tribes, having them as my family, this being my

62

home. I have a way better recollection of when we went to the fort that winter when we had no food. The government agent saw me and took me away."

Charlotte calmed. Everyone's life was heartache and there was nothing to be done about it. "Then what?" she said quietly.

"I got adopted. But it didn't last long. I stole a horse and rode as far and as fast as I could."

"How old were you?"

"I don't know. Could've been nine, or maybe ten."

"Where did you run to?"

Charlotte saw that now they had come down to the truth of it. "To Ellis. He knew all about it so I was sure he'd let me stay and he did. Now I'm a help to him, so it's even better."

"Ellis Gray," she said and turned the puzzle of him over in her mind.

Charlotte raised her head as another person headed slowly her way, his horse trailing behind him.

"Sit down," she said to Ellis. "Eat something. He did."

"Already ate, but thank you." He tethered his horse with Miller's and took a seat next to the fire. Charlotte thought that he suddenly looked older than his years, whatever those might be.

"Miller's been here talking with me for a while. It's your turn. Tell me the rest. I already know there's nothing good in it."

Ellis took a deep breath and exhaled it slowly as if he was willing all the pain to go away. "It's the old one. He grieves for how much his people suffer, how much they've lost. I understand that, but going to Washington City won't help. They didn't listen the last time, they won't listen now. He thinks they will if I'm the one making the argument." Ellis seemed to be talking to himself. "I have to go."

"What about the wagon train?"

"I'm leaving, that was obvious, but they voted on it and threw me out anyway to make it official. I told them Miller has to stay, they won't make it without him and hopefully they understand that. Now they're debating who's to be captain. Contentious as they are,

63

the probability exists that they'll still be fighting about it come morning."

"What about me? I'm in hell already so it doesn't exactly matter what you have to say."

Ellis kept his eyes steady on her. "Miller offered to be your benefactor till you got to Fort Randall. They were having none of it, never mind that there'll be a mountain of supplies waiting for them as pay for taking you on. And if you're wondering, I'm giving my fee back to you."

"And I'll spend it where?" But there was a more important point to consider. She'd thought about death before. Now she was thinking about it again, all those rivers she couldn't ford alone, how long her provisions would last.

"I see where your mind's going. I had an answer, but it'd only work if you were set on Fort Randall. That's why when you said you might have doubts, I maybe didn't react in the best possible way."

"What answer did you have?" Charlotte said, thinking she should have eaten something. She felt light-headed, dizzy.

Ellis took a moment, then spoke. "Trust me, though I know at the moment you have no cause to. Just come with me."

Charlotte couldn't even imagine what he was talking about. "Come with you where?"

"Don't ask. Get your horse saddled up and meet us back here." He stood up. His face was unreadable. "Miller's coming too."

A new and horrifying thought came to her. "I have to know. You have to tell me where we're going."

Ellis watched the sky. There'd be a beautiful sunset. No rain at least to add to everyone's miseries. He turned back to her. "To the old one. He wants to meet you."

12

Charlotte rode up over the ridge between the two of them. The mare seemed glad for the quickened pace. Ellis had posted what he said was a reliable boy to stay with her wagon. She'd quickly hidden the guns. When the boy eyed her plate of food enviously, she gave it to him.

A mile or two on the other side of the ridge, the land rolled into more forest. Ellis led them among the trees till they came to a clearing and a campfire. A pale half moon was rising in the east against the fading sky. Birds serenaded with their last song of the day accompanied by a chorus of crickets in the underbrush. The first stars appeared. Charlotte could hardly breathe.

The old one rose as they dismounted. The others remained seated. She saw that Ada had been right. Each of them wore a blanket though the day's warmth still held. She noticed however that the soft breeze carried with it no scent of cooking, no smell of roasted meat.

He was not centuries old and bent, not yet, but his face was lined with a thousand creeks and valleys. The peace medal was a silver disc, hung on a ribbon, embossed with a profile. She folded her arms to keep anyone from seeing how much her hands were shaking. Ellis stood close on one side, Miller on the other.

"He won't speak to you in English," Ellis said, "but Miller will tell you what he's saying."

The old one, however, said nothing. He just kept walking closer, all eyes on him, until he was standing in front of Charlotte, regarding her in a way that she'd never experienced before, and which had nothing to do with her hair or bruised face. She held her ground, the fight rising in her. Nobody could judge her unless they'd lived her life. Though his eyes were faded, and she could see that he too was tired, still an equal fierceness showed in his. She dared him to find her wanting.

She realized, watching his reaction, that there was no need for translators. He'd heard all that she had to say. He turned away from her, first letting his gaze rest gently on Miller, then moving to regard Ellis with some intent. Finally, he spoke and Charlotte listened, transfixed. It was a language from another place and time, an ancient tongue, like nothing she had ever heard before.

"He honors you," Miller said, "as a strong woman. He sees it in your eyes. He welcomes you to his campfire. He regrets there's not more time. He says that everything will happen when the sun rises again, and this is the way it will be." Miller paused, listening to the unraveling skein of words. "He says he is sorry that your journey will not follow the path your important father expected it to but he himself will guarantee your safety until you reach your destination."

"I told him everything," Ellis said.

Charlotte gave up. She seemed once again to have completely lost control of her life. She reached into her pocket and held out an offering to the old one. Puzzled, he took it. He looked questioningly at Miller.

"What is it?" Miller asked, equally puzzled.

"A biscuit." It was the one she'd been saving for lunch and never ate. She listened as Miller translated this, speaking the strange dialect as if it were his own, the stark realization coming to her that it truly had been his own.

They all watched as the grandfather raised the biscuit to his lips, tested the aroma, squinted at the composition of it, then slowly took a bite. He chewed thoughtfully. Charlotte feared it might have grown crusty, but the rich flavor would still be there. When the old one smiled, his face broke into even more creeks and valleys. He nodded, then reached out and touched her forehead almost as a benediction.

She sensed Ellis shaking his head.

Then the old man was speaking again. Miller paused a moment before he returned to translating.

"He says he is fortunate in his life to have grandsons, counting me and Ellis among them. He says he's chosen one to lead you

66

where you need to go, on a path that will be its own journey. He says your father if he knew would agree because there is wisdom in this approach."

Charlotte took a step back, trying hard not to cry.

"Why is he saying this?" she said, her voice barely a whisper. Even with her arms folded tightly, still the pounding of her heart felt as if it would break her ribs.

The old man seemed to understand this and waved her fears away. He beckoned behind him and a blanketed figure rose from the circle. Charlotte watched in terror, but then her eyes narrowed. The closer he came, the more she didn't know whether to run or faint or expire where she stood, which would definitely at this point, she considered, be the most useful option. Instead, she gathered what courage she had left.

"You've lost your bow and your rifle," she said bravely.

"They're still here," he said. "But where's your Colt?"

"Safely hidden away, thank you. I'm obliged for the squirrel."

"You went out and found it?"

"And cooked it."

All else was stunned silence. Charlotte could feel Ellis and Miller on either side of her trying to comprehend what had just happened. The old one stood back with an expression on his face that said all of the world except the white man's was wrapped up in the mysteries of the gods and the spirits of the earth.

13

Back at the wagon train, when Ellis tried to unsaddle Charlotte's mare as a gesture of kindness, Charlotte stepped in front of him. "It's my horse, I can take care of her." She'd stopped shaking but now she was angry, at what she hardly knew anymore. "If I'm on my own, it starts right here."

"You aren't on your own. You've got Chace, and if there were anybody better than Miller or me, it'd be him."

"Chace?"

"Chace Yellow Cloud, back there, the one you already seem to be acquainted with. Do you want to tell me about that five days later than you should have?"

"I forgot about him the minute I found out I had a whole wagon train's worth of people against me. He just showed up, we exchanged some words, and then he was gone."

"What kind of words?"

"I got the Colt and aimed it at him and he sat on his horse and didn't seem to care. Then he asked what happened to me. Then he asked if he could see the Colt and he shot a squirrel with it and rode off and I cooked the squirrel for dinner."

Ellis rubbed his face. "I can't tell you how painful this all is. If it helps, I'd put my life in his hands."

"I would too," Miller said, glad to be able to add something useful to the conversation.

"Well, I wish you'd all just put your life in each other's hands and leave me alone, though I know I can't do anything but accept it. I'm more than aware that I'll die if I don't. But you see, that's the point, there are so many ways now that I could die. The options are endless."

"Don't do that," Ellis said.

"Why not? It's the truth."

"Why don't we forget about this for a while and get some sleep? Miller and I'll bunk down here." He indicated the saddles lying on the ground.

"No, you won't." Miller felt as if he was getting his first lesson in the peculiar ways of women.

"What's that supposed to mean?"

"I want to be by myself. It's my last wish as far as you're concerned so you can just go ahead and grant it."

"You can be by yourself as much as you want in that wagon, but we're sleeping where I said, here on the ground."

"You aren't in charge of me anymore." Charlotte was aiming the anger at him, unfair as that was. "I've got guns you don't even know about. I'll keep the fire up. The wolves are gone. And it seems I shouldn't be fearing members of the tribes. So go. I've got work to do."

"You are…" Ellis began with some heat.

"Don't say it," she cautioned.

"If you're not here in the morning, it's not my fault."

"Unfortunately, I'll be here."

Miller waited until he saw what direction Ellis would take, then they both hoisted their saddles up and left. Miller tried to look back once, but Ellis was moving fast.

By the light of an oil lamp hanging from the wagon supports, Charlotte took apart her bed and went through the entire collection of books one at a time. When she was done with that, she dug into the flour barrel, rummaged in the tins of ingredients and spices and set up the tin oven over the fire. The baking alone took half the night. Toward dawn, she pried up the floorboards and found the silver. Carefully, she filled a small drawstring bag, adding in enough cotton wool so that the coins wouldn't clink against each other and give away their presence.

Miller Dawson came by before the sentinel blasted apart the quiet, before the day had even begun. Before he could say anything, she put a small loaf of molasses bread in his hands.

"Miller, you're so damned nice. There just aren't many like you. Did they find a captain?"

"For now they did but he won't last long. Just so they leave me alone to be the pilot I'm not complaining."

"Good luck with all of it then. I know you'll be stretched for hours in the day, but if you can, look out for Fiona, will you?"

"She's the one with the baby?"

"Yes."

Miller nodded.

"I wish you well," Charlotte said. "And now for just one moment I'm going to pretend I don't have principles and kiss you." She reached up, took his astonished face in her hands, and did just that. "Now hurry up out of here before I cry. And thank you for everything, Miller Dawson."

Miller got on his horse and rode away in a daze, belatedly wishing he'd known how to kiss her back. He realized Ellis hadn't told him near enough about these kinds of things.

Charlotte was sitting with a board across her knees and the ink beside her writing a letter when Ellis Gray walked slowly out from the curved line of wagons, his loaded horse trailing behind him.

"Did you sleep?" she said. He didn't look like it.

"Only some."

"I didn't sleep at all but I didn't want to. Sit down. Give me a minute and I'll make you breakfast."

"I don't need breakfast."

"Ellis, I was taught to respect my elders but if you don't sit down right now because I asked you to, I'll start screaming and I swear that's the truth."

"Feels like this is where we left off last night."

"The fire's down. If you could get it going, that'd be a help. I've just got some things left to take care of."

"I'm making the breakfast," he said. "I've got dried buffalo meat."

"Hopefully you'll still have that same dried buffalo meat tomorrow. I'll find you some ham and eggs to fry."

"And an onion if you've got it."

Charlotte closed her eyes and sighed. She dug the breakfast makings out of the wagon and quickly handed them off to him.

"I'll be back," she said. He didn't bother asking where she was going. There was no use in that.

She hadn't been able to think of some way to go about this until the doltish boys ahead of her came to mind. She found them still asleep rolled in blankets under their wagon. She kicked at the nearest form until it unfolded.

"Ouch," it said.

"Get up. I need your help but there's something in it for you."

"Just don't kick me again."

"If you get up, I won't."

A boy stood up, near his teens, hopelessly lost, probably wondering how he'd ended up here in this vast uncharted land, dragged through the mud and dust as unpaid labor on someone else's dream. Maybe, Charlotte thought, she could change his luck.

"I have some errands that need to be run immediately."

"What are they?" He eyed her uncertainly, all at once remembering what he'd heard about her.

"It's simple," she said, ignoring his hesitation. "But it pays good if you manage to do it right. If not..." she said, and willfully left the consequences unspoken.

"I'll try," he said, more afraid than he had been.

"You'll see. What's your name?"

"Edward."

"Edward what?"

"Edward Fenton."

"Okay, Edward, here's what it is. Now let me say first that being discreet is part of this. Do you even know what that means?"

Edward Fenton rose to his full height. His hair was still sticking straight up. He was the one she'd seen before. "I went to school. It means careful."

No one was what they seemed.

"Go to the wagon with the five children and it has to be quick. Find the one called Ada, the girl with the wild hair, and on any pretense you can think of bring her back here with her brother, his name's Brewster. It'll only be for a minute." Edward blinked hard,

71

concentrating. "Because, Edward, after that minute I'll be gone, and it'll be very sad for you and her if you didn't find her." As an afterthought, she added, "Tell them Ellis Gray needs them." They'd never be allowed to come if it was for her.

Edward nodded fearfully. "And as fast as you can after that, with this being a far more difficult proposition, go to the wagon where the baby was just born. The mother's name is Fiona, do you know her?"

Edward nodded. Likely he was her younger brother or her nephew or her second cousin by marriage, they all appeared to be related somehow or other.

"And however you can manage it, bring her here to me. Need I say, avoid the husband?"

Edward shook his head no, meaning she needn't say it, and was off at a run.

Charlotte hated feeling like a dictator, scaring the boy out of his wits, but she'd been true in her words, there was only so much time.

Ada came first, hurrying again as if it was Indians, Brewster staggering along sleepily behind her. Charlotte's heart broke, aware that this would be the last she ever saw of this child. Confusion was written all over Ada's face.

"What's happening?" she said, breathless. "They said you're going away."

"Funny. How is what they say always right?"

"Does it have to do with the Indians?"

"Ada, you are about a thousand times too smart for your own good. I'm not saying what it has to do with."

"Children aren't allowed to hear again."

"Exactly."

"Then it mustn't be good."

"Nothing's good or bad anymore. It's just how it is. What I wanted was to say goodbye, but also I spent the night baking and Brewster's the one to sort it all out for me." Charlotte took a sack from the back of the wagon, filled to overflowing with loaves of molasses bread, ginger cake, dried apple bread and honey cakes.

She feared at first that Brewster wouldn't be able to carry it, but he slung it over his shoulder and bent under the weight.

Charlotte ruffled Brewster's hair. "You're a wonderful child," she said. She reached back into the wagon, pulled out a tall stack of books and turned to Ada.

"These are for all of you." The girl held out her arms and Charlotte transferred the stack to her one book at a time. "I read them when I was a girl. Just don't grow up to be like me." Charlotte put her arms around both Ada and the books and hugged tight. "I'm not going to cry and you aren't either," though Ada already was.

"I don't want you to be afraid," Ada said.

Charlotte wiped away her own tears. "I won't if you won't. No matter what. Promise?"

"I promise."

Charlotte watched the two small forms with their burdens until they were out of sight.

Edward Fenton was an inspired choice for a runner. Fiona came slowly, her face pale, wrapped in a shawl and carrying the baby. She smiled gently at Charlotte and didn't even seem to question the summons.

"I hope you don't mind," Charlotte said for Ellis's benefit. She knew he must be listening. "I just wanted to see the baby one more time."

Fiona unwrapped the bundle and unexpectedly placed the baby in Charlotte's arms. Of course, Charlotte thought. She'd held infants before, but never voluntarily. It always happened like this, new mothers assuming everyone shared their same maternal joy. Charlotte cradled the tiny thing uneasily against her, amazed once again at the perfect little face and rosebud lips. Then without seeming to do it in haste, she handed the baby back and pulled Fiona to the far side of the wagon, away from the fire.

Charlotte withdrew the drawstring bag from her pocket. "Please don't take offense at this," she said, her voice low and hopefully out of range. This was just between women. She handed the bag to Fiona. "I'm going to be blunt. I don't know if you're aware of my history, thought it shows plain as day anyway, but I don't want it ever to be anyone else's history if I can help it."

Charlotte's views were confirmed. Fiona didn't seem surprised or upset in any way. Her gaze stayed evenly on Charlotte. "It's silver. Enough to see you through whatever might come. It's packed in cotton wool so that..." she hesitated. Fiona nodded. Charlotte saw that she understood perfectly. As Charlotte watched, she slipped the bag into her waistband underneath her apron.

"Thank you. I'm grateful."

"Your baby's beautiful," Charlotte said, and she meant it.

"Go with God," Fiona said. Well, that wasn't quite who it was going to be.

Edward Fenton hovered near the front of the wagon. Charlotte could smell the ham and onions frying.

"You did a fine job," she said.

"I wasn't awake at first but now I am."

"I've got one more thing and it's important."

"Yes, ma'am."

She pulled out the letter in its sealed envelope. "This needs to go to the name on the front, Tobias Duchesne, when you get to Fort Randall. He may not be there right away, but I'm asking you to find someone who can give it to him. I'm also asking you to protect the letter, carry it safe on your person, until you get there. Is that something you can do?"

"Yes, ma'am."

"I trust that's true." Charlotte handed him the letter. Then she took his other hand, opened it and poured an amount of silver into his palm. She closed his fingers around the coins. His eyes were wide. "If people know you have money, then you don't always have it anymore. And if you're foolish with it, then you don't have it anymore either. But I don't think you're foolish, Edward Fenton."

"I never was," he said with some feeling.

"Good," she said. "I'm lucky then."

<>

74

Ellis made a perfectly acceptable breakfast. He offered it to her on one of her own tin plates.

"You've been busy," he said.

"I told you I had things to do."

"What's the letter say?"

"I was counting on you being hard of hearing. You'll be in Washington talking to the old ones so what do you care?"

"I care."

"It's not your concern."

"If you'll remember correctly, it is my concern. I was being paid to get you there."

"That was yesterday."

"I'm asking you again and I want an answer. What does the letter say?"

"This must be your captain-in-charge voice. Don't worry, I'm used to that too. It says I'm safe, don't wait for me, I'll be there when I can."

"Or never."

"Or never."

"I've changed my mind," Ellis said. He'd eaten his breakfast in four mouthfuls. "I'm giving the money to Chace."

"You can give it to anybody you want. Makes no difference to me."

"But wait a minute. Do you have a real fear for Fiona?"

"Did you have to listen to every damn word? Yes, the truth is I do. Looking at her husband is like living that nightmare all over again and I think she knows it. The people who don't shy away from me, you wonder why not. And she doesn't."

"So you've taken care of everyone."

"Everyone that I can, and that's not saying much. I don't even know the rest of them." Charlotte put down her plate. "Why didn't you tell Miller about women?"

"What?"

"He doesn't know anything. He should at least know something."

"Do you get the feeling this conversation just ended? Because I do."

Now Charlotte was interested. "Are you embarrassed?"

"I'm not embarrassed. If you really want to know, I'm worried sick and completely, thoroughly exasperated."

"Why?" Charlotte said. "It's only me."

Ellis was on his feet, handing back his plate, wiping out the frying pan, putting out the fire. "That's what I was just saying."

The call went out for the wagon train to move and suddenly she was vulnerable again. This he could handle.

"We need to get going," he said.

"We do." She couldn't bear it if the wagons all pulled out and hers was left behind, still standing here alone in the quiet and dust raised up from the cattle.

"I'm not going to argue with you. I'll drive if you want. If that's not what you want, say so now."

"You drive." She was suddenly very tired.

Ellis hitched up her team and tethered his horse and the mare behind. "There's one other thing."

"What's that?" She couldn't imagine what might be left. She was done with all of this.

"We should say goodbye here, not out there."

"Oh," she said. "Then goodbye I guess."

She hadn't counted on his reaction at all. Ellis wrapped her in his arms and held her tight against him. Then he kissed the top of her head. For one brief moment, she wanted to collapse against him, lean into his strength rather than having to depend on her own. Then the moment was over and the realities of her life came back to her.

"Thank you, Ellis."

"I feel like I keep trying to apologize. There's nothing either of us could change, but I wish it had turned out some other way than this."

"Wishing won't do it. Remember? You're the one who told me that."

"You'll be safe," he said. "Safe where is the question."

Charlotte smiled up at him, her eyes brimming over. "It's an interesting question anyway," she said.

Ellis couldn't stand to even think about it.

14

Chace Yellow Cloud sat alone underneath a tree at the edge of the forest. His dappled horse grazed nearby. When he saw the wagon, he rose to his feet. He'd put on a loose soft shirt over the buckskin pants.

"They're gone already?" Ellis said.

"Not long ago and they're moving slow. They'll stay on the main road till you catch up."

Ellis swung down from the wagon and headed back to untie his horse. "I'm not looking forward to this."

"No one is," Chace said. "But he'll go even if it means going alone."

"I'm worn out. Why isn't he?"

"He thinks his time's coming and this is what he has to do first."

"So be it, then. I'm worried about the wagon train. It's got some mule-heads in it and I don't want Miller finding himself in more trouble than he can handle. None of them are worth it, that's for certain."

"Some of them are," Charlotte said. Both of them turned to look at her as if they'd forgotten she was there. Though I am involved somewhat, she thought.

"Yes," Ellis said, "but you took care of your own and fed the whole damn company and headed off your uncle for at least a while. Not bad for a night's work."

"I'll miss you," she said, "even though you were never there."

"Don't get me started again. Just say goodbye nicely."

She lifted her chin. "Goodbye, Ellis."

Ellis swung up into the saddle and Chace Yellow Cloud did the same.

"Go well, my brother," Chace said.

"Go well to you, my brother," Ellis said, and he was gone.

<>

Charlotte sat in silence, waiting for what came next. Ellis's sudden absence affected her more than she'd thought it would. With all his faults, he'd still been the constant, the one person she believed she could trust. He didn't have to treat her well, but he had. He didn't have to care, but he did. She wondered if and when he'd handed over the money so that now she would be someone else's problem instead of that burden belonging solely to him. She was sure that in her father's eyes, beyond being horrified at the turn of events, he would expect each of them to accept responsibility for the decisions they made and the outcome of those decisions. For Ellis, that meant leaving her. For Chace Yellow Cloud, she had no idea what it meant. And what kind of name was that anyway?

It all seemed so preposterous, sitting on the seat of a wagon containing all the possessions she had left in the world, having to figure out the rest of her life with a perfect stranger, not to mention *this* perfect stranger who sat on his horse apparently waiting for her to say something.

"Why are you called Chace?" she said.

"We've had this conversation already, or one very much like it."

"That was about English."

"Right. I remember now."

"Are you going to answer me?"

"About which question?"

"The second one."

"It's a white man's name," he said.

"I knew that."

"A trapper who lived with my people. He said he'd heard if you gave a child of the tribes a white man's name, that child would grow up knowing everything there was to know about the white man, and that would be a useful thing. So they gave me his name."

"Which was?"

"Chace Bridger."

"Do you regret it?"

"I don't think about it and nobody else does either that I know of except for you. But do you want to talk about something else, like where we're going for instance?"

"To Fort Randall."

"Ellis said maybe not."

Maybe not, Charlotte repeated to herself. Those two words held out such promise. "I'd be fooling myself if I believed that for even one minute."

"And what's in Fort Randall?"

"My uncle, life starting over in the desert somewhere, a new husband they didn't tell me anything about, not even his name."

"He's brave. That's something."

"Exactly what I didn't need to hear. The sooner we get there, the better."

"Something tells me you don't mean that. So just to be helpful, let's talk about what you do mean."

Why she was doing this, she couldn't understand except that in so many ways she had nothing to lose. "You're right," she said. "Sooner isn't better. I don't want to go. I don't want to live in the desert. I don't want a new husband."

Charlotte set her expression hard. "But there's no other option. When I was out there on the prairie, I thought about being on my own and going where I pleased. But I couldn't even get across the river by myself. And they don't want me in the wagon train. So Fort Randall and the desert's all there is. If that's true, then I want to take as long as possible getting there. And I don't want to meet up with any wagon trains, or be around people at all."

"I can do that," he said. "It's nothing one way or the other to me."

<>

The morning's journey proved long and tedious but at least they were moving, going somewhere. Fatigue bore down on Charlotte as the hours passed and the heat rose. They were heading far away from the road the settlers took. Chace Yellow Cloud was as good as his word in that at least. He led his horse through the tall grass

80

with the wagon following. The grass waved, bent, flowed around them, closing again as if they'd never been there.

At the noon hour, when the horses required a break, Charlotte moved wearily forward to unhitch the team. He was already there. "Get some sleep," was all he said, and she did, climbing into the wagon, gone before she'd pulled the blanket over her.

For the afternoon, without asking her he took the reins, creating a disconcerting image, his appearance so much at odds with that of the wagon. The iron wheels, board sides, plain stretched canvas spoke of a rough and simple man, a woodsman, a farmer. All this member of the tribes could possibly have in common with such people were his hands on the reins.

Charlotte saddled the mare and trailed behind, watching the dragonflies alight on tender shafts of bluegrass, listening for the sound of a bird, any bird. Once, she heard the scream of a hawk, but couldn't place him in the sky's endless pale blue reaches. Shading her eyes, she turned into the sun, and then couldn't see anything.

It was peaceful anyway, to be rolling steadily forward with the land passing under her like the waves under a ship at sea. She let her mind drift off into oblivion.

Close to the end of the afternoon, weary again, she drew the mare up alongside the wagon.

"Are we near a place to stop?" she said.

"Not much farther. When the swallows fly low like that, they're headed to water."

She'd gone into such a monotony-induced trance that she hadn't even noticed the swallows flipping dark to light as they darted through the air.

<>

"It's a very old camping place," Charlotte said. Blackened rocks and ash-colored earth gave evidence of many fires down the long years.

"This was a hunting trail for the tribes that lived here."

"Where are they now?"

"Mostly gone to the agencies, their land ceded, the old ones dead."

Charlotte held that thought in her mind while she led the horses down along the bank to stand in the clear cold water and drink their fill. She imagined her own small strange tribe one day going the same way, forcibly disbanded and removed from their land, but not without a fight. Chace Yellow Cloud untied his horse from the wagon and pulled out his bow.

"I've got food," she said. "You don't have to do that."

"I'll be back."

"Do you know something?"

"I know so many things," he said and was gone.

She picketed the horses to let them graze then gathered enough wood to start a fire. Till he came back, she didn't know what more to do. In the meantime, she washed out some petticoats and hung them over the back of the wagon to dry.

He returned with two grouse. Charlotte prepared the plump birds and roasted them over the open fire. The sunlight was beginning to filter at an angle through the trees when the tin plates were clean again.

"I have a large amount of supplies and that was intentional," Charlotte said. "All of it's meant to sustain me and my supposed benefactor, which would have been Ellis. Now, due to some unknown misfortune on your part, it's you."

"I have dried buffalo meat."

"You and everyone else. That would be a useful thing if it were actually food, which it isn't. Why is this a problem?"

"I don't think about why. It just is."

"Well here's what. I'm making you breakfast in the morning and if you don't eat it, I'll dump it on the ground. If that seems reasonable to you, fine." She put a hand to her head. She had something more important to talk about and now she'd completely lost her train of thought. Then she got it back.

"Guns," she said, noting with satisfaction his suddenly guarded expression.

"What about guns?"

"I've got more than a few. I don't understand what my father was thinking, except that maybe he wasn't." Charlotte climbed up on the seat of the wagon. "They're all here easy to get to. I'll hand them out one at a time."

"What are you doing?" he said.

"What good are they stacked up in there and you knowing nothing about them if there was ever trouble? Are you going to leave that to me?"

"I see your point."

"You saw it too quickly." But she started retrieving the guns. The first were repeating rifles.

"Wait," he said. He'd put two down on the ground without looking at them, and was holding the third. "What is this?"

Charlotte frowned. "Two are Henrys and one's a Spencer. That's the Spencer, I guess. He gave me a lecture about them but everything ran together. A seventeen-round magazine maybe? Is that possible?"

"I didn't think so, but that's what it is."

"How do you feel about it?"

"I don't even know yet."

"Listen to me. This may seem strange, but I'm giving it to you and it's like breakfast. If you don't take it, I'm putting it down on the ground and leaving it here."

"Are you always like this?"

"If you say the word difficult, I will scream, I promise you. Here, you also have to take one of the Colts. Believe it or not, I've got two."

"You're just giving me these guns."

"For purposes of safety, yours and mine both. Look at it that way." She stopped for a moment, struck. "A thought just occurred to me. The first thing they'll do is separate me from every one of those guns by about a mile anyway."

Chace Yellow Cloud still had his hands on the Spencer. "What's your father's name?" he said.

"Samuel Duchesne, but why?"

"I want to remember it."

83

The light began to fade. He brought in the horses and tied them up close to the wagon, put out the fire, prepared for the night. He laid down his saddle and unrolled a blanket. Charlotte longed for sleep. She hesitated, one hand on the back of the wagon.

"Last thing I need for you to know. Sometimes I wake up screaming." Let him do what he would with that information.

15

In the gray light before dawn, Charlotte sat bolt upright and wondered what had awakened her. Then she knew. It was the sound of the sentinel's bugle that she'd gotten enough used to hearing, or dreading, that she woke even without it.

The member of the tribes had preempted her plans for breakfast with trout fresh from the stream. She panfried them. They were delicious.

"I'm not saying anything," she said.

"Good, that solves one problem. It'll be easier traveling now but we're in disputed country. Keep your eyes open."

"Disputed how?"

"Displaced tribes put here by the government. Plus the renegades always out there somewhere on their own."

The conversation set Charlotte on edge.

Still, the slow journey by wagon produced its familiar rhythms. In the morning, she took the reins. The day was warm. Tiny insects hovered in swarming clouds. The trail stayed close to the creek meaning the swallows were always there, chittering as they rose and fell in swift, darting arcs, a flash of white followed by a band of ruddy gold and midnight blue.

She used the swallows to keep her mind focused on the present, the hard-packed trail, the quaking aspens and understory thick with the possibility of berries. The rifle lay beside her in case she spotted dinner, though she knew any hope of that was futile. First, Chace Yellow Cloud would see anything long before she did, and second, he would likely react unfavorably to a shot ringing out behind him. She trained her eyes on the passing landscape anyway, trying not to let her thoughts settle on images of displaced tribes and renegades.

Charlotte began to understand that her current benefactor was very much like her previous one. As the trail grew more visible, he grew less so. Often he traveled so far up ahead that she lost sight of him. Now and then he eased his horse off into the brush, disappearing altogether. Thus far he'd appeared again before she grew uncomfortable. He didn't seem concerned for her safety, so she decided not to be either, but it remained disconcerting nevertheless.

In the afternoon, he asked that she keep the reins. "Is something wrong?"

"No." He took his rifle instead of the bow. She could anticipate what was coming and decided not to complain. She began to drift again, allowing her mind to wander. Travel was slow but that was good. Let Fort Randall remain someone else's bad idea, off in a very hazy land far away.

Charlotte was daydreaming, entirely alone in the world, when he appeared out of nowhere with a bloody haunch tossed over the back of his horse.

"What is that?" she said.

"Deer. Part of one anyway."

"Where's the rest?"

"I left it out there. It'd attract coyotes at the least, or bear, nothing anybody wants." Bear, something that hadn't even occurred to her.

"Dinner," she said.

"But if you want to dump it on the ground that's fine too."

"Those are my words."

"I know."

Charlotte cut out steaks to fry. As the sun retreated a coolness rose up from the ground and the air smelled clean and fresh. With the meal ended, she set about cutting out more steaks and chopping up the rest for stew. If farmers and tradesmen didn't always make the best hunters apparently a member of the tribes did.

Chace occupied himself with the Spencer, examining its intricacies, clicking open the magazine, the chambers, testing its action again and again.

"Did Ellis give you the money?" Charlotte said into the quiet.

"I didn't want it."

Charlotte took a moment to let this sink in. "Why not?"

"It has no meaning to me."

"Not that it's important or anything, but if that's true why on earth are you here?"

"It's what my grandfather wanted. But also, if I'm here with you, I don't have to be in Washington City."

"And if I'm here with you, I don't have to be in Fort Randall." She suddenly saw the interesting benefits to be had by both parties.

"I've never been to Washington," she said. "To some wouldn't it be a privilege?"

"Maybe for your people. The old ones are from another world. They don't understand anything that goes on there. They can talk for hours and walk all around it, but not actually state one clear thing that speaks to the point they wanted with all their heart to make. The earth is our mother, this is true, but after a hundred repetitions the words become meaningless and the white people, accustomed to lawyers and arguments sharpened like knives, don't even listen anymore, let alone care."

"I don't know what to say."

"That's because there isn't anything left for anyone to say."

16

Deep in the black of night, Charlotte woke to the sound of screaming and realized this time it was her own. She'd taken off her narrowly buttoned shirt before retiring and now her camisole was drenched in sweat. Her heart pounded and her breath came as hard as if she'd run straight up a very steep hill with demons pursuing her. She put her hands to her face, gulping for air. Then she had to get out of the wagon as quickly as possible.

She didn't have time to calculate Chace Yellow Cloud's whereabouts. The fire was going, but he wasn't within its range. It didn't matter. She ran into the bushes and heaved until there was nothing left to come up but bitterness.

He appeared at her side with a mason jar of water. She held out her cupped hands. He poured the water and she splashed it on her face. "Drink," he said, handing her the jar. She filled her mouth, then turned away from him and spit on the ground. She filled her mouth again and swallowed large gulps.

"Thank you," she said.

"Come sit by the fire."

She was shaky, but agreed. At the back of the wagon, she reached in for a shawl to belatedly cover her lack of attire.

He'd built the flames back up. She wrapped her arms around her knees and huddled into a ball. She could feel the cold deep inside. He watched her shiver, her teeth chattering, her face ghostly pale. He gave her his blanket. When she still shivered, he went to the wagon and brought back a second one to cover her with.

"Is he there? Is that what it is?"

"I hear the gun go off. I try to stop it but I can't." She stared into the fire as the flames consumed a log and sparks shot up. "I'm sorry."

"For what? For being alive?"

"No, not for that," she said. "For everything else."

<>

She woke in the wagon at dawn and immediately the night's events came rushing back to her. Hastily, she changed into another camisole, buttoned up a high-collared shirt that had once been starched, went to brush her hair and remembered she had none, and thus subdued began her morning.

Chace was nowhere to be seen. Would he bring trout for breakfast? She didn't care. She set out the frying pan and made ham and eggs enough for two with biscuits on the side. He came up from the creek dressed but dripping wet.

"You went swimming?"

"Hardly. It's not deep enough for that, but anyway I fell in."

"You did?" She wanted to smile but wasn't sure she should.

"Happens. Those rocks are slippery. But it felt good. You should try it."

"Falling in?"

"Falling in, getting in, just sitting there."

Charlotte was instantly wary.

"I'd go somewhere else if you wanted to." She felt herself coloring and though embarrassed, acknowledged that it was at least far better than how she'd appeared in the night.

She was still wary. There were no trout. Cautiously, she held out a plate of ham and eggs. He took it with no show of concern, sat down and ate without a word being said. She handed him a biscuit. He ate that too. Maybe they had a truce. Maybe screaming in the night was the answer.

"We should stay in one place now and then," he said. "This time just for the morning."

"Why?"

"That's one way to slow down. As long as there's food and water, we've got time."

Charlotte was still not well.

"You won't go off and leave me?"

"Understand that I'm always aware of what's out there, but no, I won't go off and leave you."

89

It seemed odd, being alone in the middle of nowhere yet not actually being alone. Chace sat on the other side of the clearing, still studying the Spencer.

"How can you know what it's actually like if you haven't shot it?"

"That's better done somewhere else."

"You mean not where we are?"

"Signaling your whereabouts is hardly ever a good idea."

Something occurred to her. "I never showed you where the ammunition was. You should find what you need, keep it with you."

He waited, then a realization dawned.

"You expect me to go in there?" He nodded at the wagon.

"I keep trying to tell you, you need to know everything I know. Samuel Duchesne requires that it be that way. See if you find more things to use as weapons, just in case." In case of what, she didn't know.

She considered that it wouldn't be the nest of blankets, or the skirts and petticoats hanging on hooks, or the barrels and canisters of food. But maybe the shovel, iron poles, saw, cooking utensils, her grandmother's flatware in the dark polished box. She watched him climb in at the back and make his way uncomfortably forward, the unfamiliar smell of spices, lamp oil and lilac soap hanging in the air around him.

The guns were stacked at the front. Sitting in the narrow aisle, he ran his hand down the print on the wooden boxes next to them, found the ones he wanted, pulled them out and opened them. The cartridges were packed in straw. He reached over and a handful at a time stacked the rounds outside the front of the wagon then quickly climbed up on the seat and extricated himself.

"See?" she said. "It wasn't the seventh rung of hell or anything."

"Don't be so sure."

"I still have to find some better kind of mood and I know one thing that almost always helps. The more horse brushing I can do, the better off I'll be. Would you be interested in contributing yours?"

"I wouldn't count on him being willing."

"We'll see."

With the wagon train, there'd barely been time. Now there was so much time. She started with one of the team horses, going slow, making it last, smiling when the horse nickered softly, smiling again when the trembling began. The anxious unsettled feeling gradually left her, taking the fear with it. Putting her mind to the horses let her thoughts rest, gave her some semblance of peace.

At last, she'd finished all three and turned to the beautiful dappled horse. Chace had kept an eye on her. As she approached the horse, he was there.

"Let me get him to the wagon," he said. When he'd tied up the big gray, he stood back. Charlotte began with easy strokes. The horse startled and wrenched his neck swiftly in her direction, teeth bared. Chace stood at his head, holding the halter taut. Charlotte started over, talking softly, running her brush down the horse's neck, over his shoulder, down the legs, along his sides and flanks in long firm rhythmic strokes. His stiffened posture relaxed. His head drooped. And then there it was, that sweet nickering sound that said, in horse language, she was certain, please don't ever stop doing that.

"I think you've just ruined my horse."

"I don't suppose I can feed him oats now?"

"No, I don't suppose you can."

<>

The days came more easily with the accommodations they'd made to each other after the nightmares. He stayed closer, she was less anxious. He wanted her to ride up ahead on her mare, not trail behind as she had been, and she did so without asking why. They traveled even more slowly. Charlotte had no idea what awaited him at the end of the journey, though she meant to ask. For herself, they could be traveling backwards for all she cared, or standing still, as long as the Family was far enough away on either end.

She commented on the blessed relief, the acres of time.

"It won't be forever, though, will it?"

"No. Not unless we change direction. I could get you south on the trail to Santa Fe, but then where would you be?"

"In Santa Fe, I guess. I'm still going to pretend it's forever. Right now I'm erasing the desert and everything in it, including the uncle I can barely remember."

"The waiting one?"

"Forget about him like I am," she said evenly. "He doesn't even have a name."

Charlotte realized that she felt a deep humiliation for how much he knew about her. It was all so private, so painful. Yet the respite he provided was worth every hard revelation.

<>

The rest stops became her favorite part of any given day. She could do as she pleased. Chace Bridger Yellow Cloud made no claims on her time. He was obviously used to being alone far more than she had ever been. Sometimes, it seemed as if he hardly knew she was there.

He hunted small game, always in the vicinity, always with the bow. Once she asked to hold the bow, just to see what it was like. When she pulled back, nothing happened. The bow was strung so tight it didn't give an inch. She stared at him. How anyone managed to shoot anything with it, she couldn't begin to understand. If that had been her only means of acquiring food, she'd have starved within days. And yet he continued to quietly bring in quail, ducks, once four rabbits from a hollow tree, once, definitely by luck, she said and he denied it, a gorgeous pheasant.

She watched him draw on a doe and fawn coming to water far up across the creek. Then he slowly released the bow and lowered it. "I hope I don't regret that," he said to no one. Charlotte realized that not only was he more alone than she, but he thought about the immediate future more, always calculating.

While he dwelt necessarily on survival, Charlotte took the only chance she might ever have to concentrate on pure pleasure. She retrieved the tin oven from the wagon and baked yeast bread, the heavenly aroma wafting off into the trees. She loved having the time to prepare it, to mix, knead, allow it to rise, be punched down and then rise again. Surprisingly, Chace ate it without complaint and she wondered what he was thinking since the distance between fresh-baked bread and years-old dried buffalo meat was about halfway around the earth.

She sat under a tree and read books, some familiar, some she'd never heard of and wondered where and how her father had acquired them. And even more puzzling, why he'd given them to her. Again, it was clear in those desperate days he was hardly thinking at all, in survival mode himself on her behalf. When she got tired of reading, she sewed. When she got tired of sewing, she brushed the horses. With time still left, she lay back luxuriously and simply gazed up into the branches. She found herself sighing with contentment, all the while questioning how this was possible.

She found out then that it wasn't possible. She woke screaming again in the night. Despite her every effort, the dream only kept growing more vivid with time. She saw his face, felt the kick of the gun and the warm blood pooling on the floor. She couldn't get air, couldn't breathe.

Chace was instantly there. "Come out," he said. She was shaking too hard to speak. "Charlotte." It was the first time he had ever used her name. "You can't stay in there like that."

"I'm all right," she said in a halting voice.

"I hate to say this, but if you don't come out, I'm coming in and dragging you out."

She struggled to sit up. "Why?" Reeling, she pressed her hands against her eyes. It was still all there. She shuddered, her stomach turning. She couldn't keep doing this. She had to make it stop.

"You need to sleep out here tonight."

"Why?" she said again. She felt so confused.

"You just do. Think about what you need and bring it. Now."

She wiped at her face and tried to get her mind to work. Why was he doing this? She gathered up a shirt, a blanket, the velvet coat. That was all. Slowly she stood up and took the two steps that brought her to the back of the wagon. He reached up for what she was carrying, then waited while she climbed out. He dug into the wagon behind her for her saddle.

The night was very dark and warm but the cold inside her had returned and she was shivering. He wrapped the blanket around her.

"Are you going to be sick?"

She shook her head no. She wouldn't. She refused

"I've got water anyway. Drink some." He held out the jar. "The fire's gone out but I'll get another blanket. You'll be warm soon enough."

"I don't think so," she said, trembling.

"You will."

Chace carried her saddle over and set it down next to his. He brought the second blanket and laid it on the ground. As he watched, she arranged the velvet coat over the saddle. "Lie down," he said. She did, pulling both blankets tight around her. He lay down next to her wrapped in his own blanket. "I'm here," he said. "I won't go to sleep until you do and I won't get up till you're awake."

"All right." She turned away from him and curled into a ball. Now the tears were coming. "Are you still here?" He moved closer until his arm touched against her back. "Thank you." She closed her eyes.

17

Chace kept his gray horse alongside as they traveled.

Charlotte, holding the team in line, let out a shaky breath. "It'll never go away from me, you know."

"With time everything goes away, the things that should, the things that shouldn't." He glanced out at the horizon. "Today's a better day for traveling than sitting."

In the afternoon, Charlotte couldn't face saddling her horse so they rode on the wagon together. The air grew humid and a haze covered the sun. A family of shiny black crows set up an ear-splitting racket in the branches of a dead tree. Cicadas hummed in the nodding grasses.

"Do you want to talk?" he said.

"I don't think so," she said.

"Not about anything?"

"Like what?"

"I don't know," he said. "Pick something."

She tried to smile. "I thought you had a subject in mind."

"No. I can go for months without talking."

"I'm sure that's true." He'd rolled back the sleeves of his shirt and she liked to watch his hands on the reins. She reached out and touched one of the silver bracelets that fit close on his wrist. "I should have things so beautiful."

"Warriors are raised to have no fear, but also to wear what makes them stand out. They're proud."

"Then you need more."

"I had more, shells and beads and bear claws and feathers."

"I would give anything…"

"That's done and gone. All of it."

"But the ones on their way to Washington?"

"They'll be in their finest, everything they own. The old ones, that's who they are."

She reached up and touched the silver at his ear. "Did you ever wear anything other than hoops?" she said, and then she did smile. She was having a conversation with him about jewelry.

"I wore many things once. It's the way of the hunter, the warrior, how they dress and paint themselves, the importance of each design, each item worn, fur, a feather, a bone, a quill, where it came from, which animal or plant, the colors used and the sacred meanings behind them. The ancestors say how it should be."

No white man could possibly understand this, Charlotte thought. But the silver seemed a natural part of him, a flash of reflected light against the warmth of his skin and the unevenly cut midnight black hair. She reluctantly took her eyes away. Time to change the subject.

"Did you get gifts?"

"For wearing feathers?"

"No, I mean when you were a child. On a birthday or anything?"

"Not exactly like that but if you're asking did people give you things, yes."

"What's your favorite thing as a child that you were given?"

"I don't even have to think about it. My first bow, when I was four. My first pony, when I was six. As a boy in a tribe, those were the only two things you needed in the world and to have them made you very happy."

"Four?"

"When it would mean everything to you, be your whole life, it could never be too early."

"It was very serious then."

"In that way, yes it was."

"I don't have anything like that," she said, "but do you want to hear what my favorite gift was?"

"Sure."

"I don't think so."

"If you want to talk, I'll listen."

"Everyone had to have a horse so I'd get that anyway. But back before the Second Migration, when we had money but there were also sometimes ways to spend it, my father bought me a doll that I'd wanted ever since I could remember. It was called an Elizabeth doll and she had a china head and a little red mouth and blue eyes that opened and closed and patent leather shoes and a lace dress that came from Paris."

Chace hesitated.

"I don't know what to say."

"And she sat at the table with us," Charlotte finished. "Didn't the girls of your people have dolls?"

"Cornstalk dolls or stuffed heads on sticks and they didn't sit at tables." Then he was suddenly different.

"Charlotte," he said quietly. "Stay still. Don't be afraid, but we're going to have company." The rifle was always beside him when he rode in the wagon. "I need you to reach back and get the Colt. Keep it with you but out of sight."

Then they traveled so long in silence that she began to wonder what he was talking about. Suddenly three members of the tribes on horseback seemed to materialize like a mirage out of the tall grasses. They appeared to be merely curious, but were as fully armed as Chace Yellow Cloud had been the first time she'd seen him.

"Fox," he said. "We're lucky for that." He reined in the team.

The three sat abreast, talking amongst themselves and seemingly discussing what they saw before them. Though she hadn't thought of it in days, Charlotte became acutely aware again of her appearance. She watched their reaction as Chace began speaking to them in his strange language. A lengthy conversation ensued, interspersed with private consultations among the three, possibly a communications issue, Charlotte thought, wondering how one strange language could fit together with another strange language. She noted the quiet certainty in Chace's tone of voice, the calm he maintained that carried with it no hint of concern or threat.

Though he never turned her way, she understood that he was speaking to her. "They want to know if you're armed. I told them you were. So slowly bring up the Colt, but don't aim it anywhere near them."

"Oh my God," Charlotte said, but she did as he'd asked. She lifted the heavy pistol with two hands and pointed it far off on the other side of the trail.

More animated conversation ensued this time. Some of it at least sounded appreciative and she remembered Chace's reaction to the gun.

"They want you to shoot it. Can you do that?"

"I think so." She straightened, tried to steady herself, squinted and fired out into the trees.

"Again."

"There's no way I can aim this thing."

"There's nothing out there, don't worry about it."

She fired off three more rapid shots and thought the Indians were going to fall off their horses. Then with trembling hands she carefully lowered the gun till it was between her knees and pointing at the floor of the wagon.

More discussion followed, a back and forth that seemed far more involved. Charlotte's concern deepened.

"I'm going to put my hand on you," Chace said evenly, still not looking at her. "Don't jump when I do."

"I won't."

He laid his hand easily on her thigh and continued the conversation. Then suddenly they laughed, wheeled their horses around and were gone.

Charlotte pressed her hands to her heart. "Thank heaven," she said. "Who were they?"

"The Fox nation was peaceful anyway but now it's mostly broken. They're braves cut loose. Just wandering."

"And you know their language?"

"Not well. But enough."

"What did they want?"

"They wanted you. They offered three horses. I told them I'd paid fifteen and you were worth at least twenty."

Charlotte stared at him. "You can't be serious."

"Did you want me to sell you for three horses?"

"What if they come back with twenty?"

"They don't have enough food to eat, let alone twenty horses."

She shuddered. "That's horrifying," she said, not daring to think what would have happened if he hadn't been there.

<>

When they stopped for the day, Chace chose to be careful.

"I'll sleep now," he said, "and get up in a while. It's probably good to keep a watch tonight."

"You're thinking they'll come back."

"I'm thinking they're off in some other direction and a day's worth of riding away, but I'm going to act otherwise."

He lay down wrapped in his blanket and was instantly dead to the world, leaving Charlotte to eat alone. She sat by the fire, the rifle at her side. She considered briefly the fantastic notion that she was for this brief moment in time keeping watch over him, keeping him safe, though she imagined he knew in his sleep who was or wasn't out in the bushes in a ten-mile radius.

As the sun sank and the daylight faded, she returned to the place she'd been those several weeks ago, alone on the prairie. A barn owl's rasping call issued from a tree nearby. Skimming forms again claimed the dusk sky and she still didn't know whether they were bats or nighthawks. The image came unbidden to her of her father alone in his house with his books and all his weighty burdens. What he'd planned was surely hard enough for him to live with. She hated to think what his reaction would be if he knew where she was, and that an attempt had been made to purchase her for three horses.

Chace woke almost exactly when the first stars appeared. Charlotte handed him a plate of beans and rice. He ate in a hurry.

"I'm just going to ride some ways out, listen for a while."

Ride some ways out. What did that even mean? "I'll be anxious till you get back."

"Understood." Then he was on his horse and gone. Charlotte sat away from the fire with her back against a tree and the rifle across her knees. As she watched, something that might have been a possum ambled out into the firelight sniffing. If it had any possibility as dinner, she knew she should shoot, but that would be all Chace needed. "Shoo," she said, and threw sticks till whatever it was thought better of the whole situation and retreated.

Come back, she kept saying, her mind focused on only one person. Please come back.

He slipped back quietly into the firelight.

"That was long," she said.

"Had to be. Nothing out there. You can go to sleep now."

Charlotte's glance took in the wagon. "We still have our agreement, don't we?"

"That won't change."

The makings of a bed were simple, saddle, blanket, velvet coat, person of the tribes.

18

When all was as it should be, uneventful and undisturbed, still Chace wanted to keep moving. At midday, they stopped, rested the horses and ate a cold meal in silence. In the afternoon, Chace tied the gray to the back of the wagon and took the reins. Charlotte rode up ahead, gazing out over the prairie. How desolate it would be to live out here with no one around in any direction for hundreds of miles. Then abruptly she reined in the mare. She squinted, trying to make certain of what she was seeing. Chace had stopped the wagon behind her.

"It's a house," she said. "How can that even be?" She scanned the outlines more closely. No smoke coming from the chimney. No visible signs of people anywhere. The only sound was the wind moving through the grass. Chace had relaxed into an alert watchfulness.

"Tie up the mare and take the wagon," he said. "I just don't want to come up on anybody unexpected." Or worse, she knew. Find something she shouldn't see.

He rode the gray slowly up the track and into the yard, a rifle resting across his lap, a sign that he was armed but not looking for trouble. He led his horse even more slowly around the house, down to the creek, then around the barn. Finally, he dismounted and knocked at the door.

No one answered the knock. No sounds issued from inside. He tried the door. It was securely latched but not locked and swung silently open. The cabin was empty, only a thin layer of dust on the floor. No furniture or belongings, but no evidence that there'd been trouble here either.

He went out to the barn. It too was empty though there was still straw in the stalls and water in the trough.

"There's no one?" He nodded and she flicked the reins to move the wagon up into the clearing. She got down and stood staring at the house, mystified.

It was a perfect log cabin, thoughtfully sited, handsomely built, with strong chinked walls and even windows paned with glass. The barn held the same carefully considered dimensions and tight construction.

The enormity of such a life broke over her. Who built this house? The Family were brave but they had each other. Out here settlers would be completely alone.

"That plowed field has crops started," she said. "That means they were here not that long ago, doesn't it? How strange. Who were they? Why did they leave?"

He'd left the door open. Charlotte went inside. She ran her hand slowly over the rock fireplace, stooped to sift the ash in the hearth, felt the smooth-planked floor. She sat on the wooden bed frame built into one corner. Another just like it occupied the opposite corner. Two men? Or parents on one side, children on the other? What kind of parents? Hearty, she decided, strong, unafraid. Assuming the father had built the cabin, she saw him as a determined man with good hands. And the wife? Like all the women she knew, burdened but resilient, still able to find occasions to laugh.

She came back out. Chace was waiting. She walked over to the broad cleared field. Hardly anything was more than ankle-high, corn, beans, potatoes, peppers. She knew the seeds or cuttings for those had once traveled a long way, zealously guarded, more precious than gold. Now, the birds and various passing animals would get the entire crop.

"I'll bet they had a cow. And chickens. And a dog. And I think there were children, so maybe a pony." She was daydreaming up an entire family and how they lived.

"We could stay a while if you want. We're getting closer."

Closer. She focused on the barn. "Real shelter for the horses. They'd hardly know what to do with it."

"After all the brushing and oats I think they'd have their minds turned in that direction anyway and it wouldn't be hard to figure out." She knew he was still unhappy that she hadn't listened to him and had fed the last of the oats to his horse as well as hers. "Rain's another consideration. Coming soon."

"It's good with you, then?"

"But not to sleep in the house, if that's what you were thinking." She quietly noted the continuing thought that wherever they slept, it would be together. "Staying with the horses is the thing."

Charlotte nodded. "I wouldn't want to sleep in that house. It'd give me the shivers."

Charlotte watered the horses and led them to stalls. She stood up in the loft and threw down armfuls of sweet hay. "So upsetting," she called down to him. "Poor well-fed horses."

Returning to the wagon, she laid India rubber sheets over the books and ammunition as her father had always done, and tied down more sheets over the wagon top, knowing they wouldn't hold forever. Storms were familiar to her. On the Second Migration, it seemed as if the rain never stopped. The sky is weeping for us, the women had said.

Before the sky wept for her, Charlotte meant to collect firewood. Chace took out his bow.

"What are you going to do?" she said.

"I'm going to shoot my horse to put him out of his misery."

"What are you actually going to do?"

"Go down to the creek. Fish rise in the rain." Drops had already started to fall.

Charlotte gathered all the deadfall she could find and carried it into the house. She stacked the wood in the fireplace, lit kindling and dried grasses underneath it, brought in the pan and tin plates, left the front door open and sat with her back against the wall waiting. The rain began to fall in earnest, not torrential yet but whipped along in spirals by the wind. She could already see the rubber sheets straining at their holds. The white canvas was well-oiled. It would stay waterproof for at least a while.

Though she knew she'd made them up, the family was there by the fire with her, the practical father stitching leather for harnesses,

103

the mother in an apron darning socks, obedient children, a girl and boy like Ada and Brewster lying on their stomachs reading books.

What would they eat? Porridge. Stewed fruit. Salt bread. Rabbit. Quail. Beef maybe if a trader ever happened by. Then she remembered. Fish.

"You do not disappoint," she said as Chace appeared with a brace of trout.

"I try not to. Disappointment's never exactly my intention."

"Did you fall in again?" He was soaked.

He glanced out the door. The rain was coming down harder now. "I might as well have."

She fried up the trout with wild onion and watercress from the creek bank. They ate sitting on the floor in front of the fire while rain lashed the windowpanes.

Back in the barn, with the sky darkening and the light prematurely fading, Charlotte cleared a square of hard-packed earth and lit the oil lamp.

"What now?" Chace said. "I'm not crazy about the expression on your face."

She held out her hand. In it was a deck of cards.

"Do you know anything about these?" she said.

"Maybe," he said.

"Really? From where?"

"From when, not where. From when I was a soldier."

She nearly dropped the cards. "You were a *soldier*?"

He nodded. "With Ellis. Scout, interpreter, whatever they needed."

"Because Chace Bridger Yellow Cloud knows the white man. I can't imagine you as a soldier."

"When I'm with Ellis, it's easy. When I'm not, that's a world away."

She spread out a blanket. "Would you play?"

"I told you, I don't disappoint," he said and sat down with her.

"So what card games do you know?"

"Probably all of them that you know."

104

She glanced up from shuffling the deck. "You're pretty sure of yourself, but that won't get you very far because I only know one."

"Which is?"

"Poker."

"What kind of poker?"

"All kinds. But just for fun, with as many things wild as possible."

A pained look crossed his face. "Deuces?"

"Plus one-eyed jacks and king-with-the-ax. That's just for starters."

"No, that's more than enough. What do you want to play for?"

"Well, you don't have any money so that won't work. I wish it was acorn season. How about pieces of straw?"

"You realize that straw's all there is here, a whole barn full of it, so we've both won already."

"Right. But that won't stop us. And there's the double-ace flush rule, right?" He shook his head.

They played several hands before he stopped her.

"Either you don't know the rules or you're choosing not to play by them," he said. "That hand isn't worth anything."

"I have this king-with-the-ax."

"Yes and it still isn't worth anything, no matter what you call your king-with-the-ax."

"Maybe I'm setting you up."

"Maybe you are, but I doubt it."

"Go ahead and doubt it all you want." She then beat him four hands in a row, using the wild cards in devious ways, making a neat collection of pieces of straw.

He took the deck from her. "Let's play something else," he said.

"Something I don't know so you can win?"

"A game better suited to the situation."

"Which is?"

"Two people, one of whom is a ringer."

"What's a ringer?"

He let his eyes rest on her. "You've never played a real game of stakes poker, have you?"

"No. What's your new game?"

"What did you do? Play poker by yourself? I don't think that's possible, is it?"

"No comment," she said. Why go there? It wasn't worth it. "The new game, please."

"Blackjack." He taught her how to play it. She caught on quickly. "If you're set on not going out to the desert you could probably become a professional card player. You've already got the Colt which would be the other requirement."

"I don't want to talk about the desert. I'm pretending it doesn't exist, remember?" She was quiet for a moment. "But I want to tell you one more awful thing and then I'm done forever with awful things."

"Go ahead."

"I got five lashes for playing cards."

"Why?"

"Because cards are forbidden. They're frivolous, a mindless distraction when we're supposed to stay pure and focused."

"Seriously, were you playing by yourself?"

"No, with a group of boys, which made it even worse. They got six lashes. I was a trial for my father every time he turned around."

"He's not the one I feel for," Chace said. He waited. "I got ten for stealing a pig."

"We were raised by the same people."

"No, it was the missionaries. It was their pig. But we were very hungry."

Charlotte put down her cards. "We both know what it feels like then," she said heatedly. "Not what someone should ever think to visit on a child." Then she lightened. "But how exactly do you go about stealing a pig? Wouldn't that be hard?"

"It was hard, don't ever try it. They make all these horrible noises and they're slippery and fast. I felt like I deserved that pig after what I went through to get it."

"I'm trying hard not to laugh. I've got a very detailed picture in my mind." The image quickly faded from the pig back to the ten lashes. "What's *wrong* with people?" she said.

They kept playing but now Chace had gone quiet.

"There's something I don't understand," he said.

"What is it?"

"Who is your father? Who is this man called Samuel Duchesne?"

"If you really want to know, I'll try and tell you." She hesitated, thinking about how to explain it. "I'll start with my grandfather," she said, "my father's father, his name was Wallace. Back east a long time ago, he and three friends were out hunting when they came up on what they called the Others. All four saw them but the Others would only speak to Wallace. They told him they'd come from an important place very far away, but this wasn't the first time they'd been here. They said he should call his people the Family and keep them prepared for the next time they came, when they wouldn't be leaving again, they would stay and this would be their home. My grandfather said he understood their language because they'd been in his dreams. My father's never seen them, but they talk to him all the time and he understands their language too, though he's the only one who does. So in public we're the Family, but in private we're called the Church of the Brothers of Ezekiel. Wallace was the Founder and First Elder and when he died, Samuel took his place.

"The Family considers it a great privilege and honor that they've been chosen this way," she continued, "and they believe that we'll be prosperous and successful all our lives because we're connected to the Others, because they watch over us. Not everyone feels that this is a rational way of thinking or even has kind feelings for a group who would hold such ideas, which is why we've been driven out of the places we lived and five years ago my father had to find another one in the wilderness where no one had ever heard of us. He takes his responsibilities to the Family and to the Others very seriously.

107

"That's not everything, but maybe it's enough for now. I know it might not make any sense to you, but in every way down to his bones that's who he is."

"Does your father always say who someone marries?"

"No. That's just for me."

"Why?"

She turned away. It was a hard thing to talk about. "Because he needs an heir, someone to pass the understanding on to. And the father of that heir should have the right history, come from the right lineage."

"This person you shot had the right history?"

"Yes, he did. Which obviously meant nothing."

"And the one out in the desert?"

"I don't know. Father didn't tell me."

"So one of the strange things the Church of the Brothers of Ezekiel believes in is flogging and hanging their women?"

Charlotte concentrated on her hands. The cards blurred. "Please don't make me cry. I've done too much of that already."

She put down the cards and got to her feet. The barn doors were open enough for fresh air to get in.

"Where are you going?" Chace said.

"Just out." It wasn't a reasonable thing to do, but she needed it. The wind had let up but the rain was pouring down. The night was warm, the sky black.

She only went far enough to be in the open, to stand unhindered in the rain and let it run down her upturned face so that she wouldn't have to think about anything but being alone and drenched on the prairie, far away from anyone and anything that had to do with all of that.

He stood with a hand on either side of the door watching her.

"Are you sure you're happier out here?"

"You can't cry in the rain. For some reason it doesn't work. Come out and join me."

"Some of us are crazy and some of us aren't. I just don't want you to drown."

"If I said please?"

"My people never go out on moonless nights."

"I'll forget for a minute that there's a lantern lighting up the whole place. What's wrong with moonless nights?"

"On a raid, you can trip, lose your way, lose your horses, run into somebody you didn't want to run into. It's asking for trouble."

"And who wants that."

"Exactly."

"You're already drenched anyway, you know." It was true. He was still wet from the creek and now the rain slanted against him with the overhang of the barn roof offering no protection.

"I'm used to it. I'll wait you out."

"Your loss," she said and turned her face back to the sky. She found herself grateful just to be there, in the downpour, with the ghost family and the barn and the horses and someone who hadn't taken the money, had nothing to do with the Family, was willing to let their journey take almost forever.

She turned toward him again. It didn't take many wet barefoot steps to reach him.

"I'm going to put my hands on you," she said. "Don't jump when I do." She pressed her palms against him and bent her face into his wet shirt.

"Just for a minute." But it was longer than that. When she lifted her head and stepped back, their damp clothing pulled slowly apart.

"Thank you," she said.

He said nothing.

In the barn, Charlotte wiped her face and shook out her hair, water spraying off in every direction.

"I had visions of sleeping in the loft," she said.

"There'll be rats," he said, recovering his voice.

"But the stalls smell like cow and that's not inviting either."

Chace tested the packed dirt floor of the barn. "Put down enough straw here at the back and nobody could ask for more."

Charlotte's clothes hung on her like wet rags. "I think there's probably somebody somewhere used to sleeping in a canopy bed on a feather mattress with satin sheets and fourteen layers of down quilts who might ask for more, but not me. If this very fine straw is what you're offering, guess what, I'm taking it."

He spread straw in a thick layer and she shook several blankets out over it. He set the saddles down and held out her velvet coat.

"You remembered. We've been together too long."

"Seems like years."

"That's terrible. Should I go and put out the lamp? It'll be pitch black."

"Pitch black's better than burned down."

"Good thought." Carefully she blew out the lamp by the door and then couldn't see anything. "Keep talking so I can find you."

"I'll tell you a Creation story," he said.

"You will?"

"No. It takes two days. You said to just keep talking."

She was feeling along the floor with her bare feet. "Say one more unhelpful thing and that'll get me there."

"I don't know anything that's unhelpful."

Her toes reached the blanket. "Fine. That's over. Remind me not to hire you as a scout." She could hear him moving. "What are you doing?"

"Can't sleep in this shirt, it's making everything else wet," he said into the darkness. "Now I'm asking you the same question."

"Like you. Some layers anyway. Too bad all of them are wet." She felt her way to the nearest stall and draped her shirt and skirt over it. That left her with petticoats clinging to her legs, a damp uncomfortable camisole and gratitude for the pitch black night.

Charlotte lay down and wrapped up in her blanket. The horses shifted, snorting now and then. Rain pounded on the roof. The wind had come up again and whistled through the opening in the doors. She listened more carefully to something scurrying and considered how much she didn't want it to be a rat.

"Are you asleep?" she said over her shoulder.

"No. Are you?"

"Smart-mouthed members of the tribes. Who needs them?"

"You do," he said.

"That's true." For the first time, she violated their unspoken rules. She turned toward him, the blanket falling away. She felt him go quiet. "I won't touch you," she said, which wasn't true, her feet were on his, "but I'm asking if you'd touch me, just once."

"You can't say things like that."

"Yes I can. I just did."

"I don't even believe in that place where people burn forever in the fire, but one of us is headed there."

"It's only touching."

"There is no such thing."

"I'm good at preventing disasters. What's that sound? Are you choking?"

"Yes, I'm choking."

"Is that your answer?"

The silence had a current running through it. "No," he said. She sensed him turn and reach for her. In the dark, he found her shoulder. Slowly, he ran his hand down her bare arm, closing at the end over her wrist, staying there. Her breath caught in her throat. His hand traveled back up the length of her arm, over the curve of her shoulder, hesitating at the lacy strap of the camisole. His fingers slid under the lace and stayed there as if he was thinking something. With a word that might have been a curse, he took his hand away. She waited, silently willing him to continue. He found her again, gently touching her brow, the curve of her bruised cheekbone…"Does it hurt?" he said, "No," she whispered…the healing line of her jaw, "Here?" "No."…stopping at her mouth. He traced his fingers back and forth over her lips. She was in a trance, as still as stone.

Awakening, she moved her hands to the front of the camisole to undo it. Not hesitating for a second, he brought his hand down to cover hers, stopping her.

"No. Forget this ever happened. I need to learn. When you're safe somewhere…"

She gave a harsh laugh. "Safe. There's a word."

He started over. "When you're safe somewhere, I'll be gone."

"To where?"

"Very far away. That's nothing to do with you and everything to do with me. You have to know that."

"Seeing how you are, I think I always knew." She curled up with her knees against him and he went quiet again. "Not to make an argument," she said softly, "but how many chances do you think I'll have for happiness in my life? I'll tell you what I think. None. Except right here, right now."

"I can't let anything happen to you," he said. "Ever."

She waited again, unwilling to move, wanting to hold onto the moment. Finally, she pulled the blanket back up around her and turned away. She could sense only a deep and unsettled stillness behind her.

"Just understand that nothing will ever be your fault."

"That's your way of looking at it."

"Are you going to sleep now?"

"No, but I can't tell you how much I wish you would."

"You'll still be here?"

"I'll always be here."

"Until you're not."

"You couldn't make this more difficult if you tried," he said.

"I don't know about that," she said. "Let me sleep on it."

19

The rain held through the morning, turning all the dust into mud. In the afternoon, when the sun came out, Charlotte climbed into the wagon to inspect the damage. The outside rubber sheets had mostly blown off and were plastered against the side of the barn. The inside ones had done their job. The clothes hung on pegs were wet, the blankets left on the bed, the velvet-lined box holding her grandmother's silver, but those would all survive. The book crates were dry. She mopped up the water on the floorboards and took a cloth to everything else that was damp. The foodstuffs were preserved, that was the most important thing. She knew the uselessness of wet flour.

Chace had disappeared, though she now trusted that he was always within shouting distance. He approached her in the middle of the afternoon carrying something small, but oddly with just the ends of his fingers. He held it up.

"Do you know what this is?" he said.

She shrieked. "Do you know what that is?"

"I just asked you."

"That is a crawfish. Where did you find it?"

"The creek bank's crawling with them. They must've been flushed out by the storm."

"Show me. Though I don't know whether you'd favor them or not. We'll see."

The creek had risen in its banks, the water churning with fallen branches and debris.

"Here," Chace said.

The muddy oozing bank was alive with crawfish. "Are you afraid of them?" He looked at her. "Never mind. I forgot who I was talking to." Quickly, she ran and got a bucket from the wagon.

"Can you stand in the creek?"

"Sure, why not? I'll be wet for the rest of my life." He climbed down the bank.

"Dump as many as you can get in here." It wasn't hard. "Then it just needs to be tipped over a couple times to rinse and drain them."

With that accomplished, Chace climbed back out of the creek.

"Are these dinner?" he said. "Hope they're worth it."

"That's what I don't know. Whether you'll think so or not."

Charlotte built a fire in the cabin and set water to boiling in the Dutch oven.

"I need a cow."

"To cook crawfish?"

"For butter. Wait," she said suddenly. "Maybe I still have some." She ran back to the wagon and rummaged in the sack of flour. There it was, buried deep, still floating in its jar of water. When the water boiled in the pot, she dropped the crawfish in, counting the seconds.

"Now I have to dump them out. Well, actually, you do."

He used her heavy folded cloths to lift the Dutch oven from the fire, then stood back outside as the boiling water splattered into gullies in the already muddy ground. Charlotte showed him how to eat one, twisting off the head, pulling off the tail, removing the white sweet flesh with her fingers and dipping it into the melted butter.

"So good," she said. "Is all that taking apart too much for you?"

"On buffalo hunts the youngest ones ate slices of the raw liver while it was still steaming. When there was hunger we ate grubs. So no." He did as she had done, dipped the contents in butter and slowly put it in his mouth.

She couldn't read his face. "What do you think?"

"Better than buffalo's liver. Probably more like oats would be for a horse that hadn't ever had them before."

She smiled. "Are you serious?"

"It was worth it," he said and reached for another crawfish.

<>

They decided to stay at the cabin until they got tired of being there.

"How far?" Charlotte said. "I can't keep pretending forever. I suppose I need to know the truth."

"Not all that far. You don't have to think about it right now. But we sleep outside."

"Why?"

"There are guns and ammunition in that wagon. And it's better protection for the horses." And that other reason, she thought.

Charlotte fell back into the rhythm of their days, time slowing down to the arc of the sun across the sky and each night's phase of the rising new moon. She took a broom and swept the dust off the cabin floor, then set up her meager kitchen, the Dutch oven, frying pan and knives. She brought in two crates of books, set her cutting board across them and called it a table, though the chairs were still the hard wooden floor. She washed clothes in the creek once it calmed, even asking Chace for his shirt. He gave it to her then quickly pulled another faded one from his saddlebags and put it on.

Every day she gathered firewood and foraged in the vegetation by the creek. When she found wild plums, she made plum bread. She made corn cakes, roasted quail wrapped in bacon, chopped peppers and fried ham with beans, simmered rabbit stew till the meat fell off the bone.

Chace left her entirely for a part of one day to ride far off and fire the Spencer. He came back subdued.

"It's not good?" she said.

"It's too good." He narrowed his eyes, staring out at the horizon. "My people never stood a chance," he said to no one.

She got out the cards at every opportunity. He taught her faro and casino. In return for being forced to learn these games, she demanded the right every now and then to play poker with anything wild that she wanted. Those games made her laugh so hard she almost fell over.

Outside, they played for twigs. "I have more twigs than you'll ever have," she said.

"And then what? What are you going to do with all those twigs?"

115

"Build my very own forest and stay in it." She turned quickly away from that thought and onto another one.

"Is that how you speak English better than people who speak English? From being a soldier with Ellis and playing cards?"

"What brought that up?"

"From not wanting to talk about living alone in my own forest."

"I knew English long before I was a soldier."

"Then how did you learn it so well? I about lost my mind that first day when I saw you. I expected you'd shoot me and you just kept talking and using all those words."

"I never figured that out," he said. "Why would I shoot you?"

"I don't know. Because you wanted the horses?"

"I hadn't even thought about the horses. How you were, that was enough to think about. But to answer your question, the trapper taught me English."

"The one with your name?"

"Him. He lived as part of the tribe, that was common. He came and went, brought food and trade goods, shared what he had. I meant something to him so he had to make good on his promise. There was confusion at first because he was teaching me French, but then we got the right language.

"After that, when my people went in and out of the agencies, I was the one who could talk to the soldiers, the missionaries, beg for food. At the gathering of the tribes every year where the traders would be, I could speak for my people. I went to Washington City the first time with my grandfather because of the English. I became a soldier because of the English."

"So he was right. His name made a difference in how your life went."

"He made a difference in how my life went." There was a long pause. "He took my wife."

She searched his face, not understanding. "Your wife?"

"We'd been promised to each other since childhood. And he wasn't so old as he seemed. None of that matters. It was his right as a member of the tribe. It was her right to agree to it. I wasn't there."

"But you *had* to leave, didn't you?"

"That doesn't matter either."

She waited, watching him. "There's more." She knew him in this way if no other.

"We had a son."

"Oh please, no," she said, staring at him. "Where is he now?"

Chace took his time with it. "He was small. And he's dead. They're all dead. Even Chace Bridger."

"Chace," she said softly. "What on earth." What were they to each other? A convenience turned into a necessity that had become this never-ending pain.

"How did they die?" Her voice was only a whisper.

"After this, there is no more," he said. "Ellis's wife? She was my sister. She came home to our people thinking it would be for the birth of her child. They all died the same way." She knew now what so often brought the trouble to his eyes. She tried to hold back the tears but they spilled over. "I want to show you where, it's on the way. Almost from the beginning I've wanted to do that because I saw that you would understand."

"I hurt for you."

"Don't. It's not worth it."

"I'm grateful that you told me." She wiped her face on her sleeve. "I'm glad we're here in this peaceful place. I'm glad we have this. Tell me nothing will change between us, not until it has to."

"Nothing will change."

<>

Charlotte placed the saddles under the tree the same way they always did. But she couldn't imagine, on this one night, turning her back on him. She calmed herself, checked that her shirt was buttoned up to the neck, all the petticoats in place, nothing showing anywhere. He was already rolled in his blanket, lying on his back, eyes closed. She lay down beside him. Sensing her breathing coming from the wrong direction, he opened his eyes.

She put her arm across him. "Just for tonight," she said. "I promise no one's asking for trouble, just…"

After the briefest hesitation, he unfolded his arms and opened the blanket. She crawled over the edge and into it, close against him. He pulled the blanket back around both of them. She fell asleep listening to the night sounds and the slow steady beating of his heart.

20

The morning felt somber. From the temperature already, Charlotte knew the day would be hot. The horses grazed peaceably. She went down to the creek and washed her clothes, also using the privacy to wash herself as she did every morning. She didn't allow herself to think of an actual bathing tub filled to the brim with steaming hot water, or how it would feel to soak in it up to her neck.

How did Ada's mother do it, she wondered, taking care of five children's dirty clothes? She guessed that's why a mother wanted girls and a father wanted boys, each greedy for more help with their own large set of chores. On the Second Migration, the women to whom slovenliness was a sin would even, after all the scrubbing and rinsing, heat up their iron in the fire and press out the wrinkles on aprons and dresses. And then it would rain again, making a mockery of all that work. Not that that had any bearing on the matter. Work was a way to stay pure and focused.

Charlotte listened to a mockingbird in the highest branches of a nearby cottonwood running through its repertoire of fifteen different songs, all of them stolen. She eyed the hawk drifting in lazy circles and wondered if hawks ate mockingbirds. If one of those mindless birds happened to take up residence for the night, she knew from experience that sleep would be hard to come by. Their love of their own voice contained within it no reasonable set of hours, daylight or dark. A doe and fawn stepped out delicately from the thick brush upstream. She wondered if these were the ones Chace had spared.

He was there when she carried her wet garments back to the wagon. She studied his face but could find nothing different than any other day.

"Are you all right?" he said.

"Yes. Are you?"

He nodded and she knew they would talk no more about it.

"Ducks," he said, holding up a pair.

"I see, but what I want to know is what's that thing in your other hand."

He lifted it up by the long thin curling tail. Whatever it was woke from its stupor and began hissing wildly, snapping at the air with sharp pointy teeth.

"Possum. I found him in a tree. Do you cook them?"

"Some do, but not me. They're strange."

"I'll throw him back then." He went out into the brush and did just that.

The day grew hotter as the sun rose. Chace took it upon himself to pluck and singe the ducks, gut them, cut off their heads and feet. She found it almost hard to watch how expertly he handled a knife.

Charlotte sat under a tree with her book. When her skin became dewy with perspiration and the hair next to her scalp grew damp, she couldn't take it any longer.

"I have to," she said. She unbuttoned her shirt, took it off and wiped her face with it. The camisole was cover enough, just regrettably an undergarment rather than an outer garment. It wasn't as if he hadn't seen it before. He made no comment.

"Two days, I think," he said, "and then we should be moving on." She glanced up in surprise.

"Why? Are you restless? Have you had enough?" She wondered what he did when he was alone. Did he keep on the move all day every day? And if he did, then why? What was he heading toward, or away from?

"No. That's not it." He had piled the feathers on the chopping board.

"Can I have one?"

"You can have all of them."

"Just one. To keep."

"We've been here a while now," he said.

She put down the book. "That's not the answer."

"Somebody went by yesterday. Across the creek and up north some. Not close, but close enough."

"More members of the tribes wanting to buy women?"

"No, I'd say someone white, the horse had shoes. And more careful than those. Someone going slow and thinking about things. Just not thinking right yet."

"You have an opinion as to who this person might be, I'm guessing."

"The wagon train should be past Fort Randall and up into the mountains by now."

She tried to track where he was going, and then she knew. "Tobias would've got the letter."

"How well do you know him?"

"Not at all. I can hardly remember anything. That's why my going to him is so strange."

"Would he come looking for you?"

The idea seemed completely impossible. "He and my father didn't get along. He was more or less forced to come out here. I doubt he'd do anything more than he absolutely had to in that regard. And from what I remember of him, he was the kind to sit and read a book, not the kind to be chasing someone down all over the prairie, not even if it was me. Or maybe especially not if it was me."

Chace was silent for a minute and she didn't like the silence. She could beat him at cards but she was always ten steps behind when he concentrated on a problem.

"I'm just going to ask this. I'm not saying it's what I believe, not at the moment, but I need to know your thoughts on it. Would your father, having possibly heard about the letter, having possibly got a letter himself, would he be out here on his horse somewhere looking for you?"

Charlotte considered the person who had put this question to her, unsure of how she was ever going to let him go.

"My father has responsibilities. A lot of people depend on him, not only for guidance but for keeping them safe. I made this task even harder for him by what I've done. So though I know he cares about me, and would die a thousand deaths if he knew where I

121

was, because he wouldn't have any way of seeing who you are, I'll say no to that. He wouldn't come looking for me. He couldn't."

"Next question. Would he send someone else?"

"Now you're making me afraid."

"I have to think about these possibilities, but it could be something else entirely, something that has nothing to do with you or me at all. And the tracks lead out, away from here. They don't lead back or go in circles or anything. They're just careful, but so far as it is now, it's someone who passed on by and we'll take it that way."

"When will you feel like you're sure about it?" Given the situation, her father riding into the clearing out of nowhere was about as disastrous an occurrence as she could imagine.

"I'll go back out early in the evening." He worked on something. "Now that I'm thinking about it, here are these ducks but I don't want a fire going, smoke, the smell of anything cooking."

"We'll have the ducks for breakfast." She would eat grass and dried buffalo, which were about the same thing, if it would keep her father away.

<>

When it couldn't grow any hotter, the day did. Charlotte took off her skirt and all but one petticoat and threw them in the back of the wagon. "Apologies," she said again. Chace didn't ever seem to take issue with heat or cold or discomfort or to notice, at least this time maybe purposefully, what she was wearing. She took a bucket down to the creek and dumped cold water over her head. Any hotter and she would have to go in.

In the shade of the tree, she tried to concentrate on her book. Chace came and lay down beside her.

"What are you reading?"

"It's *Moby-Dick*."

"The book?"

"Yes. It's the name of a whale."

"It's a book about a whale named Moby-Dick."

"It's a whale that's been hunted, has all these harpoons stuck in him. He got back at the captain of a whaling boat who harpooned him, the captain's name is Ahab, by taking his leg and sinking his boat. Now Ahab is obsessed with getting revenge on the whale even if he destroys everybody else, his whole crew, and dies himself in order to do it."

"I'm having trouble seeing a buffalo with a lance still in his shoulder coming back for the one who stuck it in him."

"That's why it's just a book. It's hard going though."

"Seems like it would be."

"I'll read some of it to you. Do you want the beginning, the middle or the end?"

"I don't care. You choose."

"I'll start at the beginning like I have four other times." She turned back to the first page. "*Call me Ishmael*," she read.

"I thought this was about Moby-Dick. Who's Ishmael?"

"He's a young schoolteacher but he's not happy with his life, he's in a 'November of the soul' he says, and he's been out to sea before so he signs up to go out on this whaling boat but he doesn't know yet that Ahab is the captain and he's insane."

"I see, I guess."

Charlotte continued to read. Heat rose off her skin. The birds grew silent, no sparrows chittering, no hawk screeching, not even the lonely sound of a mourning dove. Cicadas kept up their rhythmic chorus that came to be one with the heavy air. When she turned the page and looked over, Chace was sound asleep.

She'd become as familiar with the smooth warm planes of his face as she was with her own face in the mirror, but now she noticed something she'd never quite thought about before. His hair. Cut at some point with a dull knife is what occurred to her that first time. Chopped off is what came to her now. *My people do it in grief,* he'd said. Tears came to her eyes again.

He startled awake and sat up. "This is what happens when you spend time with a woman. Out on raids, we bathed in ice cold streams, rode hard, slept little, ate nothing. And now look."

"Go bathe in an ice cold stream," she said.

"I just might," he said.

<>

There was no fire. The sun set and the moon rose, only the faintest sliver of white. The stars came out. Chace returned on his horse.

"No one. They've gone on, whoever they are. No tracks since yesterday afternoon. No stopping. No fires."

"And you mean it, one more day?"

"It'll have to be the last, but yes, one more day."

"You're not finished with this yet, are you?"

"One more day is for you but I also want to give that someone time to get farther along on his travels."

They went through their nightly routine. Settled in the darkness, Charlotte lay on her back gazing up at the million stars. She had made up her mind. A tiny light suddenly streaked across the sky.

"Did you see that?" she said. "A shooting star!"

There was nothing. And then she became aware of the silence. Slowly she turned on her side, the wrong side, toward him.

"All I've ever been good for," she said into the darkness, "is doing things I'm not supposed to do. You can choose whether you want to suffer for that like my father does or not." Having warned him, she reached out and took his hand. Slowly she turned it over and traced her fingers along the palm. Even more slowly, she picked up the hand and held it to her cheek, the one he'd touched before, the one another's hand had broken. She turned her face into his hand and pressed her lips there once, then again.

He had already shifted to face her. His hand went back to the softness of her cheek. He closed the space between them and kissed her mouth tenderly, gently, tasting her for the first time. He kissed her again, another gentle kiss that lingered. She moved even closer, curving into his body. He brushed his fingertips over her face, her closed eyes, ran his thumb over her mouth then down over her throat. She made a small sound.

He paused. She opened her eyes and reached out to touch his own mouth, his brow, his hair, then kissed him in the same way,

124

slow, lingering. Each kiss that followed was an exploration, some soft and sliding, some more urgent, others deep and never-ending. To know his mouth this way was all she asked. His arms went around her and she held him tight and the kisses kept coming over and over again, sweet, hungry, effortless, blotting out the stars, the night, time, fear, memory, everything.

It was minutes, hours, half the night. They surfaced, exhausted, kissed one last time, and went no further. With caution at least partially restored, they settled into a tangled embrace, the blankets pulled up around them again. Charlotte had only one thought, that she wanted this. Everything about their time together told her that he felt the same way.

21

Suddenly, when nothing was supposed to change, everything had changed. Charlotte held that idea warm inside her. She expected to feel nervous and shy. Instead, she was deeply calm.

She made corn cakes for breakfast, saving the ducks for dinner. They ate in silence.

Her first thought was to clean the cabin. She wanted to move out of it slowly, not all in a rush the following morning. She didn't want to feel as if she too were abandoning it. Who knew? Maybe she'd come back one day when everything else had fallen apart and this is where she would live.

She'd spread items out so far that it took some doing to get it all back into the wagon. Then she swept the cabin again, reaching up with the broom for cobwebs in the rafters. Not in my house you don't, she said to the spiders. Eventually, she knew, if no one claimed it, there would be birds' nests in the eaves, mice scurrying in the dark corners, damp rotting floorboards, the chimney falling in. But she didn't want to dwell on that. Instead she designed a chicken coop in her head and imagined where it would be, then a kitchen addition with a good cast iron cookstove, then a bathing alcove with a copper tub, and an outhouse and a smokehouse. Soon she'd come up with a whole compound. And who, she wondered, would be there to build it for her? She saw the chimney falling in again.

She washed clothes in the creek. Following that she brushed the horses. Following that, she didn't know what to do. Knitting, she told herself. Somewhere in the wagon was a shawl that she'd begun but the stitches were tiny, the yarn silken, and it was too frustrating. It would have to be *Moby-Dick* again.

The gray horse was gone. She waited, sitting under the tree, trying to comprehend Ahab or even Ishmael. Before the waiting turned into anxiety, Chace appeared. Her mind stopped focusing on the rifle by her side.

"Is there anything I should know about?" she said, trying to keep down all the other thoughts that came unbidden at the sight of him.

"Nothing. But I found this." He held it out.

"It's an eagle feather."

"It is."

"Where did you get it?"

"There've been two eagles feeding on a fish kill farther up the creek. I thought maybe I'd go back today to see if they were still there. They weren't but the feather was."

"Just lying there? An eagle feather doesn't show up every day of the week, you know."

"Some day you'll be a believer. Eagles are sacred to us. If I were to speak with my grandfather's words, I'd say it was meant to be there, I was meant to find it."

"Why?"

"Who knows why? I'm not my grandfather." He gave her the feather and sat down in the grass beside her.

"But he's like that?" she said.

"He has the old wisdom, what came before. He would tell you that the Great Spirit sends the eagle. Its wings provide shelter for the two-leggeds, it holds great power to protect. Life divides always into two parts that are opposites and that's the eagle feather also, black and white, then daylight and darkness, summer and winter, life and death. Most important is that one part has no meaning without the other."

"These things have been on your mind?"

"He's been on my mind. I hope he's still alive. Maybe he's the one who wants you to have the feather."

"Maybe he does. In exchange for the biscuit."

"I'm sure he's still thinking about that." He lay sideways to her, using part of her skirts as a pillow, a simple gesture, she considered, but one that held within it the shift in who they were.

"Do you want to hear more of *Moby-Dick*?" she said.

"What was his name again?"

"Ishmael. I'll read about when he meets Queequeg. That's a better part. At least I could get through it."

"How big is a whale, do you think?"

"As big as a house. More."

"Like ten buffalo? Fifteen?"

Charlotte frowned. "That's an odd way of looking at it."

"I wonder if the whale is to them what the buffalo was to us."

"Somewhere in this book it has to tell you what the whale is to them because it tells you everything else there is about whales, even things you never wanted to know." She started to read about the cannibal who had a body covered in tattoos and worshiped a small statue.

Since he was immune to the heat, it must have been the monotonous sound of her voice. It only took minutes before Chace was asleep.

<>

Charlotte built the evening fire outside, leaving the cabin to itself. She panfried the duck with dried apples.

"If you went to Oregon Territory, what would you do?" she said, and then was horrified that she'd brought it up. She was certain she hadn't been contemplating anything remotely like that.

"In the first place, I wouldn't go to Oregon Territory."

"Yes, but if you did, what would you do?" Since she'd opened up the subject, she might as well keep on with it.

"You mean if I had to raise things or grow things?"

"Like that, I guess, is what I'm saying."

"At the Agency, they taught my people how to grow corn and squash and beans, but the crops failed and none of that had anything to do with the buffalo. Grandfather tried to raise cattle, but they took away the land they'd given him and it shouldn't have mattered because none of that had anything to do with buffalo either. See if you can keep a tribe fed through the winter on grouse or stay warm in cow leather." He stopped, trying to redirect his thinking. "I saw goats once."

"Goats?"

"I'd never seen one before. On a raid when we were too young, stealing a herd of horses from a ranch, we came across the goats and no one knew what they were. Later, with the missionaries, I found out. If the buffalo were gone for good, and others depended on me, I'd maybe find an interest in goats."

Sometimes she thought she knew him, only to turn around and find out that she didn't know him at all. Goats?

"You know what I'd want to do?" she said.

"What?"

"Raise geese. I heard in Oregon they don't have the good kind of geese, just a big ugly wild duck with all the wrong feathers, so there's nothing to fill a mattress with."

"That's the strangest thing I ever heard."

"That there aren't any geese in Oregon?"

"No, that you have to have feathers to make a bed to sleep on. Do you want to go back to the buffalo? What a buffalo robe is? How many people needed them to stay warm in the winter and needed the food to keep from starving? How many carcasses were left out on the prairie to rot instead?" He stopped again. "Never mind. Forget I said anything."

"I'm sorry."

"No, I am. What's the point in taking it out on you?"

The evening had closed in. The thin crescent of moon hung low in the sky. Charlotte cleaned the plates and put out the fire. She splashed water on her face and rinsed out her mouth with water from the bucket.

"I'll be back," he said. She got the rifle out from under the wagon seat.

A softness settled over the land. A few ragged clouds sailed out of the west, catching the light of the dying sun. The sky turned pink, then rose, then gray. A meadowlark sang its evening song then quieted. What am I doing? she thought, aware of the places her mind was going. She could see her father pacing, on the edge of hysteria. The dear chosen child wanting only to be with one member of the tribes before their journey ended. And it would end, possibly sooner than she even knew, and in the way that they both understood. There was no usefulness to be had in denying it, in trying to believe otherwise.

These two possessions she would take from their time together, a duck feather for all that was simple and easy between them, and an eagle feather for what was complicated and beyond words. She would build a collection around them, though that was an offense within the Family also. She'd been doing such a thing with interesting objects since she was small, why, she didn't know. They didn't have any significance to her that she could recall, she just liked how they belonged together, but her father insisted on calling them altars and it upset him greatly. She couldn't count how many he'd taken apart, throwing away the acorns and seed pods, blue jay feathers, dead bees, birds' nests, pebbles from the river, dried flowers. Did he seriously believe that she could cause harm with such innocent constructions? She felt sadness for him sometimes on that count alone, the constant vigilance required to protect his faith.

Charlotte was aware of the explanation behind all this sudden turn of thought. If someone was out looking for her and had come from Fort Randall, how many days had he traveled? Not many, she guessed. Chace had told her they'd soon have to cross the creek and head north again. But north into what? At least there was this, the cabin, the barn, the surround of trees from which to look out on the vast prairie and either dream or despair. She was doing both.

In the gathering darkness, Charlotte took off her shirt and hung it over the back of the wagon, choosing among other reasons not to swelter through the night. Having the blanket around her was hot enough. She sat in her bare feet with the rifle across her knees, thinking nothing except as usual, where was he?

Then the big gray edged into the clearing. Chace swung down and led the horse to the creek, then into the barn. He picked up his blanket and went to lay it under the tree.

"Since it's the last time ever here," she said, "could we sleep in the barn?"

"What's the last time ever got to do with it?"

"To remember it by. Unless I come back out here to live someday, I'll never see it again."

"Don't talk like that," he said, and had to turn away. "It's hot in there."

"No hotter than out here. The doors can be wide open. The loft door's already open and there's sort of a breeze."

"It's dark."

"It's dark everywhere. It's night and not even a quarter moon. And it's more comfortable in there. I don't mind sleeping outside but every once in a while I'd like to turn over in the night and not have a rock in my back."

"We could put down straw out here."

"What? Is there something in there you're afraid of?"

"I told you, I was raised so that you can't have fear. Even if you have it, you can't have it."

"Maybe you're secretly afraid of the rats. Well, I'm not." That was a brave and totally false statement. "And I can take care of myself anyway."

"Except getting across a river in a wagon."

"Except that one small thing. Or if a wheel falls off or someone steals my horses."

"Or steals the whole wagon."

"That, too."

He had to have seen it coming, and likely also that this was how it would happen.

In the barn, they placed their saddles in the dark, then the blankets. All the night sounds were there along with the shuffling of the horses. Chace settled in the way he always did, on his back. Charlotte lay beside him wrapped in her blanket. A coyote howled and then another until there was a chorus echoing off the banks of the creek. She shivered.

"The coyotes were stealing the chickens. That's why the shotgun was at the door."

"It's behind you. Keep it there."

"Can you do that?"

"Sometimes."

"Like now?"

There was a long pause.

"Maybe like now."

"If time's short, we should make good use of what we have left," she said.

"Good use could be anything."

"It'd be what I considered good use."

"Why is that not a surprise?"

She turned to face him, her bare feet touching his. "I'm here," she said. "Where are you?"

"Lost."

"Chace?"

"What?"

"When I told you about suffering like my father does for the way I behave? There's more coming. I just wanted you to know."

She leaned in and kissed him gently. He reached up and slid his palms against her scalp beneath her chopped hair, holding her there, kissing her back. "I already knew," he said quietly. She shifted, fitting herself down the length of him. Her fingers felt for his mouth and she kissed him one more time.

"Touch me like you did before," she said softly. His hand went from her shoulder slowly down her bare arm to her wrist, lingering there. His fingers worked their way even more slowly back up the inside of her arm, across the lace strap, to her throat and then her mouth. She felt he was holding his breath the same way she was holding hers. Her hand went up between them to undo the lacing of the camisole. He moved to give her room. When the camisole came free, her hands went to his shirt, undoing it. He struggled out of it and she wrapped her arms around him, making a small sound as their skin touched everywhere. Suddenly he held her tight against him and kissed her hard, his strong hands in her hair, grasping her shoulders, traveling firmly down the smooth curve of her back. She sensed just the faintest tremor underneath his touch, lending more urgency to the kisses, taking them both to a place where there was no time but now, no dark or light, no beginning or end.

"Don't stop," she said. "Please don't stop." He didn't stop. As more clothes came off, his hands took all of her. She rose and twisted, crying out at his touch, then locked him into her embrace and kissed him wildly. He held her down, his mouth fiercely on hers, answering her wanting with his own, all thought gone. He kissed her deeply one last time and then they were moving together, going where he'd vowed they never would, to the edge and then over, in shattering free fall, taking possession of each other in the dark.

22

Charlotte climbed reluctantly up to the wagon seat. She didn't want to leave. She'd made the illusion of a home here, with him. She was still vibrating, still filled with a steady buzzing hum as if there were cicadas in her blood.

"Will we cross the creek today?"

"Tomorrow."

Before they left its banks, she would wash out her clothes one more time, fill the canvas bags with water, harvest edibles. She had searched over the crops in the field but nothing was close to ripe. The corn would be a feast for the birds and raccoons if left till the ears came in, but the squash blossoms were already withering on the vine.

At the last minute, she got back down and dug in the back of the wagon. As Chace waited, she took one of her iron fry pans into the house and set it in the fireplace.

"What was that for?" he said.

"In case someone else comes along and wants to cook and they don't have a pan."

He nodded, refraining from letting his eyes rest on the vast empty sweep of land all around them.

Without discussing it, they set up their traveling day as before. Charlotte took the reins in the morning, Chace stayed close, he took the reins in the afternoon and she rode the mare up ahead, keeping in sight. The skies were gray and a light rain fell, but only enough to cool off the horses and damp down the dust of the track.

Chace stopped early, holding back as much as he possibly could. Charlotte gathered wood and built a fire. She had the urge to bake. When Chace came back from hunting, he had squirrels.

"Lean day," he said.

"I've still got cornmeal left. I'll fry them in bacon grease. And I made honey cake."

"I don't know why the white man thought he needed all those guns. All they had to do was send you in to cook and none of the members of the tribes would be able to get up on their horses."

"It's not that bad."

"In that way, it is that bad."

In the evening, they played cards.

"I can't handle so many wild cards," he said.

"We'll get serious then."

"I already was serious."

"Five card stud," she said and he looked at her hard.

"We have to talk sometime," he said as he dealt out the first cards.

"Please not now."

"Okay, but soon."

She won three games out of four and had a pile of twigs.

"We should up the stakes. Play for branches or something. What I need is a town to be in. I imagine they don't let women into poker games but I could maybe be a dancehall girl."

"You could not be a dancehall girl. We're switching to blackjack."

"Why couldn't I? They put their hair up and wear those satiny kinds of dresses don't they? Do they dance? I could stand behind somebody and tell him what cards to play."

"They go upstairs."

"Upstairs?" What did that mean? And then it came to her and she felt herself flush with color. Then suddenly she was studying him. How did he know these things?

"Have you ever gone upstairs?"

"If I had, I wouldn't tell you."

"That's not fair. Why can't I know?"

"You just can't. That's long ago and far away from here."

She let her gaze rest on him. "You've lived about a hundred lives."

"Sometimes it feels like it. Are you playing or aren't you?"

135

After enough rounds of blackjack, when he had won back some of the twigs, they still sat at the fire.

"I've been thinking," Chace said, "and I've got questions again."

"Is this possibly about the Others?"

"It possibly is."

"I guess I expected that. What do you want to know?"

"Everything you can tell me."

There were an infinite number of other conversations she'd rather have but she felt she owed him this.

"They aren't from here."

"Where are they from?"

"My grandfather said they seemed to come from out of nowhere, as if they'd fallen from the sky. They told him the reason he'd heard them in dreams was so that he wouldn't be frightened. The last time they'd tried to come back, they felt that had happened, when they met up with Ezekiel in the desert and everything went wrong."

"What went wrong? Who's Ezekiel?"

"He's a prophet in the Bible. He thought he was seeing visions of God. He said they came in an immense cloud of lightning and fire and glowing metal, and each of them had four faces and four wings, with human parts and animal parts and wheels full of eyes. The Others told Wallace they'd never intended to make such an amazingly strange impression, that they only wanted to come as human beings and be among us."

"Be among us? What does that mean?"

"My father says they're not God, but they're from God, fallen Angels seeking redemption by restoring man's faith, and to do that, they have to become us. He hears their voices as songs, music that he writes down and keeps. On the wall in our meetinghouse is the only message from them that he's ever translated. It says: We weep here for how the World goes and your Life that passes touches our Hearts."

"What does the Family have to do with this?"

136

"When the Others are here to stay they'll be with us quietly until they've learned and are ready to go out, as I said, among us, among everyone. So the Family has to be the first whose faith is restored, who believe, who stay pure and focused so as to protect them wisely. We're seen as doing this not just for ourselves, or for them, but for all those who come after us."

"And your husband?"

"Those three with Wallace when the Others came are the Witnesses. He was the grandson of one of them, a First Descendant like I am. It's believed that we're different because of this. After the Witnesses come the Council of Elders, then the Believers and the Family."

"Where are you in all of that?"

"Way down at the bottom, the one they'd like to put in a closet and forget about. Two questions though are never answered. Father cuts a large circle and a design in our crops every year that can be seen from the heavens as a sign that we're keeping the faith, but he won't ever show the design or say what it means. And none of the First Descendants who are the Included ones will ever let it be known what the Witnesses and Wallace actually saw."

"Do you know?"

"I'm a First Descendant, but I can't be an Included. There are no Sisters of Ezekiel. So no, I don't." She paused for a long moment. "Samuel's a good person and I want you to know that. This isn't something he asked for. He says he was born to it, and he'll lead the Family and wait for the Others till the day he dies."

The fire was dying. An animal of some sort rustled in the brush.

"It's that possum coming back to get you," she said, glad to be done and that Chace asked no more.

"Why? I saved his life."

"You threw him into the bushes."

"He's coming because he smells bacon grease and fried squirrel."

The pale moon had crested the sky and was on its descent. There was just enough light that Charlotte could make her way to the creek and wash. She came back carrying a bucket of water and her shirt.

Chace had put out the fire and made a bed with what seemed to be all of the blankets in the wagon.

"You said rocks," he said.

"I know it's the ground. I understand there are rocks everywhere and that's the way it's supposed to be, but thank you."

He lay down and rested his head on his saddle. Charlotte sat next to him. In that other far away life she'd once led, she'd be in her father's house settling into bed with a lamp and a good book. Though not with a member of the tribes beside her, this was true.

"Do you believe in beings that come from the sky?"

"The old ones say spirits come from the sky all the time."

"Maybe the tribes are Family and you don't even know it."

"Maybe we're the Others," he said, "and you don't even know it."

She shivered. "Don't even say that. It's too scary."

"Maybe there's nothing."

"My father says you have to have faith, you have to believe, it's why we're here. All of us."

"I believe in the sun, the moon, the stars, that's it."

"You believe in your grandfather."

Chace stared out into the night. "You're right. I do."

She held out her hand and he closed his fingers into hers. More than anything, she believed in this. He ran his other hand easily along her thigh. She slid down beside him and pressed both their hands to her heart. Then she turned her face up to meet his mouth, surrendering to the warmth of his kisses. His arms went tightly around her then and they kissed as if it were the end of the world, as if the thrill of fingers touching and a mouth tasting warm scented flesh had become everything there was. She gave herself to him gladly and he took her not knowing anymore what he was doing, oblivious to the future, the past, wanting just this, to be with her, to not think about ever having to let go.

23

They crossed the creek where the banks opened out and sloped more gently. A path led down through the cottonwoods. Chace took the reins. The rocky creek bottom caused the wagon to pitch sickeningly. The mare stepped carefully along behind, seeking sure footing, and Charlotte prayed, only breathing again when they had reached the safety of the other side. They switched, with Chace keeping the reins in the morning, disappearing on the gray at noon. He gave no reason, but she knew the reason. Their journey was almost at an end. She could sense it.

Early in the afternoon, when they had come off the flat plains and into wooded hills, Chace stopped.

"How far?"

"Tomorrow we'll be due south of the fort, but some distance still."

"There's no escaping it then."

"There never was." He sat for a minute on the gray. "This is where I wanted to take you. Pull the wagon over into the trees. I'll saddle the mare."

She did what he asked. "Should I loosen the traces on the team?"

"No, we won't be long."

She rode with him up over the hills on a narrow path and then along the ridge toward a broad sheltered valley. The creek running through it was almost dry. The land spread out below them was green and peaceful.

Chace stopped at the top of the valley, his eyes following the line of the creek. She sat on the mare beside him.

"My people were here," he said, "preparing to come into the fort for the winter. The warriors were on the last buffalo hunt but there were no buffalo for half a day's ride. I was in Washington with Grandfather making another treaty that didn't turn out to be one. Ellis had gone east scouting land for a new fort for the army.

The agent said the government wanted to end the wars and stop the killing. The major at the fort promised protection and food to my people, but only if they would come in.

"A new commander took over the fort without notice, bringing with him men who were not soldiers. They were volunteers carrying out a different set of government orders that said to exterminate the tribes.

"In the dark they set up cannon on this hill. At first light they came down the valley on their horses with their guns and swords. They killed everyone, women, children, old ones, every brave left behind. They killed my son, my mother and sister, my grandmother, all of my family.

"My grandfather's brother thought there must be a misunderstanding. He had spoken to the white people's old ones. He had the peace medal like my grandfather. He honored his word to the white man and was bringing his hungry people in again before winter. He ran up the white man's stars and stripes flag, and below it the flag he knew was the signal of truce. They killed him where he stood and cut him into pieces. Then they slaughtered all the horses, set fire to the camp and left it to burn."

The tears streamed silently down Charlotte's face.

"The only place where I belong," Chace said, "is away from everyone." He stared out at the horizon.

<>

Late in the afternoon, Chace brought them to a clearing next to a small spring with trees for shelter and grass for the horses. Charlotte found brush and deadfall for a fire. This land seemed drier, less able to throw up the bounty Chace was used to finding. She decided on biscuits and gravy. She got out the tin oven. That was her skill. Before the Second Migration, she sold her baked goods regularly and put the money in the Family coffers, making her contribution, staying pure and focused. If only that were true.

They ate in silence. Nothing could erase his words and the images they brought. Charlotte knew she had to speak.

"We can talk now," she said quietly.

"I'll go crazy if I don't have any idea where you are," Chace said. "So I'm asking what your intentions might be."

"You say that as if I had a choice and I don't."

"You'll go into the fort then?"

"I will."

"And wait for your uncle?"

"Yes."

No other words came. "Ask it," she said, turned cold as stone. "Go ahead. There's one more question."

"Will you marry him?"

"What do you think?"

"I don't know."

The fierceness rose in her again, what he'd caught a glimpse of at the first, made to pause even then by what he was seeing.

"Never. They can shoot me, hang me. My father can threaten anything he wants, Tobias too. I refuse. Nobody can make me do it, and if they try, I swear I'll find a gun somewhere and do something with it and then they can put me in jail." She stopped. "This is a vow I'm making to myself, but also I'm making it to you. Remember that I'll go just as crazy not knowing where you are or even if you're still alive."

Chace turned away. When he came back to her, his eyes stayed on her healed face touched now by the sun, her butchered hair that still shone in the light.

"There are many kinds of pain. I'll be beyond the desert, in the high canyons, the last untouched land, the last emptiness. I won't die, I'm already dead. And I am about to die again."

She tried, but could find no words. She could only choke back tears. She watched him will his calm, unfazed expression to return.

"Do you have a plan for what happens after the fort?"

"Bread and geese."

"That's all of it?"

"Criticize your own plan," she said. "Leave mine alone."

"Do you have thoughts on where you'd go?"

"None. But I'll send you a letter when I figure it out. Not that you'll ever get it."

141

"You know you can't hurt me," he said. "It's not possible."

"You can't hurt me either. Well, yes you can." She gathered what strength she had. "But I said I understand and I do. I wouldn't ever try to take that from you, what you have to do and who you need to be." She fought hard to keep her emotions from showing, and succeeded, at least for the moment.

24

Charlotte tried to prepare breakfast with care, committing every motion, every ingredient to memory, but she still belonged to Chace in the night, as he had belonged to her.

She concentrated on slicing up the cornbread she'd made the day before. She set the iron skillet on the fire. When the bacon was fried, she added the slices and dried apples to the fat. Her thoughts lost among the sizzling and popping sounds, she suddenly looked up.

She was alone and there was a man on a horse in front of her. She stood up so fast she almost knocked over the pan. Quickly she took it off the fire. Where was the rifle? For once, when she needed it most, she didn't know. The man was solidly built with a sun-creased face. He wore an old plaid shirt, a vest, dusty boots, a long jacket and a gun. His rifle was holstered, she saw that.

"Who are you?" she said. "What do you want?"

His eyes were a faded gray, narrowed and aware. He didn't seem to present a rough kind of trouble, but definitely there was an air about him that suggested some kind of trouble.

"My turn first. Are you Charlotte Duchesne?"

Something in Charlotte turned cold. So this was how it would be. Ever since Ellis had brought it up, she'd been thinking about it. She was prepared. She was her father's child.

"I am. But now I need to know who's asking."

She saw him suddenly glance to his right. Her eyes followed his and there was Chace, sitting on the gray much like the first time she'd seen him. He wore the shirt now, but his knee was up over the saddle horn, the rifle across his lap. The bow was gone but the knife had reappeared. His eyes were steady on their visitor, easy, neutral.

"Abner Cross," the visitor said, turning back to Charlotte. "Federal marshal. And if you don't mind my asking, who is he?"

"How do I know that's really who you are?" Charlotte said, ignoring his question.

Abner Cross started for his shirt pocket, then thought better of it. "I'd show you but I don't feel the need to get shot doing it."

"That's not going to happen."

He took the badge out of the pocket and reached down to show her. She nodded.

"And what have you come all this way to talk to me about?"

Abner Cross glanced again at Chace, who hadn't moved.

"Let's get straight who this other party is first."

"Chace Bridger Yellow Cloud."

"And what is he to you?"

Everything. "My protection. If you want to offer me your guns for the duration of the time you're here, I imagine that would make things easier."

"No, thank you."

"Then this is where we are."

"You know why I'm here."

"I don't until you tell me. I don't count many federal marshals among my acquaintances, so that's not it."

"It's about Conner Mathis who was shot dead in his own kitchen." Charlotte was silent. "If I could sit down and just talk with you, it would be a help."

"Leave your guns and you can do anything you want."

Abner looked one more time at Chace and made a calculated decision. He slowly removed his revolver from its holster, turned it handle forward and handed it to Charlotte. Then he got down off his horse, leaving the rifle where it was.

Charlotte sat down at the fire. Abner Cross sat down as well.

"Do you have anything to say about that?" he said.

"I don't."

"Did you shoot him?"

"Everyone knows I did. You didn't need to track me over hell and all creation to find that out."

"Why did you shoot him?"

144

Charlotte stood up again. "I've been waiting for this day. You can trust Chace and you can trust me a whole lot more than you could trust Conner Mathis. I'm getting something out of the wagon and it's not going to be a gun."

She went over and reached into the back of the wagon where she kept it. She sat back down at the fire.

"Abner Cross, I don't know if you know what it's like to be married. For myself, I expected different. Even though my marriage was arranged without my consent, still I thought there would at least be some consideration and decency, some sort of understanding that would come with time. There was no such thing. He wasn't ever truthful once in his life and his anger was in his fists. Without that shotgun, I'd have been the one dead. Here," she said, holding out what was in her hand.

Abner Cross reached for it. It was a photograph. He winced. Her father had it taken as soon as he saw what had happened, dragged the Family member skilled with cameras into the horrible aftermath, knowing that it would be needed, aware of all that might come. It showed her seated in a chair, her eye swollen shut, the cheek lumpy and vividly bruised down to the jaw, her neck bearing dark marks and the torn front of her dress covered in a large black stain that was obviously blood. They had not yet had the chance to cut off her hair.

Abner Cross sighed heavily. "I have a witness," he said.

"A witness? That can't be true."

"Not a witness to the event. A witness to the intent. Someone to whom Conner Mathis mentioned, not very wisely, that he wanted to kill you."

Charlotte doubted that remark was made with any thought of what actually happened. Leave it be if it got this federal marshal removed from her presence.

"I had to find you anyway just to make sure. The days of the lawless west are over. There'll be accountability now." He glanced up at Chace one more time. "I could've got to this sooner if I ever thought you'd gone so far south of the trail as you did. That never occurred to me."

145

Charlotte studied her hands.

"One other thing and then I'll leave you in peace. Miller Dawson, he was the pilot on a wagon train that passed through there a while back, he said if I ever found you, to tell you something."

Charlotte was instantly on the alert.

"Tell me what?"

"It's about a young girl. Her name is Ada."

Charlotte considered that she was about to be hysterical. "Tell me what about Ada?"

"He said you'd want to know she's at Fort Randall."

"Why? They were going to Oregon Territory."

"They aren't going anywhere. None of this is good. I'm just passing on what I was asked to. The father died of the fever. Then the mother overturned the wagon on herself during a crossing. She and the baby and a man who tried to save them all got drowned."

"*No*. It can't be. Where are the other children? There were three more."

"They were taken in by the missionaries at the Agency but there was some trouble."

"What kind of trouble?" Charlotte said, her voice rising. She wanted to scream.

Abner Cross took one more look at Chace. "Some members of the tribes tried to burn the house down. That's all I know. Everybody's at the fort."

Charlotte stood up. "I'd ask you to stay for breakfast but you need to be on your way."

Abner Cross got up stiffly. "I already ate thanks," he said, although nothing had been offered.

"You have to do me this favor after hunting me down like a jackal."

"Do you mind before there's any talk of favors if I have my gun back?" Charlotte retrieved the gun and handed it to him. It wasn't heavy enough to be a Colt. "Now what's this favor?"

"How far is it to Fort Randall?"

"I'd be there later this morning if I rode fairly hard."

"I'm asking you to ride fairly hard then, and please tell Ada that I'll be there. It's important. Are you willing to do that for me?"

Abner Cross took in all of her. "What happened to you?" he said.

"You're the first one who's ever asked that question already knowing the answer."

"I mean your hair."

"I belong to the Family. I disobeyed my husband and that's forbidden. The women cut it off as punishment. That was in preparation for hanging me."

The marshal nodded thoughtfully. "I was just wondering. It's a shame, what you've been through."

Abner Cross holstered his gun and mounted his horse. He turned to Chace. "Nice to have made your acquaintance."

"I'd say otherwise," Chace said, "but you're entitled to your opinion."

Charlotte watched Abner's face register the surprise. He studied Chace, thinking. Then he turned his horse and started off at a walk that turned into a pace that churned up dust.

Chace got down off the gray. Charlotte sat with her head on her knees.

"You don't back down from anything." He picked up the photograph and stared at it for a long time. "Your father's a very careful man to have thought of this. But explain to me what's going on now."

"Sit down," Charlotte said and handed him a plate. She tried to calm herself. "Ada never left me alone for one minute of the days I was with the wagon train. Every time I turned around, there she was. When I made bread, there were the rest of them. The smallest one couldn't have been more than three. I didn't even remember there was a baby. Even though she was only twelve, Ada was like me, we saw eye to eye on things. The next oldest, her brother Brewster, helped me when I needed it. I can't believe this.

"Chace, I have to go to them, there's no doubt involved. Miller wouldn't have done that if they had any other choice. And I have to get there soon. Otherwise, I'll be frantic."

"It's a question of how long the horses can go without stopping," he said. "Or you can take the mare."

"You mean go on by myself without you? Never." She considered something for a moment. "But trying to burn down the house?"

"I might have burned something down myself if I could have found a way."

"Daylight and darkness," she said.

"And all the other opposites you can think of," he said. But one has no meaning without the other.

<>

She insisted they ride on the wagon together. There was no need for scouting out the next creek or tracing the paths of dragonflies. They were headed in one direction, the destination given, the outcome not in doubt.

At the noon hour, when the horses had to rest, Chace brought back two sage hens.

"Should I save them for dinner?" she said.

"I don't think so. Better now." She could hardly stand what he was saying.

They each took one to make the fixing time faster. She roasted them over the fire. When the plates were cleaned, with the last of the journey awaiting them, she stood up and her hands went to the collar of her shirt. He watched her, then undid the blanket roll from his saddle.

It was quick and fierce between them, tender and wrenching. She felt as if they were devouring each other, that no amount of what they were together would ever be enough. And then it had to be enough, the tears, the kisses, the thought-obliterating cliff edge one more time would have to be enough, would have to last forever.

<>

148

They came within sight of the fort as the sun began to cast shadows. Chace handed her the reins and got down from the wagon. He untied his gray horse from the back and swung up into the saddle. He'd put the Spencer back in the wagon but had kept the Colt if for no other reason than to remember her by. He rode up to the side of the wagon.

"I'll stay here till you get inside," he said.

"I'll wait in case you show up someday," she said. "I'll wait even if you never show up. When you're old, if you're still alive, come and find me."

His eyes held hers, never looking away. Then he backed up his horse so that she could leave. She lifted the reins. He watched until she was gone. He waited for just a moment, eyes closed, then turned the gray and headed toward the desert.

Charlotte never looked back. She couldn't. He was gone and her life now would be whatever lay ahead, moving forward alone, in this direction only.

She could manage only one impression, that the simply constructed fort still bore a close resemblance to a small town. Though the walls were high, with a guard standing watch in the blockhouse and a huge cannon inside facing the open gates, commerce appeared to be nonstop. Horsemen, soldiers, buggies, trappers, mountain men, traders, men in suspenders and women wearing sunbonnets all flowed around each other going in and out. A wagon train had circled up by the river, its herd of cattle spread out to the west. On the other side of the fort stood an Indian encampment, many of its members visible and milling about. Charlotte glanced cautiously in that direction then threaded the wagon through the foot traffic and gained entrance to the fort.

Once inside, she found herself on a large parade ground. Her eyes ran over the rest of the interior, the barracks, stables, an open forge and laundry, a storefront, a mess hall. She could see a second courtyard to the right, behind the mess hall, and a row of doors behind which might be accommodations.

A soldier approached her. He was young and eager, with an open, friendly face. Glancing up at the walkways going along the top of the walls, she realized that all of the sentries were watching her.

"Ma'am? Are you with the wagon train? Because the rest of them are all out there." He seemed puzzled.

Charlotte willed herself to speak. "I'm not with the wagon train."

The soldier looked at her wagon then out the gate, as if hoping to find some other kind of traveling group that she might be with. Oxen freighters? The mule cart bringing the mail? Nothing in the way of an answer appeared.

"You're by yourself?" Inexperienced as he was, only three months out from Virginia, still he knew that couldn't possibly be true.

Charlotte cursed inwardly. She should have thought this all out beforehand. She could see it wasn't going to be easy.

"I was with Ellis Gray's wagon train that I understand passed through here a while back."

The soldier considered this piece of information. "But Ellis Gray wasn't with them. Was he?"

"No. That's true. He was not."

"And they went on again some time ago."

"I imagine that's so."

"And you wouldn't want to try catching up with them at this point. Up in those mountains."

"I imagine that's so too."

"So you're just...here?"

"I am." She knew she wasn't helping him but she didn't yet have the composure to think of reasonable answers to his questions. In the first place, there were no reasonable answers.

"Well I'm supposed to take a census of everyone passing through so that's what I was doing." He glanced out the gate again as if hoping something had changed. Nothing had. "One wagon, I guess. Three horses. One woman." One woman, she said to herself. *Chace*. He'd be far out of sight by now. Was he riding fast? But she had to put all those thoughts out of her mind.

"That's about what there is." She was aware that she had to pull herself together. "Can I camp outside then?"

"When you're not with a wagon train?" The soldier frowned. This was getting too complicated for him. "That doesn't seem right. It wouldn't be safe, I don't think. But let me get someone who'd know." He started off, but she called him back.

"I'm not doing a very good job of this," she said. "And I apologize for that. I'll do whatever you want with the wagon. I was sent here, more or less, to find four children who were also with Ellis Gray's wagon train. I was told they'd been taken to the missionaries but to expect that now they'd be here."

151

Something clicked in the young man's mind. Sometimes he worried that he didn't have a brain at all.

"Are you Charlotte Duchesne?"

Charlotte nearly fell off the seat. Relief flooded through her, quickly replaced by wariness. How did he know? What had been said? She would have to feel her way very carefully through every step of these proceedings. She was in a fort, close to being in the hands of the military.

"I am. But you just set me back a great deal by saying that."

"Miller Dawson told me to watch for you. I don't know how I could have forgot such a thing, especially since, pardon for saying so, it's not every day of the week that a woman rides through those gates alone. Or ever, that I know of." He seemed dazed by having made such a speech.

"Do you know where I'm supposed to go?"

"They didn't tell me that. But let me find someone. I expect it'll be the colonel's wife."

Wait, she wanted to say again, but he had already run off. The colonel's wife could be nothing but more trouble. She felt as if she'd barely got out of the wagon train unscathed and now she was likely back in the same kind of disapproving company.

A bugle sounded loudly nearby and soldiers appeared from everywhere. Suddenly the empty parade ground was filled with noise, conversation, the clatter of boots on the wood walkways heading to the mess hall. Several looks were passed her way. She straightened and averted her eyes.

The young soldier came running back. She realized that she was close to becoming a problem to him. If he didn't finish with her soon he'd miss dinner.

"I'll lead your team over into the other courtyard so your wagon's out of the way," he said. "Then you can stable your horses. There's water and hay. Then Mrs. Hutchinson said to show you were the children are. Then she said if you needed to eat, there's food in the mess hall kitchen. Then she said come see her if that'd be all right with you."

Charlotte got down from the wagon. "Do you have a name I could call you by?"

"Joseph Beacham. Corporal. Infantry C. United States Army."

"Joseph Beacham. Thank you for your kindness. That's all I wanted to say."

"Yes, ma'am." Charlotte wanted to tell him to stop calling her ma'am, but she was afraid he wouldn't comprehend what she was saying any more than Miller had.

"Tell me where to find them please?"

"Sorry, I forgot again. Over there." He pointed to the doors that bordered the second parade ground. "First door. In an empty junior officer's quarters because there were four and I think, begging your pardon again ma'am, that no one knew what to do with them."

No one knew what to do with them. "I'm obliged," she said.

Charlotte unhitched the team and led them to the stalls along with the mare. She was grateful for the respite, the watering and feeding, but now she had to find them. Suddenly it seemed so hard, knowing what they'd been through.

She stopped in front of the door Joseph Beacham had indicated. She waited. Gathering all her courage and resolve, she knocked. The door opened cautiously and then flew open and Ada was in her arms, clutching her with a strangle hold, the face pale and thin now, hidden away in Charlotte's shoulder. No tears, though. And because Ada didn't cry, Charlotte refused to.

While she held Ada, Charlotte acknowledged the three others who were watching her solemnly.

"I'm here," she said. Ada took her hand and held it tight, leading Charlotte over the threshold. There were two rooms, scrubbed wood floors, a vaulted ceiling with rafters. Clean, she noted. A broad many-paned window let in light. A long farm table took up most of the space, along with a butcher block and a sideboard. A double-sided fireplace with a cooking grate stood between the rooms. A rocking chair sat by the hearth. In the other room, she could see a row of iron beds pushed up against each other.

153

"Brewster. I remember you well." She looked past him to the small boy.

"Jeremy," the small boy said. She guessed he was six.

"I saw you around the side of the wagon that day."

"When you made the bread."

"Yes, and your feet were black. Are they still black?" She bent down and picked up one of his small feet. "Oh my gosh they are. Imagine that."

"Will there be more bread?"

"So much more bread." She bent to the smallest child, a girl.

"This is Grace," Ada said. Charlotte turned to Ada, a question in her eyes. The child's face was puffy and her eyes swollen as if she'd been crying for days. "I don't know what to do anymore."

"I have to let go of your hand," Charlotte said. "Not forever, just for now."

Charlotte leaned down and picked up Grace. She balanced the little girl on her hip, one arm around her tiny waist. With her other hand, Charlotte reached down for the hem of her own petticoat and used it to blow the girl's nose.

"Grace, this is where you're going to stay. I'm not putting you down for quite some time. Is that okay with you?" For no reason that Charlotte could understand, the child shook her head yes.

"Let's see where we are," Charlotte said, sitting down in one of the rocking chairs with Grace in her lap. "What do you do for food?"

"They bring it," Ada said.

"Have you eaten yet tonight?"

"Not yet," Ada said carefully.

"Does it not always come?"

"No, it comes."

"But what?"

"But it's not always good," Brewster said. "Sometimes you're not even sure what it is." Charlotte gritted her teeth.

"That can be fixed." There was a knock.

"Here it is," Brewster said.

Ada got up and answered the door. It was Joseph Beacham. He had a large hunk of bread in one hand and a pot in the other.

"Ma'am," he said, nodding to Charlotte. She resisted the temptation one more time.

"What have you brought us?"

He frowned. "I'm not sure. Some kind of meat."

"Is it horse?" He looked horrified.

"We don't eat the horses. That I know of."

"Badger then maybe?"

"I don't know," he said. She realized she was being unfair. He put the bread and the pot on the table and fled.

Charlotte stood up and adjusted Grace on her hip. "I'll be back. Unless you all want to come with me." They did.

Charlotte thought the light would have faded. This day felt as if it had lasted at least a week. But she was mistaken, it wasn't yet anywhere near dusk. While she held Grace, she allowed all of them to climb into the wagon and inspect what was there. That would be the next job, sorting it all out again, but this immediate situation needed to be addressed first. She directed Ada where to find the ham, onions, bacon, potatoes. She wondered briefly if Joseph Beacham had any hunting abilities at all then answered her own question in the negative.

"Is there firewood?" she asked and Brewster went running for it.

They put the pot of congealed stew on the floor with the hunk of iron-hard bread beside it. It was not easy cooking and holding Grace at the same time. Every time Charlotte went to touch something, Grace's small hands got there first. Charlotte finally turned dinner over to Ada.

There was another knock at the door. "Is this Joseph Beacham again?" Ada grimaced. Brewster answered the door and it was Joseph, who appeared apologetic.

"They're always sending me somewhere for something. Pardon for bothering you again but Mrs. Hutchinson wants me to say to you that she does need a word." Charlotte imagined that Mrs. Hutchinson, whoever she was, needed more than a word, but this

155

problem could also be dealt with, somehow. She understood the questions this woman might have, and only hoped she would have answers.

"How do I find Mrs. Hutchinson?"

"She's in the offices upstairs. Ada knows." Ada grimaced again. Apparently Joseph Beacham was lacking in a certain kind of appeal.

Charlotte was gratified watching the four of them eat, even Grace.

"Now I do have to gather my wits about me and talk to Mrs. Hutchinson," she said. "Who she is?"

"She's the colonel's wife," Brewster said seriously. Charlotte thought he probably had the fort's entire chain of command committed to memory.

"And what's your opinion of her, Brewster?"

"She's the one who said to let us stay here."

"Ah."

"Though she might tell you some things," Ada said.

"And those would be what?"

"That I was ungrateful and rude to Mrs. Bixby."

"And who is Mrs. Bixby?"

"The major's wife who was supposed to take care of us but didn't really want to."

"Anything else?"

"Maybe she'll mention hateful too," Ada added.

"Impressive. I'll find out all the reasons later because I'm sure there are good ones. Can't wait to hear."

Ada let out a huge sigh of relief. "You aren't disgusted?"

"Ada, please at all times remember this. Whatever you've done, no matter how atrocious or disheartening you or anyone else thinks it may be, first thing is I trust you and second is I promise you I've done a thousand times worse."

26

The office was definitely a colonel's. An American flag stood in one corner. Citations, accolades and awards hung on the wall, along with framed photographs. Charlotte stopped, Grace still on her hip. She went around the bemused Mrs. Hutchinson to the photograph showing members of the tribes seated in all their traditional finery and eagle feathers with congressmen in dark suits behind them. *Chace.* She stared at the faces but couldn't pick out one that might be the grandfather's. Likely he wasn't in it anyway, she told herself. It could be any tribe, anywhere. Let it go.

"I apologize, I wasn't thinking for a moment," Charlotte said. She held out her free hand. "Charlotte Duchesne. I know you have questions to ask me. I would, in your place."

Mrs. Hutchinson was lovely. Older, maybe, and lined, with some sort of resignation set in around her gentle mouth. But her piled up hair was rich and lustrous, her smile was kind, and something in her eyes said that she didn't live by the rules and didn't necessarily believe anybody else should either. Charlotte also recognized that, as she'd somehow known, the woman was not a dithering idiot and this would not be easy.

"First, I am not Mrs. Hutchinson. Call me Lenore. And I see you've already got the youngest one in tow."

"Ada said she wouldn't stop crying, so I thought I'd try this. Seems to be working." Charlotte sat down with Grace. "I obviously have concerns about all of them, though."

"Myself as well. You're right, I do have questions and I'd be remiss in my responsibilities to these children if I didn't ask them."

"I understand," Charlotte said.

"First, if I may ask, how old are you?"

"Twenty-five."

Lenore actually laughed out loud. "You're no more twenty-five than I am."

"Close. Coming up." She didn't want to lose them before she even had them.

"Coming up when?"

"In five years."

"That's what I thought. You're very much like Ada. I suppose you know that."

"Yes."

"You left the wagon train. Why is that?"

"I was in the care of Ellis Gray, the captain, but he was forced by circumstances to leave. I imagine you're aware of at least some of his situation. It was already clear that single women in charge of their own wagons weren't welcome and that proved to be more than the case. They took no joy in seeing me arrive and were very glad to see me go."

"So after that you traveled by yourself?"

"A group of one sort or another came by nearly every day. People were generous and helped me when I needed it."

"A man named Abner Cross came looking for you."

"My uncle," Charlotte said.

"Also a federal marshal."

"Yes. He was out here tracking someone who'd gunned down a sheriff in Kansas and he heard that I might be in trouble. By the time he found me, I wasn't in trouble anymore."

"A man named Tobias came looking for you."

"Also my uncle."

"A lot of uncles."

"Yes."

"By the way," Lenore said. "This was the first question I wanted to ask, that anyone would want to ask, I hope it's not untoward. What happened to your hair?"

"I sold it."

"You sold it? To whom?"

"A French woman who makes hairpieces and false curls. Apparently somewhere there's a liking for that sort of thing. She quoted me a more than decent price and I needed the money."

"You didn't regret parting with it?"

158

"There was so much of it and it was heavy and wouldn't stay pinned up. I'm relieved, actually."

Lenore thought about that for a minute, nodding, then moved on. "Why were you traveling alone at all?"

Charlotte readjusted Grace on her lap. "That goes back to Tobias. A husband had been chosen for me. I was coming to meet him and get married."

"I didn't realize people did things like that anymore."

"They don't. It's just me." Charlotte knew she had to be absolutely truthful in this regard. It was too important. "I'm from the Family."

"I thought maybe that was the case."

"You've heard of them?"

"I'm from back east where everyone's heard of them."

"The idea of the Family doesn't scare you then?" She'd worried about this.

There was a silence. Grace had fallen asleep.

"Do they scare you?" Lenore said.

"No, they don't."

"You'll be marrying then? Is that what you're saying?"

"Definitely not. My mind never ran in that direction in the first place and the farther west I traveled, the more I knew for certain nothing of the sort was going to happen."

"We're speaking just between us," Lenore said, "but could you be forced into this marriage?"

Charlotte realized she had to be careful. "I will not be marrying anyone by force. Ever."

"Then, a hard question and I'm sorry to have to ask it, but I will. Are the children a useful means to success in that endeavor? A fortunate excuse, shall we say?"

"The children are not an excuse of any kind. Seeing as I'm all they have, they'll be my family, they'll be my life. And in case that's a question also, they'll be no part of that world that's called the Family."

"I understand. Thank you for clarifying that. And do you have experience in child-raising?"

159

The simple answer to that question would have been no. "The Family all rely on each other. Shared responsibility is part of everyone's duty." She had not even touched a child as small as Grace until an hour ago except when people thrust their babies at her.

"I have to ask myself a hard question as well. Is your presence a godsend that relieves all of us, including vexed Mrs. Bixby, of this burden we were not handling well? Do we just turn them over to you because we can?" Lenore worked on this for a moment. Charlotte appreciated her more with every word she spoke. "I think we should leave it this way. Let's try it and see what happens. I assume you understand this means staying here at the fort, at least for the time being."

"Yes." Where else did she have to go? "I'd expect to work. To earn our keep."

"What are you thinking you'd work at?" Lenore said, somewhat taken aback by this suggestion.

"I've been told people like my bread," Charlotte said. She stopped for just a moment, her mind gone elsewhere.

"Well that's certainly an interesting idea. Get settled in and then I suppose anything's possible, especially considering that the food for the soldiers here is dreadful." Lenore stood up. "I have good instincts about people," she said. "You'll do right by these children, I know it. Thank God. They've been through too much. However it happened, the best thing for them so far is that you've come."

Charlotte hoped she could hold everything together and not reverse that opinion in any way. She'd been trying to stand herself with some difficulty, awkwardly shifting Grace from her lap to her shoulder. The child was dear but sound asleep she was as heavy as a bag of rocks.

Charlotte turned at the door. "I appreciate your faith in me," she said. "I promise I won't let you down.

< >

The light was finally beginning to fade. Charlotte knocked at the door and Ada let her in.

160

"Was it bad?" Ada said before Charlotte could even get Grace into bed.

"It was not bad. Mrs. Bixby was described as being vexed. No reason given and I didn't ask for one. That part is thankfully over. We go on from here."

Ada sank down onto the bench and burst into tears. Charlotte put an arm gently around her. "You've taken on all of them. Now let me do it for a while. I'm good at it. Blow your nose. You can use my petticoat if you want. Grace already has." Ada laughed through the tears.

"So, Grace won't have much to do with this, apparently, since she's sound asleep, but Mrs. Hutchinson said I could stay and take care of you. She trusts that I won't give you bad habits or ruin your minds, but what does she know. In any case, I need everyone to have an opinion, yes or no. Let me remind you that saying no is always an option, one that I use all the time."

"Yes," Ada said.

"Yes," Brewster said, "but is there more?"

"Wait. Jeremy gets his turn."

"Yes," Jeremy said, looking confused as to what he was having an opinion on.

"Here's the way I see it so far then, but if anyone has a better idea, I'm listening. Always. We'll have school, I'm thinking, and we'll do our own cooking so as to avoid whatever's in that pot. I'll make bread, I hope, to earn our keep. If any of you have any other schemes involving our welfare, don't keep them to yourself. We'll wash every day and do laundry and take care of the horses. That's as far as I've got. Is that enough for you, Brewster, for the moment anyway?"

"It's enough." She could tell he was worried sick about the future. She was fully aware that if she let herself think about it for even one minute, she'd be worried too.

"Now if it's all right I've got to bring some of my belongings in from the wagon. I'll be back."

When she walked out the door, Brewster followed her. She shook her head. Where had these children come from?

161

Charlotte transferred blankets, the saddle, the velvet coat, everything she needed for sleep with one exception. She brought cooking utensils and enough food for breakfast. The oil lamps. Two buckets of water from the well and a bar of her lilac soap. Somewhere in the wagon was a metal bathing tub that they'd make good use of. She'd find it later.

Last and most important were the guns. While Brewster watched, she broke open each gun, clicked through the chambers, made absolutely certain all of them were empty. The Spencer was still there. Why hadn't he taken it, she wondered.

In the room, everyone stared in awe.

"Those are yours?" Ada said.

Charlotte wanted to mention her father, if only to say they were his not hers, but mentioning anyone's father, or mother, didn't seem right, not just yet anyway. It occurred to her also that Grace could never be called the baby. Another child was the baby, another child who was gone.

"They are mine and I double-checked that they're not loaded." She picked up the Colt. "This is the best revolver you'll ever find." She handed it to Ada and it sank to the floor.

"It's so heavy. Who could shoot this thing?"

Someone who's gone. "Maybe in the future we'll try practicing with it. Right now everything goes under the bed and stays there." That would be all she'd need, for Mrs. Hutchinson to find out there was an arsenal in the room.

Suddenly the bugle sounded and there was a commotion in the courtyard.

"What in the name of heaven is that?"

"Retreat and roll call," Brewster said.

"Do you know everything?"

"I try to," he said earnestly. "They play taps later on and that's my favorite part."

"It's sad," Ada said. "But it's my favorite part too."

Charlotte realized she needed to put her arms around them all the time.

162

27

"And this is reveille, I'll bet," Charlotte said, suddenly awake. At least there was daylight coming through the window, much better than the predawn wake-up call of the wagon train. She'd ended up sleeping with Grace, whose blue eyes were now staring straight into hers.

"Where are your things?" she asked at breakfast. The rooms were completely devoid of personal objects.

"What things?" Ada said.

"Your belongings. Your clothes."

"They're in the wagon," Brewster said, but his voice was quiet.

Charlotte had to work through what this might mean, that the wagon was still intact, here somehow, with possessions left in it that maybe they hadn't touched.

"It's outside next to the abandoned ones," Ada said.

"You haven't taken anything out of it? But why?"

"Maybe we wouldn't be staying," she said softly.

"I know it might be hard to go in there. Everything will be hard for a long time, count on it. But we can go get your belongings because we are staying, that's a given. If you really want to know, Mrs. Hutchinson insists on it."

"That part's not so hard anymore. We've been in there lots."

Charlotte found their meager cache of clothes and Jeremy's boots which he hadn't worn in months. Ada opened a chest to show her the carefully folded Sunday clothes, the ones meant to be saved until they'd reached Oregon Territory.

"We kept Ma and Pa's clothes. But we gave away Alice's. It seemed better like that."

Charlotte glanced up at Ada questioningly. Then she knew. Alice was the baby.

"Are there books you want?"

"We only had what you gave us and we had to throw them out. Most of the food got thrown out, but you can go through and see what's left that you could use."

Charlotte retrieved a pepper-wrapped ham, dried apples, lard, a jar of honey. Lamp oil. Candles. She quickly wore down, going through another woman's possessions, someone who would never need them again.

<>

They hung up their clothes on the hooks that lined the walls and each slid their one pair of boots under the beds. Charlotte considered that it wasn't home, but it could become a home.

They had hardly begun to sort out the morning when the bugle blew again.

"What is it now?"

"Infantry drill," Brewster said.

"Okay, how do you know these things?"

"I watch."

"Then let's all go out and watch. I suppose we should have some idea of where we live." In a fort. With soldiers. How strange.

Sheltered under the wraparound portico that the sentries walked, Charlotte and her charges took in the drills. Men in blue with rifles on their shoulders and packs on their backs marched here and there, back and forth. They presented their rifles, then took them back. Orders were barked. Feet shuffled. Voices shouted in unison.

The bugler trumpeted one more time. "Good God, it never ends," Charlotte said. "What now?"

"Cavalry."

"Horses," Jeremy whispered and his eyes lit up. True to Brewster's word, the horse soldiers mounted, aligned themselves in formation and galloped out the open gate.

"Where are they going?"

"Out to reconnoiter. At least that's what someone told me, but I don't know what that word means."

"I have a dictionary somewhere. We'll look it up."

164

<>

Charlotte was already finding the fort claustrophobic, the walls too high, all the activity too disconcerting. She realized that she had become used to the silence of the plains and a bugle blowing every five minutes, being around so much ordered chaos, all of it was jarring.

A picnic seemed the perfect solution. She put food in a basket and asked Brewster to roll up two of her blankets.

"Have you been outside the fort?" she said.

"Mrs. Bixby wouldn't let us," Ada said. "She said we'd get kidnapped but I think that would've been what she was most hoping for."

Charlotte's eyebrows raised. "You do not like this woman."

"I guess I do have strong feelings. Can we talk about something else?"

The river behind the fort ran clear and fast. Upstream, the women from the wagon train were hard at work on their laundry, pounding piles of clothes into submission on the rocks. The smell of bacon and warm bread wafted through the air.

The day welcomed them, wide blue sky overhead, pleasantly warm in the shade. Crickets chirped in the grasses. They sat in a circle on the blankets and passed the food around. Everyone was quiet, even Ada.

"So tell me all about the fort."

"There're horses," Jeremy said helpfully.

"The soldiers think it's monotonous," Ada said. "Joseph Beacham told me he's never been so bored. He thought they would go out to fight Indians every day but all they do is work at things he did back home, like cutting hay and chopping wood. At least that's what he said."

"So Joseph Beacham comes and talks to you? That's nice, isn't it?"

"He tripped during infantry drill and fell flat on his face."

"We didn't laugh," Brewster said.

"No, that's true," Ada said. "It would have been terrible to laugh. But it was funny."

165

"He's not Miller Dawson is what you're saying."

"No," Ada said slowly, "he's not Miller Dawson."

"There's different people coming and going every day," Brewster said. "Because of so many wagon trains and this is right before the mountains."

"Some of them leave everything they've got. Wagons, cookstoves, brass beds, rocking chairs."

"Because the mountains are hard."

Charlotte stared at them both in amazement.

"They need to sell their cattle too, sometimes, and sheep and milk cows," Ada said. "We bought a milk cow."

"What?"

"We had Pa's money. Brewster and me talked about it, it seemed like a milk cow was a good investment."

"It was, wasn't it?" Brewster said.

Charlotte rested her chin on Grace's head. "Probably the best investment anyone could think of."

"Ma was worried for the baby that we didn't have one."

"That's why we did it," Brewster said and the silence was there again.

"I have a churn," Charlotte offered. Why her father had included a churn when she herself didn't have a milk cow was a question beyond answering. "We'll make cheese. We'll have cream. We'll have butter." *Butter brought back the crawfish and those brought back his face, his hands.*

"Is it in the stables?"

"Along with our horse."

"You have a horse?" Charlotte felt like she had to keep rearranging her expectations every time one of them spoke.

"The wagon train people took the team because they needed it, but we kept the riding horse."

"It's the one we'd had since ever we could remember."

"Cairo," Ada said.

"That's the name of your horse? Cairo?"

"Pa said it was the most ordinary horse he'd ever seen so it needed a fancy name. He told us Cairo was in Egypt, and Egypt

166

was in Africa, and Africa was so far away he could hardly stand to think about it."

Charlotte mourned for the people who'd imparted so much good to these children.

"Now I want to know about the missionary lady." She watched their faces grow serious.

"Miller and some of the women took us there," Ada said. "They'd talked to her and she agreed to keep us."

"But she already had other orphans."

"And she said small children were too much trouble. She said she didn't want Grace."

"So she tried to give Grace back."

"Miller started yelling. Then the women joined together for a talk and we stayed, Grace stayed, and then they rode off but I don't think Miller wanted to."

"There were Indians," Jeremy said. Charlotte began to see that these two subjects were very dear to his heart, Indians and horses.

"It's the Agency," Ada said, "where the members of the tribes are supposed to live because they don't have their land anymore. And the missionaries are in charge because they're supposed to be trustworthy and God-fearing and do the right thing."

"But she didn't like Indians," Brewster said. "They stole her crops and tracked dirt on her carpets so she didn't let them in the house."

"She almost didn't let us in the house either. She said wagon train children were filthy and ill-mannered."

"And we all slept in one bed," Jeremy said, his eyes wide.

"And some of us cried," Brewster said, "and it kept people awake."

"Some of us did," Jeremy admitted.

Charlotte could barely contain herself. "How long were you there?"

Ada smiled ruefully. "Two days. The second day some of the Indians, younger ones I think, tried to burn the house down."

"Why?"

"Because of how she treated them."

"Because if they got the house to burn down then maybe she'd go away and we'd go away and they could have their land back and live in peace. After that, she was done with us. It was almost like she blamed us for all the trouble. So her husband got out our wagon that Miller had left for us and hitched up his horses to it and drove us straight to the fort and went away again that same night, never said goodbye or anything. We told him we'd pray for him."

"Actually we didn't do that," Brewster said.

"And he didn't tell us he'd pray for us either."

"That brings us to Mrs. Bixby," Charlotte said.

"She doesn't like us either."

"She gave us candy," Jeremy said.

"That was the first day. But that didn't happen again. She didn't know what to do with us at all. She told us we weren't allowed inside all day, and we weren't allowed outside the fort."

"That's how we know about the drilling and the cavalry and everything," Brewster said.

"That's all we've done. She'd come into our room after dinner to see that we'd eaten and were all still there and told us not to light the fire or any candles and then she was gone. In the morning she'd come around to find out if we all lived through the night so she didn't have to go report anything bad to Mrs. Hutchinson."

"She shouts," Brewster said.

"Well, not at us, she wasn't ever around long enough. She shouts at her husband, though."

Charlotte blew out a long breath.

"I don't think she likes him," Brewster said, frowning.

"I don't think she likes anybody," Ada said. "She has a servant and he drives her out in her carriage every day because she hates this place, but he's not allowed to go anywhere near the Indians."

Charlotte regarded their innocent faces and held on tighter to Grace. "It'll be different now," she said. "I promise."

<>

In her own wagon, Charlotte dug through the boxes till she found the stack of identical blank journals. She knew her father had included them with the firm expectation that when she at last produced an heir, she would record every precious and enlightened minute of its day. Since that wasn't going to happen, she instead carried the journals back to the room. Brewster and Ada had already transferred the crates of books and were now attempting to divide them up into piles, although with such a strange mix, the nature of each pile did not immediately become clear.

"*Frankenstein*," Ada said. "What is that?"

"It's a novel about a scientist who creates a monster. The important point for now is that it's fiction, so it goes over there. And poetry, if you can tell that it is, goes over here. Geography, this pile, history, that pile. And start any other piles you think might make sense."

"Here we are," Charlotte said. She bent down, balancing Grace and reached into one of the crates. "School books!" She held them up. "Spelling, arithmetic, grammar, penmanship. Aren't they a lucky find?"

The looks she got back didn't say that anyone agreed they were a lucky find.

"I was joking. I don't even know where they came from. But we will read every day. I include myself in this. And we'll read to Jeremy and Grace. And we'll write and write and write."

Jeremy looked up at the mention of his name. He'd been sitting at the table mesmerized by *The Children's Book of Quadrupeds*.

"What'll we write?" Brewster asked.

"Lots of things." She handed a journal each to Brewster and Ada, set aside one for Jeremy and kept one for herself. There was even a journal left over for Grace, though Charlotte couldn't bear to think that far into the future.

"These are for you to keep. We'll write in them every day, but no one ever has to know what you wrote, or see it even, if that's the way you want it to be. We'll write stories too, and sketches and letters." This was how her father had raised her. This was how she would raise them. It was all she knew.

"Who will we write letters to?"

"Anybody you want. Sometimes you don't even have to send them, you just write them. For instance, you could write a letter to

Mrs. Bixby. That would hopefully be one you didn't actually send."
Brewster appeared confused but Ada smiled.

"It's just an idea. Another idea is that we have to write to
Miller Dawson right away, all of us, to tell him we're fine, and give
a copy of that letter to every wagon train that passes through here
headed to Oregon Territory. And here," she reached down for
another volume, "is the dictionary." She handed it to Brewster.
He paged through till he'd found the word.

"'Reconnoiter'," he said. "'To explore an area in order to
gather information, especially about the strength and positioning of
enemy forces.'" His brow knit together. "Mostly that doesn't look
like what they're doing."

"I agree, but at least we found out what the word means."

28

Charlotte found that she was moving purposefully without fully examining the origin of any of her actions. After dinner, while her charges watched carefully, she put a plank on the sideboard top. On the worn but level slab of wood, she set a smooth river rock that she'd kept from the creek. She balanced a playing card upright against the rock, the king-with-the-ax, then placed two long feathers lengthwise in front of it, one duck, one eagle. Then she lit a candle and stood it nearby.

"What is this?" Ada said.

"I've always liked to put things together that mean something to me."

"These mean something to you now?"

"More than you could ever know."

"Wait, can I ask a question?"

"No, you can't. But for this one, it's just the beginning. It'll only be finished when it's got special things from all of us." She picked the duck feather back up and handed it to Grace who ran it through her fingers over and over again.

Without saying anything, Jeremy left his book, got down from the table and went into the other room. Everyone looked after him, puzzled. When he returned, he was holding the tiniest bird nest Charlotte had ever seen, the fine straw-colored wispy grasses woven around and around into a perfect, delicate bowl.

"What kind of nest is that?"

"I don't know," he said. "I found it in a bush. Can I put it up there?"

"Yes, of course you can." She watched, her eyes shining, as he stood on a chair and carefully placed his contribution, his small face beaming with pride.

Ada had been sitting deep in thought. "It's an altar," she said.

Charlotte couldn't avoid mentioning her family this time. "That's what my father always said. He'd take them apart as fast as I made them. But I didn't have altars in mind at all."

"Is your father still alive?"

Charlotte remained uncertain how to handle these subjects that touched so dearly on all they'd lost. She decided she couldn't avoid every mention of anything, that wouldn't even be natural. And this was Ada.

"Yes. He's still alive."

"Was he there when you got trampled by wild horses?"

"Do you never forget anything?"

"I don't think so. At least I try not to."

"I would very much appreciate it if you'd forget that, all of it."

"You mean the true parts or the not true parts?"

"You do realize that I'm an adult and you're only twelve years old, don't you? I could take away all your privileges if you had any, which you don't, so that argument won't work." Charlotte thought for a moment. "I could forbid you to ever speak to Joseph Beacham again."

Ada laughed.

"But she's not twelve," Brewster said.

"You're not?"

"I was twelve," Ada said.

"Now she's thirteen."

"Thirteen?" Charlotte was completely taken aback. The child was so thin. Then it occurred to her. "Wait. When was your birthday?"

Ada was blinking hard. "Five days ago."

"Five days?" Good grief, did it never end? "And I'll bet Mrs. Bixby threw you the biggest party ever with presents and firecrackers and a huge cake that she made herself that had real birthday candles on it."

"The cake was chocolate. And she gave me new boots and a petticoat with lace on it and ribbons for my hair and my first ear drops and a flute."

"A flute?" Brewster said.

172

"I was running out of things to make up."

"What I would give for a chicken," Charlotte said.

"That would be my real present? A chicken?"

"No. I'd need a chicken for the eggs to make the real birthday cake. But I'll think of something." And she knew she would.

<>

The next day, with Grace on her hip, Charlotte began to delegate.

"Ada and Jeremy, I need three eggs. Can you please see if anyone in this whole godforsaken place has a chicken?" She threw a pointed glance just as Ada opened her mouth to speak. "And I don't want to hear about swearing. Brewster, I need you for a whole other mission. The sutler's store has steel-tipped pens and ink, but no paper. Can you use your enterprising talents and find us paper to write on? Meanwhile, Grace and I are going to conduct a search of our own. We'll meet back here and please make it less than an hour or I'll get frantic just like Mrs. Bixby and think you've been kidnapped. Only I truly will be frantic."

Charlotte thought she would never get used to the clockwork schedule of the fort. Just as she was about to start out, the bugle blew and the soldiers appeared running from every corner onto the parade ground in full uniform to perform their drills. She stood still till they'd all gone around her, some now casting frank glances at the woman with butchered hair holding the blue-eyed child. When it was safe and she trusted that she wouldn't get knocked down, she moved on.

She carefully toured the entire inside perimeter, peering into every door that it seemed permissible to peer into, checking hidden nooks and corners, any place that resembled storage or quarters going unused. Finally, she located what she'd been hoping for, a tiny schoolroom. Charlotte's instincts told her there had to have been, at one time or another, officers with children and therefore a place for schooling. And here it was, dusty, shuttered, definitely, for the moment at least, abandoned so that she could take what she wanted while feeling hardly any guilt at all.

She was glad to be the last back instead of the first. Ada and Jeremy hadn't turned up a chicken. Brewster, on the other hand, true to form, had won the prize, a thick stack of impressive bond with the letterhead of the United States Army.

"Brewster, will we be in trouble? How did you come up with this?"

"I went to Mrs. Hutchinson. She's the one who gave it to me."

"Of course you went to Mrs. Hutchinson. Why bother with all the little people? Just go to the top."

"It's good, isn't it?" he said.

"It's grand. And so are you. But we should start the journals right away." She picked up a slate and a piece of chalk. "This is what I found. I wanted to write down the date, because that's what makes it a journal. Now I realize I have no idea what the date is."

Brewster took the slate and chalk from her and wrote the date.

"Young man, someday you will do great things."

"Because I know the date?"

"No, for a whole list of reasons that I'm not going to let you know about, not just yet."

In the afternoon, Charlotte followed the part of her instructional plan that said go outside, away from the fort and everything in it, away from books and journals and pens and slates. She retrieved the pickets from the wagon.

"Today we'll start setting the horses out to pasture. And the cow."

"The cow?" Ada said.

"If you were a cow, wouldn't you like to eat the fresh rich grass down by the river?"

"I never exactly thought about what it would be like to be a cow."

Charlotte served another picnic lunch while the animals grazed peacefully. When Charlotte stood up with Grace on her hip, Grace said one word. "Down."

Charlotte laughed.

"Good job," Ada said.

"I guess."

174

<>

In the evening, while Brewster read out loud with Grace in his lap in the rocking chair, Charlotte made rice with peppers and sausage and baked an eggless but nevertheless inspired chocolate cake. She thanked the gods for rising soda, with which almost anything was possible. When dinner was done, she lined the entire center of the table with candles, placing the cake in the middle. The room lit up with a warm glow, shadows dancing off the walls. She inserted one smaller candle into the cake itself.

"You have to make a wish. But think about it first. A birthday wish is very important."

"Do you think it counts five days afterwards?"

"Absolutely it counts." Ada squeezed her eyes shut then opened them again and blew out the candle while Charlotte wondered what wish could possibly make up for all that was lost. Then Charlotte cut the cake into slices and the forks flew.

"And now for the present."

"But this was the present. That we got to have my birthday."

"Your thirteenth birthday, that's the difference. You only get to be thirteen once." She slid a small box across the table.

Ada picked it up. "What is it?"

"Usually the way this works is that you have to open it to find out. That's what presents are all about."

Slowly, Ada opened the box. Then she gasped.

"It really is gold ear drops."

Charlotte waited just a moment, trying to keep her emotions in check, which was always hard these days. "My father gave them to me when I turned thirteen. He meant it as a very special and important gift, and it was. Now I'm giving them to you."

"Are you sure?"

"I am very sure. Put them on."

Ada fastened the tiny gold drops at her ears. When she looked up, Charlotte had to compose herself again. The drops turned a child with wild hair and a heart-shaped face into the vision of the beautiful woman she would become.

175

"Thank you," Ada said and threw her arms around Charlotte's neck.

Ada sat back down and held the box, looking into the candlelight. She wiped her eyes.

"Would we ever get to meet your father?" she said out of nowhere.

Charlotte felt herself grow pale. "He's very far away," she said. And good thing. "If he were ever here so that you could meet him, that would be a very frightening day."

"It would?"

"Trust me, it would."

"Does this have to do with where you went that you won't talk about?"

"Oh my gosh, I hadn't realized. Question time is over. No more. None. This time I know what the bugle's going to blow and thankfully it'll be taps."

<>

In the morning, they wrote in their journals then started on sketches. "For the first one, we'll all write on the same topic. Just to see how it goes. What'll it be?"

"Horses," Jeremy said without hesitation. Charlotte stared at him. She was certain that he didn't even know what a sketch was and he didn't know how to write.

"Horses it is. I'll write about the mare."

"Horses wouldn't have been my first choice," Ada said. "I guess I'll write about Jack."

"Who's Jack?"

"Miller Dawson's horse," Ada said and kept her eyes down.

"I'll write about the cavalry horses," Brewster said.

"And I'll write about Cairo," Jeremy said. "I even know some of the words." Charlotte smiled.

In the afternoon as they were preparing to take the animals out, the bugle sounded.

"Target practice," Brewster said.

"How lovely. Let's find out where that is and go in the other direction."

176

They were seated in a circle, the horses and cow grazing peacefully around them and Grace playing in the grass.

"We should talk," Charlotte said, her voice turned serious. The time had come. They all watched her. "It's not good not to talk." She'd so recently experienced what it meant to have someone ask and listen and care. "I know it's hard, but we're all in this together now. Tell me about the wagon train."

There was silence. Ada pulled Jeremy onto her lap and put her arms around him. The silence grew longer.

Brewster was the one who broke it. "Pa got the fever," he said. "He was only sick for two days before he died. They helped us bury him. We put rocks over the grave to keep out the wolves. Ada made a marker."

"With his name on it like the one we saw." Charlotte nodded. She could still see all the women huddled around it on the trail.

"Ma wasn't so good after that. But there was trouble."

"From Fiona's husband," Ada said and her young girl's face had turned hard. "They made him the captain just because he was so loud and bossy. He said a woman like Ma with that many children would keep them all from getting over the mountains in time and people would die because of it. We had a river to cross and the men had to stop and help us, but he got lots of people upset about it and they said we should turn back." She stopped and laid her cheek on top of Jeremy's head.

"When we got to the next river, Ma wouldn't let anybody help her. She had her choler up, that's what she called it when she got angry. Miller Dawson said there were strong currents, so he'd strung a line across from one side to the other that people could follow. I put Jeremy on my back and held onto the line. Lots of people did it that way. Ada took Grace and Ma came behind her in the wagon." Then Brewster stopped. Jeremy suddenly turned his face into Ada's shirt.

"The wagon pitched onto its side and the horses panicked," Ada said. "Ma lost her hold, the baby was tied to her front and they both fell into the river. Then Logan Feeney jumped in to save them and he drowned too. The men all came to get hold of the horses and pull the wagon up onto the bank." Charlotte closed her eyes. Ada's face was wet.

"All except the one who had made her do it," Brewster said. "He didn't help at all."

There was silence again.

This time Ada broke it. "Miller Dawson stayed with us that night and didn't let go of any of us even though probably no one thought that was the right thing for him to be doing. He didn't care."

"The women brought us food. Then the council told us about the missionaries and said that's where we were supposed to go and Miller and the women took us there. The wagon train was still at the fort when we came back from the missionaries and nobody could believe it. That's when Miller said he'd find you."

"I'm so sorry," Charlotte said. "For everything."

Brewster bowed his head. Ada wiped her eyes.

"What's going to happen to us now?"

"It'd be better if we didn't have to think about it so much," Brewster said. "It'd just be better if we knew."

"What do you want to happen?"

"Would we live here at the fort?"

"No. At least not forever. Would you call some place back east home?"

"Not anymore," Brewster said. He looked at Ada. "If there was a way to do it, we'd be more set on going to Oregon Territory like Ma and Pa wanted to."

"Is that possible?"

"We'll make it possible," Charlotte said. "We'll find a way, that's all. We've got time yet to figure it out." And then, when the decision was made, she would have to write that letter telling him where she'd gone, the letter that would never get to him.

29

The arrangement on the sideboard slowly accumulated new items.

Brewster held up a small black much-used notebook. "Is it all right if I add this?" he said to Charlotte. "It belonged to Pa."

"Yes," she said gently. "What is it?"

"It's his numbers book. That's how he worked everything out. Feet, inches, dollars, acres, pounds, bushels, he never wanted to forget how to do anything or make it or what it cost or how long it took so he wrote it all down. For Oregon Territory it shows everything he bought and what he was going to do with it when we got there."

He placed the notebook carefully next to the king-with-the-ax.

"That's how he made our life good," Ada said. "Ma never understood that book at all. She did things her own way." Ada held up a handkerchief embroidered with lace and violets. "This was hers." She lifted it to her face and inhaled deeply. "Hyacinth. Ma used to pin it to her shirt because Pa liked the smell so much." The beautiful scent immediately drifted out into the room.

"If you closed it up tight, it might last longer."

"I know. But I like it this way. I like smelling it in the room."

Jeremy's new offering was a discarded snakeskin and Charlotte remembered her dead bees. The eagle feather still stood out. *Where are you? In what high lonely place?*

They began their own writing. Ada took Charlotte's suggestion and composed a long letter to Mrs. Bixby that she worked on for most of one morning, crossing out, starting over, the pen digging deep against the expensive bond of the letterhead. Brewster wrote a long list of questions addressed very endearingly, Charlotte thought, to the bugler. Without anybody taking particular notice, Grace began drawing pictures on her slate.

Charlotte showed them her father's way of brushing the horses and they took turns bringing on the nickering. She provided

Jeremy with a stool and a second brush from the stable master so that he could be in heaven too, doing his small part alongside the others.

At night in front of the fire, she waded into the next subject on her list.

"As I've said before, I'll only be comfortable if we're earning our keep. The bread will hopefully be one thing. Should be others, though."

"Brewster will come up with something," Ada said. "He always does." The concentration on Brewster's face said he was already working at it.

The last necessity on Charlotte's agenda was to take Ada aside.

"We're going for a walk. Brewster, can you take charge? It won't be for very long."

Brewster grew stern. If she didn't know by now that he could take charge, he didn't understand when she ever would. She laughed and hugged him though she'd been made very aware that he wasn't fond of being hugged.

"Where are we going?" Ada said outside.

"Nowhere in particular. But there are some things I need to tell you."

"Finally."

"Just because you're thirteen doesn't mean you get to be all mouth."

"You know I never talked to anyone else but you, ever."

"I heard something like that from Ellis Gray," Charlotte said. She hadn't thought of him in so long.

"I liked him."

"So did I."

"Maybe someday we'll see him again."

"And maybe we won't. But here, this is what I wanted you to know."

Charlotte took the stark photograph out of her pocket and handed it to Ada. They were beyond the gates of the fort, walking into the sunset. Another wagon train had circled next to the fort and the smell of cattle was strong in the air. Ada touched the photograph gently with her fingers.

"It's not for the others to know," Charlotte said. "They're too young. But you're close to being a woman now, so it's time to talk more openly with you about these kinds of things."

"Tell me," Ada said.

"I was married to someone. I didn't choose him. He was chosen for me. Why doesn't matter, but he was the wrong person for anyone to choose. It got so we hated each other more than anyone could believe and one night he came after me. There was a shotgun. When I got the chance, I used it. He's buried now, dead and gone."

"It's so awful."

"Please don't cry. There've been enough tears shed. But obviously I'd done a horrible wrong and nobody asked questions about why. The women held me down and cut my hair for disobeying my husband and the Elders decided I should be hanged for killing him. My father, who's important in that world, bargained for my life. The wagon has everything my father put in it while I was on trial. There were no wild horses, but no one wants to offer up such a truth to a twelve-year-old. Can you see that?"

"Yes. Thank you for treating me like an adult. I am now, you know, whatever you might think."

Charlotte put an arm around her. "In some ways. But you don't want it to be in every way, not yet."

"Will you tell me where you were?"

"I can't. But I will some day."

"Soon?"

"I don't know," Charlotte said. "When the time's right." When you're eighty-two.

30

"I need to skip school this morning," Brewster said. "I have to see some people and I could talk about the bread if you want."

"You'd negotiate for me?"

"I was thinking I would."

"And you'd do a better job?"

"I might."

"Out of the mouths of babes," Charlotte said. "When's your birthday?"

"In fifty-seven days."

"I meant approximately, but all right. I'll have to start looking now for something besides gold ear bobs."

Brewster returned in the afternoon and they went out to the grass by the river, although the sky said rain was coming.

"I hope it's okay to ask you this. Could you make all those different kinds of breads you did before so I could show them to the quartermaster?"

"I'm always willing to make bread. But why? Is there trouble?"

"No, it's not like that. He was just curious and it'd be that much better if I had the bread with me."

"We'll be going in early anyway. I'll start this afternoon."

Brewster hesitated. "Will there maybe be some left over?"

"I think there'll always be some left over."

But at their quarters, the door was open, which made Charlotte pause. She held back the children and stepped cautiously into the room. Seated at the table was a man as tall as her father but younger and leaner, his dark hair disheveled, his face marked by sad eyes and a drooping moustache. Maybe he was still missing the big wife.

"Uncle Tobias," she said.

"You remember me," he said, "and I haven't seen you since you were a child. I wouldn't have known you except you're the spitting image of your mother." Charlotte closed her eyes. This was all she needed. She could feel the presence of the children in the doorway.

"I suppose you have things you want to say to me."

"I suppose I have things Samuel wants me to say. At least now I can tell him I found you. If letters could burst into flames, his would have been doing that. He was frantic. Pardon my asking, but where in God's name have you been?"

"So many places." She turned and motioned the four of them into the room. Ada had picked up Grace. "This is my Uncle Tobias. Tobias, I want you to meet my children. They didn't start out to be mine, but fate's taken us in that direction. This is Ada, Brewster, Jeremy and Grace."

"There's a husband waiting for you," Tobias said quietly. "Out in the desert. There are responsibilities involved. You of all people know that. You're his daughter."

"I'm not going. That husband's going to have to find someone else, though I doubt he'll shed many tears over it. You can try using force if you want, but I promise you I'll put up more of a fight than you'd ever hope for."

"Force? Look at you. There's been enough of that already. That's not who we're supposed to be."

"Let all of them back there know that."

Charlotte could feel the wide eyes behind her. Thank heaven she'd told Ada, just in time.

Tobias scanned slowly around the room, seeing the papers tacked up on the walls, books piled up in the corners, plates and cups stacked on the sideboard, the cooking grate in the fireplace. Then his eyes rested on each of the children in turn. Charlotte considered that he seemed gentler than her father, so much quieter.

He studied the young woman who shared his history. "I don't understand anything," he said. "I assume you realize that. But I don't see that I can do much about it either, at least at the moment. So I guess for now I'll just head on out again."

"Wouldn't you at least like to stay for dinner?"

He considered for a moment. "I didn't want to intrude. But I believe I would, thank you. And I have fresh-caught fish if you want them."

"Fresh-caught fish? I can't think of anything better." Fish immediately brought back *the creek, the trout, the rain.*

While she made dinner, Charlotte watched Tobias out of the corner of her eye. He spent some time examining the writing papers on the wall while Brewster read out loud. He helped Ada set the table. He seemed comfortable in his own skin, Charlotte decided, on good terms with the world.

"You used to do that," he said, nodding at the wall.

"And Samuel was stern. Exacting, you might say." He nodded.

"Is it all right if I ask you something?" Brewster said. Charlotte wondered what obtuse person could have ever thought these children ill-mannered.

"Please do."

"Where did you come from?"

"The desert."

"Do you mind if I have other questions?" Tobias smiled and Brewster continued. "How do you live in the desert? What do you do for food?"

"The truth is, people've been living in the desert for thousands of years, so there are all kinds of ways. Helps to have folk who know what they're doing, though. There's some game, mule deer, jackrabbits, things like that. There're also hidden springs and once you've found them you can irrigate and grow a goodly number of crops. You just have to like it dry and sometimes very hot."

"And do you?"

"I got used to it. It's not so bad. If you build right, it stays cooler inside and that's something."

"I don't know," Brewster said. "I think I'm glad Pa wasn't headed to the desert."

Tobias glanced at Charlotte and she hoped he understood.

"Where was your Pa headed?"

"If he'd lived, he was set on all of us going to Oregon Territory."

184

After dinner, outside with Tobias, Charlotte closed the door behind her.

"Are you leaving tonight?" she said.

"No. I'll camp by the river and leave in the morning."

"I'll get up early and bake bread. Can you stay till then and I'll give you some? These days, it's about what I have to make my way with."

"I'll stay then." He turned to her. In the fading light, he was the ghost of her father. She shivered. "So they lost both parents?"

"Just a short time ago."

"That's hard. It's why you're here?"

"I'm all they have and Tobias, I'm not leaving them for anything."

"But where were you? Samuel set you on a path and now everything's got all turned around from where it was. I have to be able to tell him something."

"I know," Charlotte said. "You're caught in between us and I regret that. I wouldn't want to be in your place. But I've told you all I have to tell."

"Nothing more, you're sure?"

"Seriously, nothing more."

Tobias sighed deeply. "If that's the way it is then," he said. "Just understand that I can't give up. You're aware of that, aren't you?"

"Yes, I am. Come by in the morning."

"I'll be glad to."

"I'm grateful to have met up with you again," she said.

"I'm grateful that you're alive," he said.

<>

In the morning, Charlotte gave him breakfast and two loaves of molasses bread, then walked him out to his horse.

"Truthfully, how is it in the desert?" she said.

"It's peaceful, not near so much commotion as living with the whole Family."

"Did you ever marry again?"

"You remember about that."

185

"I was very young, but yes, I remember, mostly because Father shouted so much over it."

"He does have his opinions. But no, I never remarried. I missed her for a very long time, and then one day I didn't anymore. I'm content living by myself. I don't mind it. If you think about it, Samuel's the same way, though he had you. You're a fine young woman. He did right by you, or you by him, I don't know which."

"Thank you."

"I won't be saying goodbye," Tobias said as he mounted his horse. "Because I'll likely be back. As a matter of fact, I think you can count on it."

"There's a place at the table and you're always welcome. But just know that I'm set in my ways as much as he is and nothing's going to change."

"I'll be seeing you," he said and gave her his sad smile.

31

"The quartermaster likes your bread," Brewster said at dinner. "But you can come and talk to him yourself. He says he wants all the bread you can give him, part to use for meals and part to sell in the sutler's store. You'd buy what you need for it at what it costs them and then you'd get the profits from what they sell and payment for what they use as credit in the store. That's the part you'd want to see if you agreed with. And you'd want an understanding of numbers, how much bread we're talking about. And he's thinking you'd use the cookstove in the mess hall. It's yours whenever you want it."

"Brewster," Charlotte said. "I'm not following anything you're saying. If I go to the quartermaster, you're coming with me."

"But I found out there's more. Do you know how many soldiers here can't read or write?"

"I don't have any idea at all."

"Lots. There's a couple that hardly even speak English. And some that were never on a horse or shot a gun before, but that's a whole other thing. So you know what all those soldiers can't do?"

"No, what?"

"Send letters home. But they could if someone wrote letters for them. I could do that. Mrs. Hutchinson said I could. So could Ada."

"You went to the top again."

"Do you know what else they need?"

"I guess I don't at all," Charlotte said. She was trying hard not to laugh.

"They've got terrible boots that are mostly too big and don't have a right and a left so their socks rub and get holes all the time and their feet hurt."

"They need socks?"

"Ma used to knit us socks."

"I can knit socks," Ada said firmly. "And write letters. And whatever else needs doing."

"If you can knit socks, so can I."

"It wouldn't be a lot of money," Brewster said. "I don't think the soldiers can afford to pay much. But it'd be some for the letters. And the socks would be more credit at the store."

"I can brush the horses," Jeremy said.

"They're our horses. We're supposed to brush our own horses. Anyway, that's what I have for now."

"I believe the problem of earning our keep has just been solved," Charlotte said. "Brewster, thank you."

<>

Their days fell into a rhythm. They continued to post their writing along with Jeremy's collections of words and Grace's drawings. Without even meaning to, Brewster turned his journal into his own numbers book, recording how much they spent, how many credits they had at the general store, the dimensions of the rooms they lived in, how much firewood they used in a day. Charlotte just stared at him.

Charlotte baked three mornings a week at the huge cast iron cookstove in the mess hall and began to know the soldiers, discovering which of them were homesick or lovelorn and which were glad to be so far from home. She was thankful that, although many were her age, none of them questioned her presence or appearance or anything else about her. Since there was no assigned cook, the soldiers took turns in the kitchen, which went a great way toward explaining the quality of their meals. She noted how different it was for the officers, who had their own cook and dining room. Poor Mrs. Bixby, Charlotte thought. Heaven forbid that she would ever have to prepare a meal with her own tender hands, or knit a sock.

Charlotte showed Brewster and Ada the unused schoolroom. It seemed the perfect place, official yet private. The first letter-writings for the soldiers were awkward, Brewster admitted, because he was so young. But his hand flowed impressively across the page and one trusting customer passed that view on to another. Ada came upon a different sort of trouble. For her, the soldiers were often young and embarrassed about being in her presence, a pretty almost-grown girl, first because they required such help and then because of the sentiments they often wished to express in the letters to someone back home. She treated them with a newfound quiet and sympathy that also gained their trust. Charlotte only worried that a few of them might fall in love. When the mountain men wanted to write a letter, Charlotte gave notice that she was to be alerted and she showed up herself to take on the task.

Jeremy took complete charge of brushing the horses and milking the cow. Charlotte grew tender watching him. He was still only six.

Sometimes, later in the night, when Charlotte stepped out onto the porch for air, she could hear the muffled conversation in the bar and games room above the mess hall after all the bugling was done for the day. Just to amuse herself, she toyed lightly with the idea now and then of vastly improving some of their fortune at cards and maybe making a little more money of her own. But the thought of cards brought back *deuces wild, the horses shuffling in the barn, his mouth, his hands*, and she couldn't bear it.

They read a chapter a night of a book about three Scottish boys shipwrecked on a Pacific Island.

"I'll listen to it," Ada said, "but don't girls ever get shipwrecked?"

When they'd finished the island adventures, Charlotte found another about a man and a dog living outside a fort in the west.

"I think we could have written this book," she said. "We just don't have a dog, that's all."

"Maybe we could get one," Jeremy offered.

There were mangy dogs roaming all over the fort. "Actually, forget I brought that up."

Charlotte made sure they were learning, eating enough, keeping clean, staying busy. She didn't try to relieve them of their sorrow. No one could do that. There was only one problem, Charlotte conceded, and it belonged to her.

She could manage reveille and Grace's blue eyes opening right in front of her face at exactly the same moment every morning. She could manage breakfast, buckwheat cakes, sausage and apples, porridge with honey. After breakfast was what she couldn't manage. Without any explanation, she would find herself running out the door, across the parade ground, out through the fort's open gates and around the corner, past the latrines, hopefully down to the banks of the river and into the bushes before she lost whatever breakfast she'd just eaten.

32

The wagon trains continued to pass through, one after the other, day after endless day. As the summer wore on, they camped farther and farther out to find grass for their cattle and horses. The fort had moved to restrict its own grazing lands before they were completely stripped by the onslaught. Men from the wagon trains came into the fort seeking supplies if they'd run perilously low, a smithy to fix a wheel or shoe a horse, a carpenter's shop where an axle could be retooled or a broken wagon tongue repaired. Some of the men, the less God-fearing among them, also took a moment to put a foot up at the bar and enjoy just one solitary throat-burning glass of whiskey.

The women arrived to sell off or simply abandon their heirloom furniture that had already been soaked, knocked about, portaged and dragged up cliffs on a rope. No piece of furniture, they'd decided, however sentimental, was worth all that onerous weight and work and trouble. Charlotte sometimes wondered what was left by the time they got to Oregon.

She began to understand also how money and connections spoke. The Family connections would never get her invited to dinner anywhere, quite the opposite, but often certain dignified parties from the wagon trains would arrive on foot, or in a delicate carriage that had been pulled all the way from Missouri, to dine with the Colonel and his lovely wife, and the Major and his not so lovely wife, and the junior officers who owned the required dress uniforms but had no wives at all. These more privileged men, just a day off the trail, wore handsome frocked coats and silk vests. The ladies' skirts rustled and ear bobs were in evidence.

"The world divides," Charlotte told Ada, watching one of these processions while they folded sun-dried laundry on the porch.

"Why don't we ever get invited to dine with the Colonel?"

"Something tells me the Colonel would prefer to be as far away from our kind of company as possible."

"What does he know?"

"Exactly."

< >

It was a revelation even to themselves how quickly Charlotte and Ada could knit socks. By the time they were done, everyone in the company owned a new pair and some had extras. Then Ada conceived the brilliant idea of making mufflers for the winter with the Army unit's insignia knitted into one end. Lenore said even the Colonel wanted one. In the rest of her time Ada concentrated on the letter-writing which soon turned into many requests not just for the letters, but for acquiring the skills necessary to write those letters.

Charlotte consulted with Lenore.

"The previous chaplain used to teach reading and writing for the men who needed it," Lenore said. "That was before the trouble." She paused. "You know that's why the Colonel's here, don't you? He wouldn't normally be posted to a fort in the middle of nowhere."

"I didn't realize."

"A tragedy and a disgrace the Army won't soon recover from."

Charlotte bowed her head, seeing Chace stare down the empty valley.

Lenore frowned inwardly. Then she straightened and put away her thoughts. "By all means, use the schoolroom. I'll get you more paper. Can you imagine? Letterhead's one of the few things out here that Congress is willing to pay for."

"Thank you," Charlotte said. "And I do want you to know that every time one of those mountain men shows up, they get me instead of Ada."

Lenore laughed. "More than they bargained for."

"Definitely. Or they get the both of us, which is even worse."

< >

August heat rose up from the ground, stifling in the rooms with one window and one door. Just when the heat seemed unbearable, a thunderstorm rolled across the prairie, blasting rain against the buildings, turning the parade ground into a churning sea of mud.

192

When the lightning cracked directly overhead and thunder coming right on top of it shook the ground, everyone held onto each other. Then the wind came up to a roar and hail beat against the windows, piling up in misshapen balls of ice on the porch. Within days the blazing heat returned along with a full moon that lit the darkened rooms with an eerie midnight glow.

The vegetables and melons in the fort's garden came ripe. Charlotte showed the young kitchen soldiers how to pickle carrots and onions, how to roast corn. Raspberries covered the canes on the bank above the river and raspberry bread appeared and quickly disappeared from the sutler's store. Any wagon trains pushing through this late with the mountains still ahead of them were regarded with dismay. So many graves along the trail resulted from bad luck, so why add to the already unfavorable odds with just plain bad decisions.

Brewster's birthday arrived and it seemed he'd grown at least three inches while waiting for it. Grace knew her numbers. Jeremy could write sentences. Ada was regaining her original self, losing the reserve and sadness that had haunted her, acquiring a shape and the amazing but certainly more annoying accompaniments of womanhood.

While Charlotte baked and gave cooking instructions in the mess hall, she also slowly went about learning who could possibly shoot a rifle and hit something. With that information in hand plus some monetary exchange, she managed to secure fourteen quail for Brewster's birthday celebration.

"*Fourteen,*" Brewster said, regarding her with sincere appreciation. "For my birthday?" He sat down and seemed momentarily overwhelmed. Then he rallied. "I don't think even I could have done that." Charlotte raised an eyebrow, then laughed.

As a chicken had still not made its appearance, Charlotte baked another eggless chocolate cake, this time with raspberry filling. She roasted the quail with bacon. She cooked wild greens and rice. It was a feast. Candles filled the table again and the room glowed.

"Happy eleventh birthday," Charlotte said.

"I made it," Brewster said solemnly, which gave Charlotte pause.

"Eleven going on twenty-five. I think you ought to run for an office of some sort. We'll find one that takes eleven-year-olds. But in the meantime..."

Charlotte reached under the bed and brought out one of the Henrys. "I know you have your Pa's shotgun but this is different. It's from my father again. He gave this rifle to me on, well, another occasion, and I'm giving it to you for your birthday." She retrieved a box from the sideboard. "Ammunition. And plenty more where that came from. I'll tell you what I know about the gun, which is about two sentences' worth, and then you're on your own."

Brewster laid his hands on the rifle and suddenly blinked back tears. Ada and Charlotte found themselves doing the same. Jeremy moved closer hoping that he would at least get to touch it.

33

September arrived, the moon when the calves grow hair. Summer died and the grasses went to seed. The days grew shorter and Charlotte couldn't get her skirts to close. She was aware that she had grown temporarily gaunt from losing too many breakfasts and a few dinners as well. Now, as that particular siege relented, she realized that in places where she'd been pleasingly slender before, she'd somehow become disconcertingly wide. In order to appear decently clothed, she kept carefully inching up the waistbands to where they would come together. Then she found another solution.

"Why are you wearing an apron?" Ada said.

"Didn't all those women on the wagon train wear aprons? I know they did. It's what women do."

"But not you. You're not like them."

"Here's what," Charlotte said. "I cook over a fire, I haul in my own wood and bake in that smoky oven in the mess hall. I keep running into all those carcasses they hang up in there. I do laundry. I'm out in the garden. How many decent clothes do you think I have? That's what an apron does, it protects them. And I'll have you know, I actually have two." She'd found them in the wagon, a miracle, though it summed up her father's wishes for her, even with her appearance back then, to be like the other women. If they had aprons, she should have aprons. She'd cut up the bonnet to make part of a dress for Grace. But the aprons, what else was she supposed to do?

Charlotte could feel Ada studying her, dwelling on the issue. The answer hadn't come to her yet, in part, Charlotte knew, because Ada couldn't discover any way that such a thing would be possible.

Ada looked perplexed when Charlotte finally broke down and announced the news.

"You have questions. That's understandable, given the situation."

"I don't even know what to ask. Doesn't there have to be a…."

"Yes, of course there does. This isn't the Second Coming. Oh my Lord, you didn't just hear me say that."

"So…" Ada said.

"So I can't tell you anything."

Ada was quiet. "Will you go away?"

"Ada, it never occurred to me you'd think that. No, I'm not going anywhere. Nothing changes. We stay exactly how we are." But then it did occur to her that she had just become the definition of a fallen woman, a perfect example for an impressionable if somewhat precociously cynical thirteen-year-old girl.

The old Ada returned. "Do you even know how to have a baby?"

"No idea. Do you know?"

"Of course I do."

"Of course you do."

Ada narrowed her eyes, this child with the naïve but pointed insights. "When you left, where did you go?"

Charlotte put a finger to her lips. "Shhh," she said.

"What's the use of questions if I can't even ask them?"

"Questions won't do any good at this point. I'm just going to need your help with having this baby, that's all."

<>

"Well," Lenore said.

Charlotte was sitting in the familiar chair, staring at the familiar plaques and photographs on the walls.

"Where does your husband go all the time?" Charlotte said. Major Bixby was often the only one in charge though a tall, barking sergeant appeared to actually be running the fort.

"Out on expeditions. This time it's with a delegation from Washington City discussing solutions to the problems in the territories. Along with a hunting trip where I've no doubt by now they've killed everything in sight."

"Do you get lonely?"

"Actually I don't. Do you?"

Charlotte knew it was a serious question. She realized she wasn't here to chat. This would be the enquiry she'd been dreading. In her worst moments, she saw herself being summarily banished from the fort for conduct immoral and unbecoming of a woman with someone else's children to raise.

"It's hard to be lonely when there's not ever a moment that you're even alone," she said. "But that's not what you're asking."

"No."

Charlotte raised her chin. "I didn't do anything wrong," she said.

"What did you do?"

This would be the only moment, the only time that she would give in. The stakes were too high to do anything else.

"I came to care for someone. Enough for it to be permanent. Forever."

"Yet you seem to be very much on your own."

"And I'll continue to be. I don't see that changing."

"If it did change, how would that affect the children? You understand where my responsibility lies. We've talked about this."

"I do understand. It's my responsibility too and I take it very seriously. They could only possibly be affected for the good in it."

"You stand by this person, even though absent?"

"In every way."

Lenore sat in her husband's chair, the tips of her fingers pressed together, and studied Charlotte. "How is your father going to feel about this?"

"My father?"

"Yes, Samuel Duchesne."

Charlotte's mouth flew open. "How do you know about that?"

"I told you I came from back east and was aware of the Family. What I didn't tell you was that I knew your father many years ago, before you were born. Charlotte, my love, I also knew Tobias."

Charlotte did some rapid calculations and decided she was about to be mortified. "What are you telling me?" she said.

"That when Tobias came looking for you the first time and you weren't here, we sat down and had a long talk."

"About?"

"Everything. And now I want so much to hear about the woman you sold your hair to. That was fascinating."

Charlotte congratulated herself on being correct. Mortification was at hand. She felt her face grow hot. "Then you can't possibly have any faith left in me at all."

"Quite the contrary. You were very passionate about the children and I was impressed at the lengths you'd go to keep them."

"I still feel the same way. And I wouldn't ever bring anyone into their life who wouldn't place their welfare exactly where I place it, before my own. Though I assure you, there's no possibility of that happening."

Charlotte closed her eyes. It was even more of a humiliation that Lenore apparently knew all the details of her past. Then another thought occurred to her.

"Did you know my mother?"

"I never met her, though I knew who she was, everyone did. She was considered very brave for being willing to marry him with all that entailed." Lenore sighed. "I'm only telling you this because the Colonel's so far away and naturally it shall be between you and myself, as so many things are it seems, but I had wanted to be the brave one."

"You?" Charlotte said. "My father?" She was stunned.

"Your father," Lenore said and smiled. "Imagine that. But he loved her very much and everyone else was lost to him. However, this isn't bringing us any closer to that larger question. What is he going to do when he receives this information, which of course sooner or later he will?"

"Likely accept it. What else can he do?"

"You'll have to let me know because I'll be concerned. And in the meantime, you do have enough help, don't you?"

"More than enough."

Lenore smiled again. "And obviously with your vast experience you're perfectly capable of getting a child born."

"Absolutely. And if I weren't that wouldn't stop me anyway."

"As it hasn't yet. You've done an admirable job."

"Anyone would."

"That's not entirely true. I'll tell you this, I'm grateful every day that I trusted my instincts."

"So am I."

Charlotte was at the door when Lenore spoke again. "She was beautiful, Charlotte, and if Tobias hasn't told you then I will. You look just like her."

<>

The sergeant granted permission for Charlotte to take Brewster out to the target practice range. He stared enviously first at the Henry and then at the box of ammunition.

"Any time you'd want to spare that," he said. "Those rifles we got couldn't hit a slow-moving mule from ten feet and you don't get but about three chances at it anyway."

Then Charlotte had to hurry Brewster off because the sergeant, who wasn't all that old, had begun staring at her, trying to put together the pieces and not coming up with any explanation that worked.

"Here's what I know," she said. "How to load it." She showed Brewster, but he already seemed very familiar with the concept. "Then it has a kick that you've got to account for, but you probably know that too."

She heard Chace's voice. *It sights high.*

"Shut up," she said.

"What?' Brewster said, confused.

"Not you. Sorry. I really am losing my mind. Pay no attention. It sights high, though."

It didn't take much work for Brewster to become accurate.

"This irritates me," Charlotte said. "That's great at a hundred paces, you're very good, but what squirrel sits at a hundred paces and waits for you to shoot him? We'll have to find a way to get you some live practice."

"I love this rifle," Brewster said. She realized her thoughts were in some other place entirely. She hugged him even though he squeezed his eyes shut and flinched.

"Good, I'm glad. And it never kills anyone to be hugged."

He waited. "I've been having something on my mind. I hope it's okay to say."

"It's always okay. You can say anything to me."

"Well," he said slowly. "This is what I was thinking. I didn't want to talk to Ada about it. I just thought I should ask you. Are you going to…"

"Yes," she said. "And no, I'm not leaving, nothing's changing, yes, I do not know how to have a baby. Anything else you wanted to know?"

Brewster was completely flustered. "I don't think so."

<>

Next she had to help Ada. They sat in the schoolroom together, once more facing the mountain man, Jenkins McPherson. They already knew most of his life story since he liked nothing better, he assured them frequently, than talking to two pretty young ladies. Just keep reading, Charlotte thought. That's what we're here for.

Despite his rough appearance, he confided matter-of-factly that he wasn't even really a mountain man anymore, no beaver left, no market for it anyway, the passes well traveled, the wilderness next to gone. What he knew, he said, was the Indian lands, so he'd become a scout, a tracker, a guide, a sign language expert, an explorer, sometimes based out of the fort, sometimes ignoring the fort altogether. His one wish though was to be able to read a book and write a letter, not such a different wish than any of the others. He didn't know his age exactly, having been on his own one way or another for so long. Charlotte thought if he were to get cleaned up, shaved and shorn, he might actually still be short of old by a lot and not totally horrible-looking.

"I'm not able to read this *Moby-Dick*," he said, putting the book down on the desk that he was barely able to fit into.

"It's difficult," Charlotte said. "To raise the reading level is all."

"Difficult, yes, but I've got so many quarrels with the author that I can't see straight."

"You do?"

"Yes, so I'm respectfully returning it back to your possession."

"Here, try out another then. It's about a man marooned on an island, sort of like a mountain man without the mountain."

"We read it out loud," Ada said. "It was hard, but good."

"Reading what's hard is how you learn," Charlotte said.

She realized that Jenkins McPherson was watching both of them and not thinking about whether a book was hard or good.

He turned to Ada. "Miss," he said. "I'd like to ask for your hand in marriage."

Ada turned fifteen different shades of crimson. Charlotte gasped. "Do you realize I'm sitting right here?"

"I do, no disrespect meant. But she's sitting right there and I've been thinking on asking her for some time now."

"No disrespect meant?" Charlotte was sure that in about one minute her voice would be rising to a level no one wanted to hear. "She's *thirteen*."

"How old do you think I was when I got out into those woods, having to find my own dinner, my own bed, learn by myself about the world and how it all worked?"

Now he had done it. "Jenkins McPherson, don't tell me about any of this. I don't want to hear it. We all of us have our very sad life story. Before you go shooting your mouth off you should maybe ask somebody else how things have gone for them lately. Or ever."

"I think maybe you're a bit tetchy because you're in the family way," he said, looking less than certain now about this whole affair.

"I'm a bit tetchy, as you call it, *because she's thirteen!*" Charlotte said, getting to that untenable level.

Charlotte felt Ada put a hand on her arm. Then Ada herself was speaking and far more calmly.

"Thank you, sir, for your kind offer," she said. "I regret to inform you that I am not matrimonially disposed at this time."

"I appreciate the care you took with stating that," he said. He stood up. "I still need to learn to read and write the best I can. That's the only future I got now. I'd like to hope I'd retain my welcome here."

"You will," Ada said. "Always."

Charlotte stood by, stunned. Just like that, one of her children was no longer a child. "How is it that you're the calm one and I'm the wild one?"

"I don't know."

"You handled that beautifully. I'd say you just made a friend for life."

Ada gazed out into space. "My first marriage proposal," she said and Charlotte was surprised to hear almost a wistfulness in her voice.

"You're planning on having more than a few?"

Ada came back to earth. "No. But it was a moment, anyway. I never had anyone ask to marry me before."

"Can I just say one more time that you're thirteen? And were you honestly aware of the person doing the asking? Promise me that next time you want that kind of moment you'll pick someone even remotely acceptable."

"I wonder what kind of dress I'd wear."

"Please stop," Charlotte said, "or I'm going to get the vapors like that old lady in the wagon train."

Without saying anything, Ada put her arms around Charlotte's neck and hugged her tight.

34

The moon of the falling leaves arrived and broad areas of color showed among the trees. Wild geese congregated in the fields. Formations of ducks flew high. The cicadas quieted but the great horned owl's haunting call still echoed in the night.

In this muted season of harvest and dying back, Charlotte felt as if she and the pumpkins in the garden were the only ones growing larger all the time. She had artfully added length to her skirts so that the hiked up waistband didn't leave a scandalous swath of petticoats. She knew she was, to some eyes at least, scandalous enough without a show of undergarments to compound the affront. The only good thing, she considered, was that her hair was filling in, curling down the back of her neck and over her ears, gently framing her face. Ada managed with more luck than skill to shape it so that it now retained some semblance of deliberation rather than vengeful wielding of scissors.

It was late afternoon. Charlotte had used some of their credits at the sutler's store to buy a cut of beef and a hearty stew simmered over the fire in the fireplace. It was Brewster's turn again to read out loud. Grace rested contentedly in his lap. Ada sat at the table knitting with Jeremy beside her drawing.

The door opened without a knock, letting in the slanting sunlight. And in the doorway suddenly stood Ellis Gray with Miller Dawson behind him. Brewster and Ada stood up quickly without knowing why. Grace found herself upright on the floor instead of sitting in someone's lap. Jeremy struggled off the bench because if everyone else was standing, he thought he should be too.

"Thank God, you're here," Ellis said, taking in all four of them. "Miller got your letter but no one knew what came after that, whether you stayed or…" He was obviously struggling with his emotions. Ada stepped forward and he stared at her. This was not the wild child he had known, the one without shoes or a hairbrush, the one who wouldn't speak.

"You've grown up," he said, but then was even overcome by that statement.

"Captain Gray," she said. "We wanted to see you again. You were good to our parents and you gave us the best people to be with. Miller Dawson stood by us for as long as he could without anyone ever asking him to. Then he promised Charlotte would come, and she did."

"That doesn't help my part in this. But Miller and I thank you for your kind words."

Charlotte realized he was not wanting to see what he was seeing. Miller obviously didn't understand what he was seeing either, but was now so embarrassed that he couldn't get his bearings anyway.

"Please, everybody sit back down," Ellis said. He hadn't meant to make it sound so much like a command, but he realized he was in a state.

"I don't believe I'm in the mood for sitting," Charlotte said, meeting his eyes.

"Here we are again," he said. "Just like the old days I tried to forget about. Seems like some things haven't changed at all in the time I've been gone and other things have changed more than anyone had a right to expect."

"Hello, Ellis," she said. "I'm glad to see you too. Ask me what you have to ask."

"I have just one shred of hope. Did you go out to the desert?"

"I did not."

"Not even for two days or a week or something like that?"

"Not even for one minute."

"Damn it to hell."

"You realize there are children present."

"Step outside then. You and I need to talk."

"I won't step outside. There's nothing you can say. There's nothing to talk about."

Miller backed up. This was all very familiar to him.

"You know what I want to do?" Ellis said. "I want to pull this door off its hinges and throw it on the porch and smash it into a thousand pieces."

"That's interesting," she said. "It won't help anything, though."

"Jesus Christ, will you just get outside?"

"Not till you calm down."

"I don't think I'll ever calm down again."

"It's not that bad," Charlotte said.

Ellis rubbed his hands over his face. "Not that bad. A four-day blizzard's not that bad. A rattlesnake in your boot's not that bad. This? There are no words." Miller took two more steps back. Ada and Brewster held onto each other.

"I hate it when you shout."

"I hate it when you do stupid things. We're going to talk if I have to bodily remove you from the house."

"I'm only relenting because, if I could remind you yet again, there are children and you're making a scene."

Outside, one hand on her elbow, he hustled her down the porch, across the parade ground and out through the front gate, leaving Miller standing with his hat in his hand having no idea what to do next.

"Hold on," Ellis said. "I have to be able to breathe." He left her, walked in a large circle and came back. "That's a little better at least. Now, enlighten me as to what's going on."

"What you see is what's going on. That's all there is."

"God in heaven, I don't even know where to start."

"There's nowhere to start. This is it. I'm sorry you're not handling it well."

"Handling it well? I want to shoot myself."

Charlotte stopped and stared at him. "You're taking responsibility? That's a very strange thing to do."

"Yes, I'm taking responsibility. It started with me."

"Ellis, I don't think you understand how any of this works. And as I recall, it didn't start with you at all, it started with your grandfather. Personally, I've been thinking about that and I don't believe he'd be near as upset as you are."

205

"He couldn't be upset. He's dead."

Charlotte stopped again. "Oh no. When? Did he get to Washington City?"

"It was on the way back. He knew it was coming."

"I'm sorry," she said.

"He got near enough to home. That's something. We could bury him the way he wanted."

"Did the meetings do any good?"

"Of course not. But we weren't talking about him, we were talking about you."

Charlotte was finding it increasingly difficult to entertain this subject no matter who entered the conversation. She was aware that her discomfort showed and that Ellis saw it. In response, he put one arm firmly around her shoulder and held her close as they walked. She hugged herself in the chill of the fading afternoon sun and matched her stride to his slower pace.

"You have to speak," he said.

"I can't tell you anything," she said. "I just can't do it."

"How long were you out there?"

"I didn't want to ever reach the fort. I didn't want any of what the future held for me. But you knew that. I said I would appreciate if it just took some time."

"Why aren't we at least mentioning his name?"

"Because I won't. Not to you. Not to anybody."

"I know we've talked about how wishing doesn't mean one goddamn thing, but do you wish this had turned out differently?"

"It's impossible to make you see," she said, "and there's nothing to be done about that. I will tell you this much. The answer to your question is no. Every minute of my day is spent being grateful for this child that's coming and that I'm here for the other four."

"I can't imagine it's been easy, that part of it."

"Nothing's easy. We've talked about that too."

Charlotte felt him pause.

"I have two questions that I have to ask and you have to answer," he said. "First, do you know where he is?"

"Out there somewhere." She struggled inwardly. "He told me things. He showed me the valley. We both understood that when he left he wouldn't be back. He always made me aware of that. There was never anything hidden between us."

"There's the second question then. Does he know?"

"No." She wrapped her arms more tightly around herself.

"Let's turn around and go back," Ellis said.

"We should. Miller will think we killed each other."

And then there was silence. As they drew near to the fort the sun was sliding behind the trees and the air was growing cold.

"Charlotte?" Ellis said.

"Yes?" She thought they'd reached some sort of peace, but his voice was tense.

"I'm going after him."

"You can't. He's out there for a reason. He has to live his own life. Leave him be."

"I'll choose to ignore what you know and go with what I know."

"That's not fair to anybody. Least of all him."

"No more," Ellis said. "Be quiet, though I'm aware that's not something that comes naturally to you. I'm leaving."

"When?" she said, panicked.

"Right now. Tell Miller where I've gone."

<>

Ten days later Charlotte looked up from reading to Jeremy and Grace and there was Ellis, alone.

"I couldn't find him. I tried."

"I didn't want you to find him. Sit down, I'll get you something to eat. You're exhausted."

At least it was over. Now she could allow her mind to return to the schedule of their days, the schooling and bread baking, the chores and knitting, the horse and cow grazing.

He removed his coat and sat down wearily at the table. "He'll know I was out there."

"Don't. Please," Charlotte said. "I can't take any more."

"I left signs, messages."

"Like what? Telegrams? Four-page letters nailed to a tree?"

"There are no trees, there's nothing in those high canyons. No, it's what scouts and trackers do and he's better at it than anybody living or dead. He'll come across them."

"Ellis, stop talking. I made a life here and now I have to get back to it as if you never showed up and started yelling."

"I'll just say one more thing and then I'm done. Look at me." She did. "I'm pretty sure that, because you're so stubborn, when you commit to something, or someone, it's for good. If you didn't feel things so strongly, or have such a vile temper, I wouldn't have gone."

"So now it's my fault?"

"My going is no one's fault. It's because I care about you."

She didn't mean to blush. "And who cares about you, Ellis?"

"Someone does. Or at least I think they do."

"Besides me?" she said, surprised.

"Thank God besides you." Ellis took a sealed letter out of his shirt and put it on the table.

Her studied glance went from the letter to him and back again. "What is that all about? And why haven't you opened it?"

"I'm afraid to open it."

Charlotte stared at him. "You are? Then who is it from?"

"I don't know why I'm telling you this. It's from someone I met in Missouri."

"The way you're acting it has to be a woman. Come out with the rest of it."

Ellis leaned his head on his hands. "Her name's Isabelle," he said. "She's got two daughters. Small, like Grace."

"And the husband?"

"Dead. Got kicked in the head trying to break a horse."

"And there you were being so charming, women swooning all over the place…"

"Women were never swooning."

"I beg to differ. And yet she's still in Missouri."

"She had to think about it. Me. Oregon Territory. Then I was in a different place than I said I'd be, so this letter took some time getting to me."

"Do you want me to read it and tell you what it says?"

"That's the last thing I want."

Charlotte let her eyes rest fondly on him. "So if life finally decides to be good to you, you might get that green land in Oregon Territory you talked about and even a fine woman and her two daughters to go with it."

"Or get thrown to the ground and trampled."

"Or that," she said. "I'll pray for you."

"That scares me more than a little."

Charlotte smiled. "You're a good man, you know. My father's trust wasn't in any way misplaced."

Ellis laid his head on the table. The mention of her father brought back everything, the wagon train, Washington City, the burial, her being here in this condition, Chace out there who knew where. "Don't," he said. "Now I'm the one who can't take it."

35

With winter approaching, half the cavalry unit of the fort was reassigned to Texas. Lenore's husband, a bearded and hearty man, reappeared leading a contingent of officers and servants, five supply wagons, a cooking wagon, ten extra horses, and an entire train of mules loaded down with tents and furnishings and game. Charlotte watched Lenore descend the stairs from their quarters to greet him. She observed his half-smile, the touch of an arm, then attention turned in another direction. Charlotte thought he seemed far less than eager to give up the camaraderie of the plains and resume the dull bugle-blowing, endless parade-marching, target-shooting existence of an out-of-the-way fort, nodding by the fire with a wife, even an exceptional one. Charlotte consigned him to the trash heap of men who didn't deserve what they had.

<>

Ellis and Miller settled back easily into the barracks and life at the fort. They gave their time to whatever job was needed, shoeing horses, sewing harnesses, splitting logs, chopping wood, making repairs. Twice, having heard of trouble at Fort Pence, Colonel Hutchinson sent them to investigate. On another memorable occasion, the Colonel invited them to his office for a frank discussion of the Indian lands over cigars and brandy. Miller, with deep experience of the land that had been his home but no experience at all with social situations, got sick from the cigar and then drunk on the brandy.

Both of them respected the privacy Charlotte had built around the children. They came to dinner on Wednesdays and Sundays but otherwise stayed away, leaving her furious. At least when you come, she told them, be early enough for reading time so that they see a man now and then. Ellis pointed out that they lived in a whole fort full of men, but they began to dutifully appear at reading time and take their proper turns. Charlotte even forced the issue of a sketch.

"Listen to me," she said. "Children always need willing adults and good examples to follow. It's important."

"A sketch?" Miller said. He'd never heard of a sketch before. He could only read because Chace had taught him.

"It's writing about whatever you feel like, pick a subject. It doesn't have to be long. It helps if it's something you care about, like Jeremy writes about horses almost every time."

Miller nodded. Now he understood. He was also aware, however, that Ada was watching him and that tended to make him not think quite straight.

"You don't have to say what you decide. Though usually we do."

"And they're on government stationery," Ellis said, noting with interest the pages on the wall.

"Lenore gave it to us. That way, if you want very much to let someone know something, you can and it's official."

"Tempting."

"I'm going to write on the Colt pistol," Charlotte said. Ellis narrowed his eyes at her, but said nothing. What Colt pistol? Something else he didn't remember her mentioning to him.

"Brewster?" she said.

"My Henry rifle." Charlotte smiled.

"Ada?"

"Jenkins McPherson." Charlotte stopped smiling.

"Ellis?"

"You forgot me," Jeremy said.

"Good. Let him take his turn while I try and think of something."

"My pants," Jeremy said.

"Your pants?"

"It's that they have these special buttons on them now." The ones she'd found in his mother's button box, with curious anchors on them.

"Ellis? I'm back to you."

"Dried buffalo meat."

Charlotte tried hard not to burst out laughing. "Miller?"

"No one's ever asked me to write a sketch before in my whole entire life," he said. "I just found out what one is."

"It's only a poor man's way of schooling, that's all. Just make up a subject. That's what the rest of us are doing. For example, dried buffalo meat."

"Jack, then, my horse," Miller said and Jeremy smiled. Ada prayed that Charlotte wouldn't mention the sketch about Miller's horse already up on the wall, the first one Ada had written because she couldn't come right out and write about Miller.

<>

On a Wednesday evening in the middle of a rainstorm while they were eating dinner together a knock came at the door. Charlotte froze with her fork halfway to her mouth and turned pale. She put the fork down and folded her hands tightly in her lap.

"Ellis, please?"

He nodded and went to the door. It was Tobias, soaking wet, his hair plastered to his head, rain dripping off his waterproofs. Charlotte felt herself exhale. She took a moment to recover, but then realized that her problems had just begun. Might as well take them on directly, she told herself, and stood up for the full effect.

"Tobias," she said. "You're back."

"I said I'd be." He was appreciating the warm familial scene before him, the table, the fire, the food, and not actually focusing on her yet.

"Get off your wet things. Is your horse still out there?"

"I put him in the stables." He struggled with his long damp coat then went out and hung it over the porch railing. Gratefully he took the towel she offered to dry his hair. When he handed the towel back, for the first time his eyes rested fully on her and his face showed the shock.

"There are things I didn't know about."

"Yes."

"Thanks be to God and everyone else that I didn't bring him with me." Dinner had halted entirely.

"Who?" she said, completely alarmed.

"Your intended."

"Good Lord. Surely you weren't thinking of doing that."

"I was thinking of it very seriously. I figured to maybe force the issue."

"That would have forced it all right. I apologize again to you for being in the awful place you're in."

Tobias let his gaze fall more carefully on the people at the table. "I just don't understand," he said. "Is one of you...?"

Ellis immediately held his open palms in the air, indicating that he wasn't the responsible party, not for this part of it anyway. Miller looked around panicked, thinking this man had to be talking to someone else besides himself.

"Well, then..." Tobias said. His voice drifted off. He shook his head, seeming totally bewildered.

Charlotte quickly spoke. "You've already met the children. This is Ellis Gray and Miller Dawson." They both reached out and shook hands, Ellis hoping Tobias was bad at remembering names.

"Tobias Duchesne is my uncle. Tobias, seat yourself and I'll get you a plate. We even have brandy tonight as Miller needs some practice in drinking. After all that rain and damp, a little brandy might take the chill off."

Tobias could think of nothing better than a glass of brandy or maybe two. It was Ellis Gray's wagon train. It was Ellis Gray who left and no one seemed to know why. But now here he was and there she was with apparently no hard feelings, only this whole other situation to contend with. He wondered why he hadn't just said no to Samuel and stayed in the desert.

The dinner conversation picked up again, revolving strictly around safe topics. Charlotte was grateful to Tobias for not mentioning her father, the Family, or anything about the wagon train. And he'd drained the brandy. When the plates were clean and Grace was yawning, Ellis and Miller stood up, ready to depart.

"There's plenty of room in the barracks," Ellis said. "Stay with us. And if you're so inclined, I have no doubt that we could find a card game and maybe even some whiskey."

What was Ellis doing? Charlotte thought. He knew about the Family. Pure and focused. Brandy was bad enough. Cards and whiskey would never even be considered.

"I wouldn't mind," Tobias said and Charlotte stared at him in disbelief. He was one of the Elders.

"Cards are forbidden," she said. "You can get lashes for that."

"I did once."

"I did too."

The room grew silent again. Tobias held her with his eyes for a long moment. "You did?" He narrowed his eyes. "Ah, the Family."

In the morning when Tobias came to say goodbye, he had grown calm and thoughtful.

"I believe you and I are cut from the same cloth," he said.

"Not what they were hoping for."

"Not even close, but that's not always a bad thing. There's a need for some differences. Least that's what I keep trying to tell your father."

"Does he listen?"

"No, but he's set on his path. He does what he has to do." Tobias regarded her with concern. "Will you be all right?"

"I will. But I'll find a way to let you know."

"I'd appreciate that." He paused. "Was it poker?"

"It was."

"Are you good?"

"I am."

"That's our legacy then." He smiled and bent to kiss her cheek. "Pass it on."

"I will," she said. "Pure and focused."

"Always."

<>

Ada found Charlotte with books spread on the floor all around her. "What are you doing?"

214

"Searching for something. I know I saw it but I don't remember where."

"What is it?"

"Wait till I find it," Charlotte said. "It's perfect."

"Perfect for what? And how are you going to get back up off the floor?"

"You're going to help me, I guess. You know when Ellis and Miller wrote their sketches and we all said what we'd write about? Do you remember what you said?"

Ada thought for a moment. "Was it Jenkins McPherson?"

"It was. And right then I realized that you saw him in a whole different light than I did."

"I had to see him in a different light. He asked me to marry him."

"No, I mean, him wanting to read and write. I didn't take that seriously. You did."

"Because he was serious."

"See? That's what I mean. Do you know what a good person you are?"

"I am not a good person," Ada said. "I refuse to be."

"Well, that's wonderful, but I think you are in spite of all your best intentions. It's a book about the Oregon Trail."

They sifted through the endless volumes till Ada held one up in her hand. "Is this it?"

Charlotte took it from her and opened the cover, thumbing through the pages. "It is. Look. It's got chapter after chapter, written by someone who was right here and not all that long ago."

"And we're giving this book to Jenkins McPherson," Ada said. Suddenly it came to her. "Because maybe he's in it."

"Or at the very least it'd be familiar to him. This is everything he's been telling us about."

"And maybe someday he could write his own."

"You're way more generous than I'd be in believing he'd get that far, but stranger things have happened."

"He's gone for a while though."

"He is?" Charlotte said. "How do you know?"

Ada blushed. "He came and said goodbye."

"Bastard. When I wasn't there. Did he propose again?"

"Oh good, a new swear word."

"No it isn't and stop keeping track."

Then Ada ducked. "It's possible he did," she said.

Charlotte pursed her lips, thinking. "We might have to enlist someone stronger than me if he really does want to keep up with the schooling."

Ada stood up and held out her hands to try and help Charlotte up. It was a struggle. "We may have to enlist someone stronger than me if you keep deciding to sit on the floor."

"Have I told you how I feel about thirteen-year-old girls?" Charlotte said.

36

Charlotte began taking long walks outside the fort in the afternoons. She felt the need to keep moving and the cold air was a balm, freshening her senses that dulled with too much time spent over hot stoves and handiwork. The flocks of geese had begun their migration in earnest, rising up out of the fields, their calls carrying far into the night.

The leaves turned more quickly, leaving the forest dark and bare. The rushes along the riverbanks withered and bent. The fort's vast kitchen garden offered up only stubble and faded debris from the summer crop. Now the winter vegetables took hold, the pumpkins huge on the vines, the potatoes and turnips maturing in their own time, buried in the cold earth. Autumn winds blew fierce some days across the plains, coming from the north, touched with the frigid breath of winter ice and snow.

Charlotte tried to take someone with her whenever possible. She realized that it was neither seemly nor prudent for a woman to be alone so far outside the gates, though there had been no trouble from any quarter and all around lay only silence. Ellis, Miller, Brewster all accompanied her when they could, as glad as she was for a break in the day.

On Sunday, Charlotte grew restless earlier than usual. It being the Sabbath, the routine of the fort was suspended and the chaplain attempted to gather at least a handful of the faithful for services, though he didn't always succeed. The card tables and refreshments of an alcoholic nature provided him with unfair competition though he never complained. The rest of his life was easy, far from the strictures of the mother church.

Brewster and Jeremy bent over their books on the floor by the fire. Charlotte considered that they bore a perfect resemblance to the children she'd imagined living in the abandoned cabin. The thought was pleasing to her.

"Ada," she said. "Walk with me?"

"I hope it won't rain. You go out in any weather."

"Have you been outside at all today? Try and find a cloud."

"I'll go, then. And you know I don't mind."

"I do know." Ada still chafed at the questions that went unanswered, but she forgave easily and was glad for all the other questions that did have answers. Charlotte meant for Ada to grow up far less innocent of the truths of life than Miller was.

Charlotte worked her way into her velvet coat, which no longer had a prayer of buttoning down the front, and wrapped a large shawl around her. Ada, without even being conscious of it anymore, pulled on her mother's coat and the knitted scarf with the military insignia that Joseph Beacham had embarrassingly presented to her, completely oblivious as to its origin.

"On the way back we should see if there're more winter squash ready," Charlotte said.

"They're so heavy now."

"We'll only take two each. I want to experiment with some savories."

They went across the hard-packed parade ground and out through the gates, nodding to the guard on duty as they passed by. Outside, they stopped to take in the broad plain, the rough worn track, the forest beyond, the meadow reaching down to the river, the huge sky. The smell of wood smoke hung in the air.

It was Ada who realized it first.

"Charlotte," she said, and put a hand on Charlotte's arm.

There it was in the distance, the big gray. The horse and its rider kept coming and Charlotte couldn't move. She felt as if Ada's hand was the only thing holding her up.

"Should we go back inside?" Ada said.

The rider was shrouded in a blanket as the old ones had been, though his midnight black hair and the silver at his ears were clearly visible. There was no sign of the rifle or the bow. Behind him, he led a mule carrying an antelope and a pile of small game that Charlotte knew a swift arrow had brought down.

"Ada," Charlotte said slowly. She couldn't take her eyes from the gray. "This is him."

"Who? What do you mean? He's…"

"I know. I know everything, all of it."

"Oh my God."

Charlotte took a fraction of a second to acknowledge that Ada sounded just like her. What had she done to this child? The gray was still advancing, but more slowly now. "Stay here for just one minute. I'll be back. I promise."

As Ada watched, Charlotte began to walk forward. The gray stopped. Chace took off the blanket and let it fall behind him. Once their eyes met, his never left hers. He swung his leg over the front of the saddle and slid off the horse.

Charlotte was briefly aware of his changed attire, worn boots beneath the buckskin pants, a uniform jacket over the faded shirt. She kept coming, holding him with her gaze as he was holding her. He stood, waiting. She closed the distance between them.

Here was the face she'd held in her memory, in her heart. His eyes were as troubled as when they'd first met. She wondered if they always would be.

"It's you," she said softly.

"It is, but I need to know that it's okay."

"You aren't old yet."

"I feel like I am."

"I thought the canyons were where you wanted to be."

"So did I. But it wasn't the truth."

She reached up to touch him. "It's more than okay," she said. "I've been waiting for it. Praying for it."

He took her hand and held it against him, then wove his fingers into her hair. His mouth found hers gently, the kissing thoughtful, long and slow. She pressed her hands into the front of his coat and the kisses grew more intense, filled with wanting, until they were both lost in the longing and pain there was between them, the warmth and tenderness, all that they'd been to each other.

Ada almost felt she had to turn away. She'd never in her life seen someone kissed like that. The sight sent strange sensations all up and down her and made her toes curl in their boots. She couldn't understand at all what was happening, who this person was, where he'd come from, anything.

When the kissing ended, still neither of them let go.

"There's just one important thing I need," Charlotte said. "Tell me you're here to stay."

"I'm here to stay. I won't leave you again. Ever."

She took his hands and laid them under hers against the tight hard outward curve of her belly.

"Do you regret this?" she said, her heart momentarily stopped.

"How could I regret it?" he said. "It means more to me than you'll ever know. I didn't start out to have it happen though."

"You tried hard to resist," she said, smiling though her eyes were filled with tears. "And I appreciate that."

"If it hadn't been for the barn. And the rain…"

"Night was the problem. If it hadn't ever got dark…"

He took her face in his hands and kissed her again. "It's all coming back to me now," he said.

"And that's a good thing?"

"It is."

She was trying hard to keep herself together. "Come with me then. I've left Ada back there too long. She's likely out of her mind wondering what's going on."

They started walking, close, touching. Chace led the gray by the reins with the mule following behind.

"They don't know?" he said.

"They have no idea about anything."

"Are Ellis and Miller here?"

"Yes."

"I'll stay where they are then, as long as Colonel Hutchinson lets me in."

"Why wouldn't he?"

"I've sometimes been a problem to him."

"Now you tell me. Not always opposites."

"No, not always."

<>

Ada had so many conflicting emotions running up against each other inside her that she couldn't think straight. He was a member of the tribes. He wore silver in his ears and at his wrists, but also a uniform jacket. And he'd just spent enough time kissing Charlotte that Ada felt like she wanted to faint. None of it made any sense.

"Ada," Charlotte said. "This is Chace. Chace Bridger Yellow Cloud."

Chace held his hand out and Ada shook it but she was unsteady. After what she'd seen, she felt strange and unnerved touching him. She quickly took her hand back as if it had been burned.

"I can't even ask anything. It's all too confusing."

"I was up on the ridge that day," Chace said. "I saw you running."

"You did?"

"I was trying to find where the rifles were, but you went across all of that."

"Why were you there? The old men looked so sad."

"The old ones were sad. One of them was my grandfather. He wanted to go one last time to Washington and try to talk to the white people's old ones about his land and how he wanted to keep it."

"Did they go?"

"They did, and they took Ellis with them."

"They took him because he lost his wife?"

Charlotte held her breath. Chace might have just met his match.

"Yes. They wanted him to speak for them."

"And did he?"

"I don't know."

"Do you think they got their land back?"

"No."

"But what does that have to do with you?"

"Charlotte's father asked Ellis to get her safely to Fort Randall."

"Paid," Charlotte said.

"Paid Ellis. With him gone, she couldn't stay with the wagon train. My grandfather said I was now the one responsible for getting her to Fort Randall."

Charlotte didn't see what was coming.

"My father died of the fever, but my mother drowned in the river crossing," Ada said. "I know it wasn't his fault, but Captain Gray wasn't there to save her."

Chace never flinched. "So many died and Ellis couldn't save them. No one could."

"Your people? This is what you're saying?"

"Yes."

"Then you know what it feels like."

"Every day of my life."

"It hurts. You want to hate someone."

"I tried that," he said. "It doesn't work, so I have to find another way."

Ada didn't turn away from the truth in his eyes.

"Will you let me know when that happens?" she said.

"It just did."

37

The guard on duty did a double take.

"Chace," he said. "Is that you?"

"Sergeant Brower."

"You've been gone a long time," the guard said, remembering.

Chace nodded. "I have."

They walked across the parade ground. Chace tied the gray and the mule up at the railing.

"Are you ready?" Charlotte said.

Chace turned to Ada, catching her by surprise. "Are you ready?" he said.

"I think so." She had never dreamed this was who he'd be. "No, I am," she said. "I'm ready."

Charlotte opened the door. The room was warm from the heat of the fire. Grace sat in the rocking chair thinking she was reading to herself. Brewster and Jeremy looked up from their books. Quickly they stood up. Jeremy's eyes were as wide as an owl's. Brewster glanced at Ada hoping for answers, but she still wore a somewhat stunned expression herself.

"Ada?" Charlotte said.

"This is Chace Bridger Yellow Cloud," Ada said. "He was with the old men on the ridge that day." She turned to Chace. "This is Brewster. And Jeremy, and Grace."

Chace shook Brewster's hand, then Jeremy's. Jeremy appeared about as close to fainting as Ada had.

"Is this…?" Brewster said. He didn't even know what words to use.

"It is, yes," Charlotte said.

It only took Brewster a moment of studying to make his decision. Jeremy had to sit down. Grace watched silently.

"I'm glad to meet you," Chace said. "I only know what I know, which isn't much."

Brewster and Jeremy startled at the sound of his voice. Brewster opened his mouth to ask, but thought better of it. Charlotte was aware that without seeming to cast one glance around, Chace had seen the entire room and everything in it. He walked over to the sideboard, lightly ruffling Jeremy's hair in passing. Carefully, he reached in and picked up the eagle feather. He ran the feather thoughtfully through his hand then returned it to its place in front of the king-with-the-ax.

Grace had kept track of his every move. "Those are the bluest eyes I ever saw," he said. She reached up for the silver at his wrists. He held out his hand to let her touch it.

Somehow what should have been awkward wasn't awkward at all.

"I've got to unload the horse and mule and get them in the stables."

Brewster didn't hesitate. "I'll help. If you want help, that is."

"I'd be glad for the help."

"I'm helping too," Jeremy said. He wasn't about to let this person get out of his sight.

"Is that all right?" Brewster said.

"It is."

"I brush the horses every day," Jeremy said.

"Do you ride?"

Jeremy stopped. This was a question too large to even contemplate. "I don't ride."

"Do you ride?" Chace said to Brewster.

"I don't. Well, I haven't."

"Do you have saddles?"

"Only one that was Pa's."

"The mare's still here, isn't she?" Chace said to Charlotte. She nodded. "And that's good with you? We'll ride then. But right now I've got an antelope that I have to do something with."

When they were gone, Ada sank down onto a bench at the table. She still couldn't get over it all. "He was just out there, coming on his horse. Did you know he'd be here?"

"Never, though Ellis did go looking for him."

"They know each other?"

"They do. They know each other well."

"Will he live with us?"

"Not right now," Charlotte said. "But Ada, here's the truth. He's my life."

"And we're your life."

"Without question."

"And very important to you."

"Absolutely."

"I think I'm still in shock," Ada said. "It's just not what I ever expected."

"Do you think I expected it? Or that he did?"

"How did this ever happen?"

"We only had each other to be with. Spending all that time together, you can come to have feelings for a person, to care about them more than you ever believed possible."

"Then what?"

"Then one day I realized I didn't want to get to Fort Randall at all because I didn't want him to ever leave."

"But he did leave."

"He had to. I always knew that."

"Why?"

Charlotte could do nothing but say it. "On that day when Ellis lost his wife, Chace lost everyone, even his child."

"A child? Was it small?"

"Yes."

"That same way?"

Charlotte nodded. "He showed me the valley where they were. He felt like he shouldn't be with people anymore, that he should be alone."

Ada's eyes filled. Charlotte sat down and put an arm around her.

"Maybe he needs us," Ada said.

"Maybe he does."

After a long moment, Ada spoke again. "I never knew there could be that kind of kissing."

What to do with this? Charlotte thought.

"I can't talk about that yet," she said. "I promise you I will. No matter what else, though, it's not till you find the right one."

"Do you think Ma and Pa ever kissed like that?"

Charlotte closed her eyes. If this was what being a parent was like, she didn't see how anyone ever got through it.

"Ada, all I know is that people sometimes turn out different after they have a family and maybe not always an easy life. I'll bet when your mother and father were courting they did some fine kissing. That's what makes you want to…get married." No more. The kissing part was hard enough to explain.

<>

Jeremy and Brewster came back with ducks but Chace wasn't with them. Jeremy held out a pheasant feather.

"He said to give this to you."

"Is the rest of the pheasant somewhere?" But she could see that Jeremy had enough to think about already. "Never mind. Did you take care of the horses?"

"Just the gray one. The mule went away."

"Where would a mule go?"

"He's trading it," Brewster said.

"To whom? For what?"

"I don't know."

Charlotte's eyes lit with a smile. Nothing had changed. The pheasant feather was beautiful. She put it next to the others on the sideboard.

She tried to prepare the ducks for dinner even though her hands were shaking. Ada set the table using Charlotte's silver from the velvet-lined box, china instead of tin plates, the candles and oil lamps.

"Is it someone's birthday and no one told me?"

"It's even more special than that," Ada said. "Isn't it?" Charlotte went over and hugged her and refused to cry. "I don't put the candles out for just anyone."

226

"What should we do?" Charlotte said. She felt that everyone was nervous. "Try reading time again?" The consensus was yes, definitely reading time.

Ada sat with Grace in the rocking chair and picked up where they had left off in a book about a whole family marooned on an island, a favorite topic. As her voice rose and fell, the door opened and Chace was back. Ada paused.

"Keep going," he said. "I didn't mean to interrupt." The fire was roaring. He took off the uniform jacket and sat down next to Jeremy, his eyes resting on Charlotte over the candlelight. The door opened again and reading time was over for good. Ellis and Miller stepped into the room and both stopped as if they'd walked into a wall. Chace stood up.

"Two weeks I looked for you," Ellis said.

"I saw your tracks. I got your messages."

"Did you go to the valley? Did you find him?"

"I did and you know how much I'm obliged to you, for all of that."

Ellis stepped forward and they closed each other in a warm embrace. "I'm glad you're back," Ellis said, and his voice was rough with emotion.

Chace turned to Miller. Miller, for a moment lost for words, then spoke in the strange language and Chace answered him in the same odd tongue. This time Brewster's eyes grew wide. Miller, Ada thought. How could this even be? Then Chace held Miller hard. When he let go, Miller had to wipe his eyes with his sleeve.

"Too much," Chace said. "It's been too much."

"Well, here we are," Ellis said, "come for Sunday dinner."

The ducks, grilled in the fireplace, served up a fine meal.

"How did it go?" Chace said.

"You want to talk about it here? Now?"

"We're all family," Charlotte said. "Consider for a minute."

"I guess that's true."

"How did what go?" Ada said.

"Washington City."

227

Brewster frowned. "That's where you went? It must be far. To the other side of the country."

"It was far but we had good horses and the last part of the way we rode on a train."

"Was that same agent with you?" Chace said. "The one from Fort Pence?"

"Yes he was, talking loud and saying nothing as usual. I wish they'd pay me to do as little as he does. When we got there they put us up in a hotel that had feather beds and gas lamps. There was a dinner with starched tablecloths and oysters and beefsteak and goose and wine in crystal goblets."

"Were there congressmen this time?"

"Yes, more than a few, but what good are any of them? I said everything I was supposed to say and might as well have been talking to the man in the moon. The committee people listened and nodded and wrote things down every once in a while. Then everybody shook hands, Grandfather gave his gifts, they gave him another piece of paper with a lot of writing and seals and things on it and it was over. We took the train back to the horses and rode as far as we could."

Chace waited. "Was his dying easy?"

"He asked to be helped off his horse, said this is where it'll be, took his blanket, climbed up to the hilltop, laid down and closed his eyes. That was it. He was gone. We wrapped him in his blanket, took him to the valley and tied him up on a platform in the trees. When I met up with Miller again we went back and put those buffalo skulls at the bottom the way he'd asked."

"He got to be old," Ada said quietly. "That's something."

"True," Ellis said. "Though being old, he saw too much. I wish he'd known you. He took to Charlotte right away and you're two of a kind."

"Charlotte met him?" Ada said in disbelief.

"She did."

"She gave him a biscuit," Miller said and everyone looked at him. "No one could explain to him what it was." Again, Ada was studying Miller.

228

"If it's all right to ask," Brewster said, "what's an oyster?"

"It's a shellfish," Ellis said. "It's small, and they pry it open and inside there's this slimy thing that you swallow and they tell you it tastes like the ocean but who ever tasted the ocean?"

"Is it worse than buffalo liver?" Miller asked. He'd always had to work to get that down.

"Yes, it's worse."

"Is the train really fast?" Brewster said.

"Compared to a horse, yes sir, it is. Makes a month's journey into a handful of days."

"Then someday maybe there won't be any more wagon trains going to Oregon Territory," Brewster said and Chace regarded him with interest.

Ellis glanced at Charlotte. Grace was having trouble keeping her eyes open. "Is it time?" he said.

"Might be."

He and Miller reached for their coats and Chace reached for his.

"I give up," Ellis said. "What are you doing?"

"Coming with you."

"Why?"

Miller watched closely. This was another conversation he wasn't going to understand.

"Because it's not right to change everything all at once."

Ellis turned to Charlotte. "We talked about it," she said.

"What do I know? Do you know anything Miller?"

"I really don't," Miller said.

38

In the morning, Charlotte glanced up from baking bread in the mess hall kitchen and Chace was standing watching her. Her hand flew to her heart.

"You scared me. It's not real to me yet that you're here."

"Sometime I'll tell you where I've been and you'll know how real it is to me. The dreams didn't come back, did they?"

"No, and I'll owe you for that forever."

"Your hair's grown some."

"People still look at me."

"Let them."

She nodded at the woolen uniform jacket. "I can't get used to seeing you in that."

"Helps with coming back into this world, but also it's all I had."

"Chace, they want to keep on going to Oregon Territory."

"I already talked to Ellis and Miller about it."

"You did?"

"Ellis got word that a wagon train from back east would hire him for getting over the mountains. Miller and I'd divide up the scouting between us so the other one could stay with the wagon."

"You're serious that you'd go?"

"I promise you I don't know one living thing about goats or geese, or wagon trains either, but I'm good at what I do know."

"Ellis said you're better than anybody living or dead."

"That's Ellis. Can you spare some time?"

"Yes, soon," she said. "I'm almost done."

He sat down on the table with his boot heels resting on the bench.

The bugle sounded and noise issued from the parade ground. "I suppose that's familiar to you," she said.

Chace looked out the door of the mess hall. "Assembly of the guard duty. You get used to it."

"Brewster's learned all of it. He's like that."

"They're easy to be around."

"Are you relieved?"

"I wasn't ever worried. I trust you."

"If that's true, you're only the second person who ever has. There's something on your mind, though. What is it?"

"There's a lot of silence out there in the high country. So much of it that sometimes you begin to hear voices."

"Oh, no. Voices aren't good, are they?"

"My people's voices. And the old ones tell you when that happens, you always listen."

"Did you?"

"You have to."

"What did the voices say?"

"They said I was wrong. They said that's not what I was supposed to be doing, living and dying in the empty canyons."

"What were you supposed to be doing?"

"Finding a wife."

Charlotte hesitated for only one heartbeat. "What kind of wife?" she said.

"The kind that plays cutthroat poker and fries squirrels. And has four children."

"Or five."

"Or five. And owns a Colt she can't shoot."

"Unfair."

"And is worth twenty horses."

"Are you talking about me?"

"I'm fairly certain there isn't anyone else who fits that description."

"Because you realize, all things considered, I may not be the best marriage material there ever was."

"Between the two of us, which one is? Think about it."

"Chace, I don't have to think about it."

"Then can you go with me now?"

"Go where?"

"To the chaplain," he said.

Charlotte stared at him. "Today?" she said. "Right now?"

231

"If that's okay with you."

"I just wasn't prepared, that's all."

"There are things you need to do first?"

"Only get used to the idea this is actually happening." The heat from the cookstove was suddenly intense. She felt the flush rising in her cheeks.

"I'm concerned about what you're getting into," she said. "I'm not a member of the tribes."

"I wish you'd told me that sooner."

"But won't that change everything for you?"

"I didn't care about it back then where we were, and I don't care about it now. But there's the other side. I am a member of the tribes and there's no doubt about how much that changes life for you. It'll be there all the time. If you think people look at you now, just wait. And we'll always know that we came from very different places."

"I suppose that's true," Charlotte said, "but I don't care about any of it either. Or maybe it makes you even more important to me." She had to turn away. She bent to the oven and retrieved more loaves of bread, then came back to him. "There's one more thing and it's serious. You have to know it. It seems to me I'd be marrying myself out of the Family by doing this. But what if the horrible truth is that you'd be marrying yourself into it?"

"We have the voices and the old ones have visitors from the sky, but there are songs too. The rocks have a song, the fire has a song, all the four-leggeds have songs, the earth has a song. I bring my grandfather's words with me, and his songs and his spirit also."

"So nobody should worry about the Family is what you're saying. I won't then. In that case, I'm ready. Do you know where the chaplain even is?"

"He wasn't hard to find. I'd say he has some time on his hands."

"I have a favor to ask. Could we keep it just to ourselves for a while? That would mean a great deal to me."

"However you want it to be."

232

"There's one person who does have to know, though. I can't forget. The Colonel's wife."

"He's already aware that I'm here."

"Yes, but she's the one who agreed that I could keep the children even when I wasn't entirely honest with her."

"How weren't you honest?"

"I told her I sold my hair for money and the federal marshal was my uncle."

"Not much different than poker."

"Thank you for seeing it that way."

Her expression was gentle as she let her gaze rest on him.

"Really," she said, "is this strange to you?"

"No stranger than anything else. And it's better this way than my people's way, where I'd have to pay your father that same twenty horses, and I don't have them. I'd have to take you and carry you off, then defend our position when he came after us."

"You'd do it though, wouldn't you?"

"Not even a question. It'd just be a lot of work, that's all."

"The white people's way is easier then."

"Much," he said.

"That's something anyway."

Charlotte put on her coat. Forgive me, my sad, lovely father, but I found the right one, the good one, and I'm making this decision on my own.

None of the soldier cooks had appeared yet. She moved in between his knees. "I'm going to cause you trouble again," she said. "Kiss me just once." She closed her eyes as he took her face in his hands and spent time kissing her more than once.

<>

"You must think I never leave this office," Lenore said.

"I know that loud sergeant does something," Charlotte said, "but you're right, I believe you're running the fort and that suits everyone just fine."

"It wouldn't suit the government just fine. I'd have to write them a letter on your stationery explaining myself, and also exactly where the Colonel had got to."

"Hire Brewster. He'll write the letter for you."

"I don't know why I wouldn't. I depend on all of you for everything. You know you can't leave until at least spring or the whole place would fall apart."

"There's nowhere to even go till spring. But I did want to mention about the all-of-us part."

"Yes?" Lenore said. "I'm suddenly very interested. There are more of you? Possibly someone who arrived on Sunday and made his presence known to the Colonel?"

"Possibly."

"This is him then.

"It is."

"And everything in that conversation still stands?"

"Very much so."

"Of course it all left me stunned. I had no idea. Apparently the Colonel thinks highly of him even though it seems they've sometimes been adversaries. But apart from all of that, I need to ask and have you answer with your head, not your heart. Are you sure about this?"

"I've never been more sure of anything," Charlotte said, "but that's my heart saying it too. He's the one I want in my life and the only one there'll ever be. For now, he's living in the barracks with Ellis and Miller and the children will make their own decision, but I have no concerns about that either. You'll see."

"I'll take your word for it then."

"My real word."

"Yes," Lenore said, laughing. "That one. And Charlotte? I'm happy for you."

39

Chace located the saddles he wanted and took Jeremy and Brewster out one at a time. Jeremy rode his new Indian pony, the one Chace had traded the mule for. They rode far down the wagon track and back, then out again. Chace talked about the reins, the saddle, about the movement of the horse, the feel of it. Jeremy never stopped smiling. Brewster rode his own horse and took naturally to the saddle. Chace moved more quickly and soon they were cantering easily along the trail toward the mountains, Brewster not smiling at all, only concentrating.

The next time Chace rode with Jeremy, he picked up the pace. The next time he rode with Brewster, the Henry came along.

"What about me?" Ada said.

"What are you doing right now? We'll take Charlotte's shotgun."

"We will?"

When he went out with Ada, he lifted Grace onto the saddle in front of him.

Chace read to them, though he took issue with the rocking chair. He brushed the horses with Jeremy and came back having learned how to milk a cow. "That's what's strange," he said. He loosened the tension on his bow and began teaching Brewster how to use it.

"Jenkins McPherson is back," Ada said. "He wants to start learning again."

"Nice that he tells you before anyone else," Charlotte said. "Give him the book. You can tell him it's from me though he won't believe it. But Chace goes with you."

Chace sat in the schoolroom on one of the low benches, relaxed, with his legs stretched out.

"Don't I know you?" Jenkins said.

"Don't think so."

"No, that's not it. I know that name."

"I got it from a white man," Chace said.

"A trapper. I used to run into him. Don't anymore. Is Yellow Cloud your grandfather?"

"Was."

"Sorry. I knew him too. And what are you to this one?"

"Why don't you ask me?" Ada said.

Jenkins smiled and shook his head. "You see?" he said. "That's what I'm talking about. Fine, then. What's he to you?"

"He's my father now."

"Doesn't exactly have the years for that, does he?"

"Maybe not. He's good at it, though. He's teaching me how to shoot." Jenkins McPherson raised one eyebrow. "Here's a book for you," she said. "It's from Charlotte."

"What is it?"

"The man who wrote it, Fraser Drummond, was a city man from back east who traveled through here. It's about his trip and everything he saw and did."

Jenkins held up a hand. "Sister, don't be telling me about Fraser Drummond."

"You knew him?"

"Saved his life. Twice. He was sickly and his eyesight gave out now and then. He'd think he was coming up over the rise chasing a buffalo herd, wasn't no buffalo herd, it was a bunch of wild, screaming, meaner than the devil…" He stopped, considering the present situation.

"No offense taken," Chace said.

"Not your tribe though. But this Fraser, that's what he kept doing, wandering into dangerous places where he never should of been. Lucky he made it back east to write his fool book."

"Are you maybe in it?" Ada said. "That's the thought Charlotte had."

"And a fine thought it is. Extend her my appreciation. I better damn well be in it somewhere for all the trouble he caused me."

"Good. How many pages do you want to read at first?"

"I've got to give you a number? Lord in heaven. Thirty."

"Done," Ada said. "Write down every word you don't know. I've got a dictionary."

"Then what?" Jenkins said more gently, returning to his true cause.

"Then I guess maybe you'll start writing your own book." Seeing the way he looked at her, she hastily added, "That's what Charlotte thought, anyway."

"Will you help me?"

Now Ada was flustered, realizing she'd gone too far.

"We'll both help you," Chace said calmly.

"You can read and write?"

"I told you. I've got a white man's name."

"What do you think mine is?" Jenkins turned his attention back to the book, paging carefully through it. "I'm much obliged for this thoughtfulness," he said. His glance went again to Chace and then back to Ada. "But if you don't mind, Miss, I believe I'd be best advised to put off asking for your hand again. Least for today."

<>

Instead of writing a sketch, Chase took paper, dipped a pen in ink and began to draw. First one buffalo appeared, swiftly, in graceful clean black lines, then another, and another until there was a whole herd covering many pages of army letterhead. Ada took each one as he finished and laid them out end to end.

"Those are a lot of buffalo," Jeremy said.

"This is the way the old ones draw it," Chace said. Quickly he filled a sheet with buffalo running off the edge and behind them lines of stick figures on stick horses brandishing bows and lances. "It goes better with paint." Then he drew the stick figures on horses coming back the other way with the buffalo stacked on dragging poles behind.

"But what do you do with buffalo?" Ada said. "Do you eat it? Is it like deer?" She frowned at the drawings. "We didn't have buffalo back east. Not that I ever knew of."

"It's the same idea as deer, just doesn't taste the same. You can roast it or eat some parts raw, and yes when you dry it, it does have

237

some resemblance to boot leather," Chace said without taking his eyes from the paper. "But it gives more than that. Beds, shelter, fuel for the fire, weapons, clothing, rope for the horses, the string on a bow, the bag that holds water, the ladle for the soup and there is soup to be had, just not ducks wrapped in bacon. You can even make a boat out of what you get from a buffalo, if you ever have a need for a boat."

"Those are a lot of buffalo," Jeremy said again. "Can we put them up?"

"Absolutely," Charlotte said. She closed her eyes, thanked whatever gods had brought him to her, and began to tack the buffalo drawings up one after the other in a line that spanned the wall from one end to the other while Ada and Brewster sat thinking.

"How do you get rope?" Brewster said. He'd given up the caution of asking if he could ask questions.

"Depending on what kind of rope you want, you'd either take parts of the muscle, that's what you'd use to string a bow, or you'd cut rawhide into strips and soak them for something like a halter."

"What holds water?" Ada said.

"The bladder, the part inside that holds their water."

"How is it your bed?"

"You wrap up in a pile of buffalo robes and that's your bed."

"They're warm," Brewster said. "I guess they would be."

"They've kept the people of the tribes warm for a thousand years." Chace was quiet for a moment, his eyes on the drawings on the wall. "When the hunt's over, for what the buffalo's given, for how much it means to your people, you say a prayer. Always. You give thanks."

And then there was silence in the room again.

40

Chace handed Charlotte an opened letter. She only needed to look at his face. "Whatever it is, it's not good," she said.

"Depends. I was with Colonel Hutchinson last night. He wanted to know some things, but then he always wants to know some things. In passing, he mentioned having some curiosity about this."

"I guess he doesn't think to consult his wife in these matters." She knew what it was without even having to ask. She unfolded the page and read. It was from her father to the commanding officer of the fort, announcing his imminent arrival.

"It was bound to happen," Chace said. "After everything that's gone on, he had to come."

"I don't want to think about it. What do you suppose imminent means?"

"Maybe weeks. Likely not though."

"Days?"

"At least now you have some warning."

"I'd almost rather just have him show up out of the blue and then say whatever comes out of my mouth when I see him."

"I'd say that's the first and most important reason he had for writing the letter. He won't win anything by taking you on and he must be more aware of that than anybody."

"Thank you for your high opinion," she said. He reached out and ran his hand gently down her arm, stopping at her wrist. It took a moment for her breath to return. "Ellis and Miller have to know, though. Can you get them to dinner tonight?"

"That's never very hard."

When he was gone, Ada sighed. "Does he touch you like that all the time?"

"Ada, I don't even know what to do with your questions anymore. I'm no good at this."

Ada was thoughtful for a moment, her mind elsewhere. "I wonder if Miller's ever kissed a girl. He's so shy."

Charlotte started to say something else, then changed her mind. What difference did it make anymore? "Well, Ada, let me first tell you one more time not to grow up like me. Then I'm going to let you know, just for information's sake, that Miller has kissed someone, or rather, I should say, someone kissed him. And it was me."

"*What?* You didn't. That's crazy. But did he kiss good? Did he kiss like Chace kisses you?"

"Good Lord, no. With Miller it was innocent." She realized what she'd just said. "I mean…" she said and stopped. "Oh never mind. Though Miller's close to me in age he's obviously had no experience at all. It was when I had to leave the wagon train, that morning. He'd talked me through all of what was going on with Ellis, stood beside me when we met the grandfather. I was so thankful for how kind he was. So I did kiss him, once, quick, and I told him beforehand I was going to do it. That was all."

"What did he do?"

"He didn't do anything. He was shocked."

"But he could learn to kiss, couldn't he?"

"Anybody can learn to kiss. At least I think so. And it seems some people are just born knowing how."

"So he helped you too."

"That's what I mean," Charlotte said, "about making sure it's the right one before you decide on doing anything. If you ask me, there's hardly a person with a better heart anywhere than Miller."

"Do you think someday he'd talk to me?"

"I'd say all you need is somewhere quiet and only to ask him things, the way you do. But don't be forgetting that you're still only thirteen. And you know if things got out of hand, I wouldn't let Miller forget it either."

"That's something I don't want to ever have happen."

"Good," Charlotte said.

"I've got another question maybe you won't answer."

"I answer lots of your questions."

"Can I ask about the letter Chace brought you?"

Charlotte put her fingers to her temples. "For a minute it all went away. Here, of course." She handed Ada the letter.

"Oh my gosh," Ada said, reading quickly through it. "He's coming."

"Apparently he is."

"Soon, even?"

"Yes."

Ada studied the page. "He has beautiful handwriting."

"He has lots of beautiful things about him. Sometimes I just wish he was somebody else's father. And undoubtedly there've been times when he wished I was somebody else's daughter." She reflected for a moment. "Like now."

"What'll we do?" Ada said.

"I don't know. We'll talk about it at dinner tonight. It'll concern Ellis as much as anybody."

"Because he left you."

"Yes and Samuel would have no way of understanding that."

"That's his name? Samuel?"

"It is. Samuel Duchesne." First Elder of the Church of the Brothers of Ezekiel, God help us all.

<>

Charlotte smoothed the letter out in the middle of the table.

"Colonel Hutchinson received this from my father," she said. "You can read it if you want, but he's on his way."

"Who's on his way?" Ellis said.

"My father is. He's coming here."

"Shit. That can't even be. Nobody heard me say that."

"I did," Jeremy said.

"How's he traveling? Not on his own. Not out here."

"He's with the Brigadier General's party," Chace said.

"The General. Coming out to inspect the forts again, wanting to see everybody using a napkin and the right fork even though we have the worst guns ever dumped off on an infantry division. What was his name?"

"Bascombe."

"That's right."

"I don't remember him," Miller said.

"He weighs about three hundred pounds," Ellis said. "And wore his dress uniform and a sword to visit the latrine. That one."

"Now I remember."

"Does your father just miss you?" Ada said.

"Oh, I highly doubt that's all of it," Charlotte said, "since the chances are that he's heard from Tobias. I imagine he'll have some fairly large topics he wants to discuss, one of them being what exactly it is I think I'm going to do since nothing worked out the way he'd planned."

"Well, we're agreed on that, aren't we?" Ellis said. "We're going to Oregon Territory."

"Everybody?" Ada said. "We are?"

"It's mostly all settled."

"There's a wagon train?"

"There is, out of Missouri. We'd pick it up here and take it over the mountains, Chace and Miller and me."

Ada turned to Chace, her expression one of disbelief. "You'll go? No question?"

"No question."

"Won't it be hard to leave here?"

"It won't be hard."

"Why not? You said you'd tell me."

"If you stay with it long enough, you figure out that the world didn't end and you're still in it, so you should do something about that."

"Do you just forget then?"

"You don't ever forget," Chace said. "You just try and keep hold of what was good."

"You can do that?"

"It means too much not to."

"Then I can do it too."

"If we're talking about Oregon," Brewster said, "there'll be things to think about. Like building a house."

242

"I've never built a house," Ellis said, "but Chace and I helped build Fort Pence."

"That should count for something."

"Thank you, Brewster. And I suppose you've built three or four in your young life. It wouldn't surprise me."

"I haven't," Brewster said seriously, "but I've got this." He stood up and brought back the small black book from the sideboard. He opened it to a page and handed it to Chace. "It says how to build a cabin. The drawings and measurements come first, then the directions."

"That was your Pa's?" Ellis said. Brewster nodded.

Chace paged slowly through the small book studying the finely drawn lines of each careful entry.

"There's everything in here," he said.

"That was his way," Ada said. "And he'd planned out how the new cabin would be even better than our old one."

"There'd be planting to do," Brewster said. "We'd need seeds, cuttings, things like that."

"Who is this boy?" Ellis said.

"I have seeds," Charlotte said. "And we'll have slips and bulbs and roots and cuttings, all kinds of things by the time we leave."

"We only have one cow," Brewster said. "We could use another one or maybe two more would be good."

"Jesus Christ," Ellis said. "Jeremy, you didn't hear that either. Miller and I've traveled with about as many cows as we can stand, I think. Maybe when the railroad's built the cows can come by train."

"Brewster," Chace said, still thinking. "Do you do this too? Do you have your own book?"

Brewster held up his journal. "Charlotte gave it to me. I didn't mean for it to turn out like Pa's, it just went that way."

"Could you pass the cornbread please?" Miller said. All the talk was making his head hurt. Getting to Oregon Territory was easy compared to the thought of living there, having an actual home. Would they all stay together which he thought meant living with Ada? Were there wagon trains, and if there were, would he and

243

Ellis still lead them?   He wanted to know but he wasn't ready to find out yet.

"Could we ask you and Chace questions sometime?" Ada said.

Miller cast his eyes down on his plate. "What kind of questions is she talking about?" he said to no one. Now his head hurt even more.

"Do you mean about the tribes?" Chace said.

Ada nodded. "To know how it was. To know what you'd be leaving."

"There's time if you want to do that. And only one request."

"Anything," Ada said. Charlotte could hardly bear the certainty in her voice.

"Remember what's been said."

"We will, I promise."

"We don't have a book," he said.

Finally, Miller understood what someone was saying. He still held in his mind all the nights around the fire with the old ones telling the stories one more time so that no one would ever forget.

41

The afternoon sun was mellow and almost warm though the breeze was cold. Charlotte sat in the meadow watching Grace play her own game with a handful of sticks and wondering when those little fingers would make their first attempt at a wildflower bracelet.

"Charlotte?" The deep voice came from above her. Then there was the matter of possibly ever getting to her feet.

"I can't do it," she said. "I should've never sat down. For the time being, you'll have to sit down with me."

Samuel lowered himself to the ground next to her.

"Father," she said and reached out for him. He wrapped her in his arms and kissed her forehead.

"My daughter," he said.

"So we meet again. When you left me out there on the wagon trail, I didn't think we ever would."

"We don't need to revisit that painful time."

"Why should we when we have so many other fine topics to discuss?" She glanced behind him. "How did you get here? I don't suppose you walked."

"No. The General's company has my baggage and horses and they're still back there somewhere. For myself, it was important to travel the last part on foot, just to let everything come slowly. And then here you were."

"I do need to tell you one thing right away, Father. Tobias came to see me twice, he was very kind, and I discovered I'm quite fond of him. Sometime we'll have to talk about why he tried to leave the Family in the first place."

"I doubt we'll be having that conversation. Who is this child? I confess I'm having a great deal of trouble understanding what's going on in your life."

"This is Grace, the youngest of the four in my care now. Ada, the oldest at thirteen, asked if when you showed up, they should call you Grandfather. You might take that with a grain of salt since she's just like me, but there the question is and it could be thought of as an honor."

"Then you knew I was coming."

"Yes."

"And how did you feel about that?"

"Unhappy that I'd created the need. Mistrustful of what you might attempt. On the other hand, I wanted to see you."

"And I wanted so very much to see you. When Tobias wrote that you had all these children, and then that you were with child yourself, to keep my sanity I stopped believing him. I see now, much to my chagrin, that he was truthful in every way."

"Where are you staying?" Charlotte said, sidestepping his comments entirely.

"The General said guest quarters. What does that mean exactly?"

"Don't count on luxury."

"I don't know. So far I've been quite impressed with the level of comfort the military provides."

Grace held out her hands and Charlotte stopped for a moment to brush off all the clinging blades of grass. "Father, does the name Lenore mean anything to you?"

"In what way?"

"Back east where the Family originally belonged. Before you married Mother."

Samuel grew thoughtful. "Yes," he said after a long moment. "The name does mean something."

"I thought it might. She's the wife of Colonel Hutchinson, who commands the fort."

And still lovely, she wanted to say. And her husband's never here.

"Lenore from all those years ago? Charlotte, the world's a smaller place than we ever realize."

"Maybe." Though with him here it suddenly seemed huge and full of obstacles. "More importantly, she's the one who had faith in me, who allowed me to take on everything that I have."

Charlotte felt she had to keep speaking all in a rush to stop him from asking questions. "But what I'd like most is for you to come to dinner tonight. The children and I have our own rooms and everyone will be there."

"I have a sudden need to know what's meant by everyone."

"Miller Dawson, the pilot of the wagon train and before you ask, no, he's not the one, he's younger than me and would die at the thought. Ellis Gray and it's not him either, though I do have a very deep affection for him."

"He swore to me."

"He had no choice."

"Everyone has a choice."

Charlotte made a small choking sound. "I can't believe you're saying that to me, of all people. I never had a choice in anything and look how that turned out."

"I'm still waiting then," Samuel said.

"Chace."

"Yes?"

"Chace Bridger."

"And who is this Chace Bridger?"

"Chace Bridger Yellow Cloud who is everything to me." It was done. Let Samuel pass out in the grass or consult his conscience, his Believers, his Others, whatever he felt he had to do.

"Tobias said this person wasn't here."

"He is now."

"I see," he said. He spent some time brushing off the front of his coat until he could collect his thoughts. When he spoke, his voice was steady. "I believe I'll go now to find my belongings, but I'll be there. For dinner." He got to his feet.

"Will it be you who comes, Father, or the First Elder?" Charlotte said. "It would just be useful to know ahead of time."

"I'm both," he said, "and that can't be helped."

<>

All they could do was wait. The bread was warm out of the oven. An aromatic haunch of venison lay sliced on a platter. The oil lamps created a soft glow. Everyone had washed up at least to some degree.

Charlotte noted that Chace had gone watchful, become unreadable. Miller was fretful. Ellis couldn't sit down. He paced around in the tight quarters where there really was no room to pace.

"Maybe he won't come," Ellis said.

"And where do you think he'd go instead?"

"To Colonel Hutchinson's for brandy and cigars."

"Which is where you'd like to be?"

"Only without Colonel Hutchinson."

"Should you go and have a glass of whiskey?"

"I already did."

"When we were waiting for the bounty hunters to show," Chace said, "we sat on that hill for five days."

"That's what this is like?" Ellis said.

"You get through it is what I mean."

"I remember how that went. Sometimes you don't."

"The waiting I mean."

"You're not seeing how bad this could be."

Then Samuel was there in the doorway. His boots shone as if from a recent polishing. He wore a long jacket, waistcoat and cravat. He looked distinguished but fatigued as he entered the room.

"Father," Charlotte said and went to him.

"So this is everyone," he said, taking in the faces among the candlelight.

"This is my father, Samuel Duchesne," she said. "You've met Grace." Charlotte moved to the table. "Jeremy," she said, laying a hand on his head. "Ada. Brewster."

Samuel held up his hand in greeting. "Ada? I don't mind being called Grandfather. In fact, once I got used to it, I think it would give me great pleasure."

Charlotte felt herself relax just slightly. Although the worst was yet to come, it seemed the First Elder was being quiet.

She moved down the table. "Miller Dawson. The pilot I told you about." Charlotte put a hand on Ellis's arm. "Ellis Gray."

"We've met," Samuel said, reaching out to shake hands.

"We have. And the wagon train folk gladly took your supplies but I'm returning the money."

"Why? Charlotte's here and safe. That's what I asked."

"Still, no one felt the need to take it."

Charlotte moved farther down the table to where Chace was standing. "Chace Yellow Cloud," she said.

Samuel held out his hand again. "This afternoon I only had a name. I'm glad to put a face to it. So you're the one who brought my daughter to safety."

"You could say that," Chace said, "though she's fairly resourceful on her own."

One more time, Charlotte saw the registered surprise at Chace's words.

"I'm grateful. It was one of the hardest things I ever had to do, to leave her there."

"I can't see how it wouldn't be."

Charlotte could see her father trying to think his way through this changed and unanticipated circumstance.

"We've waited dinner for you," she said. "So it'd likely be best if we could all sit down and start in."

"I apologize for being late," Samuel said, not yet taking his eyes from Chace. "The Colonel offered me a brandy and seeing as he's my host, I found I couldn't refuse."

Brandy? Was the Family all going to hell? But this wasn't the time to worry about that. While Ada cut the bread and piled roasted potatoes into a bowl, Charlotte forked slices of venison onto the plates with gravy and passed them around.

Before Ada reached him, Samuel picked up his plate and turned it over. Charlotte watched his face soften. "Your mother's china." He set the plate back carefully in front of him.

It only took a few bites however before his eyes were raised again. "Captain Gray. May I call you Ellis?"

"Of course," Ellis said.

"I'd be grateful if you'd tell me…"

"It's long and complicated."

"But I'm the only one here who has no idea. Is this not true?"

Ellis shifted uncomfortably. "It is true. And I suppose I do owe it to you. I'll give you what I can, but I have to start some time back." He turned his gaze away from Chace and Miller. "There was a massacre of the People Touched By The River, committed by the military two years ago. The three of us sitting here one way or another lost almost everyone we cared about. My slain wife was a member of that tribe. Her grandfather and the old ones of the tribe came to me when the wagon train was five days west of where I found Charlotte. He asked that I go with him to Washington City to try and explain one more time how much his people had suffered. When the old ones ask, you don't refuse. With me gone, the wagon train turned Charlotte out. Grandfather met her and made his decision. He handed the responsibility for her safety to Chace, his grandson, his namesake, my brother and Miller's as well." There was silence around the table.

After a long moment, Samuel spoke. "Where is he now?"

"Who?"

"Your grandfather."

"He died before we could get back home. He's wrapped up in a tree in the valley, the way he wanted to be, with buffalo skulls to protect him on his journey."

"I'm sorry for his passing. I would have liked to meet him."

Charlotte put a plate of greens on the table. Keep eating. Let's not talk anymore. But her father's attention had turned to Chace.

"I have to ask. And if this is the chosen forum, and you're among those closest to you, then I'll apologize for my bluntness and put the question to you now. What are your intentions toward my daughter?"

Chace glanced at Charlotte and her color went even higher than was indicated by the warmth of the room. She gave a barely perceptible nod. "She's my wife," he said. Ada dropped her fork.

"I assume there was an event that made it so. When did that take place?"

"Two weeks ago."

"May I ask who performed the ceremony, if that's what we're speaking of?"

"That is what we're speaking of. The fort chaplain."

"And there were witnesses?"

"Father, stop," Charlotte said.

"I need to know."

"Sergeant Brower," Chace said, "and I missed the other one's name."

Charlotte supplied the answer. "Joseph Beacham." Ada's mouth dropped open.

"So it's irrevocable?"

"The words haven't changed, Father. They're the same as when you said them yourself."

Samuel was still directing his comments to Chace. "Then I'm presuming you're well enough acquainted with Charlotte to realize that not only were obligations attached to her, but those obligations went far beyond her personal situation or even mine."

"I was there with her," Chace said. "I saw what she'd been through. The only obligation I recognize is mine to her."

Samuel bowed his head. When he was ready to speak again, his remarks were addressed to everyone. "What are your plans? Where will you live? It can't possibly be here in this fort."

"We're heading to Oregon Territory, Grandfather," Ada said. She was holding tightly to Charlotte's hand. "When the passes are clear."

"Oregon Territory," Samuel said softly. "Could you go any farther away?" He paused for another moment and Charlotte could see his waning resolve. "Would you even consider the desert? Charlotte has family there."

Charlotte almost laughed out loud. Poor Tobias, he was her one fragile link to the desert, along with a nameless conscript no longer bound to a doomed marriage.

"I've been there," Chace said. There was silence again.

"I meant where Tobias lives."

"That's what I meant too. When I came down out of the canyons, they were hard to miss. There's nothing else around them anywhere. I want to show you something." He went to the sideboard, puzzled looks following him, and returned with stationery, a pen and ink. He sat back down, moved his plate away and quickly drew a design within a larger circle. Then he slid it across the table. Everyone's eyes were on the drawing. Samuel gasped.

"Do you know what this is?" Chace said.

"Yes. But how do you?"

"I understand you make them out of your crops, but Tobias never had to. This one built with stones was there long before he ever arrived."

"Why?" Samuel said. "How could that be?"

"That was the land of the tribes once and before that, the old ones say it was the First People's land, and before that, not even the old ones could tell you, though they would guess it belonged to the spirits that come down from the sky."

Samuel sat back, appearing weary. He cast his gaze from face to face around the table, inwardly framing his thoughts. He came back to Chace. "There's the child and I see now that you comprehend everything. The child will be a member of the Family."

"And of the People Touched By The River. This is just the truth, nothing more."

Charlotte stayed silent, keeping her own thoughts to herself.

"But in the end," Chace said, "be aware that I haven't ever intended to cause you grief in any way."

"Though you may be surprised to hear me say it, I am aware. However, I now find myself utterly at a loss. Sleeping on all of this is the only solution I can think of at the moment." Samuel took the napkin from his lap, folded it, and stood up. "It's been a long day and now it's time. I must take my leave. Thank you everyone for your kindnesses, both to Charlotte and to me. I look forward to continuing these conversations. And with that, I wish you all a good night."

As soon as the door shut, there was commotion of another sort. "You're *married?*" Ada shrieked.

"My thoughts exactly," Ellis said.

"And you didn't even *tell* me? You didn't invite us? Who stood up for you? Where was your dress? You could have worn my gold ear drops. *Joseph Beacham?*"

"I was never at a wedding," Miller said.

"*I never was either.*"

"Small and quiet was just the way it needed to be," Charlotte said. Chace was watching her. "For the ones getting married anyway."

"Now it'll be me baking the cake," Ada said. "You'll have to tell me how to do it."

"No cake."

"There'll be a cake. And a party. Do you think Grandfather will come?"

"I'm unsure of anything about Grandfather right now," Charlotte said.

42

Breakfast alone with Samuel in his room was a revelation, elegant furniture, embossed official china, pork cutlets, French coffee.

"Delicious," Charlotte said. "If this is breakfast, I can't wait to see lunch."

"It seems there's a fairly large gap, perhaps call it a canyon, between the ranks," Samuel said.

"Whatever it is, I'm very glad, for the moment anyway, to be on your side of it."

He let his eyes rest on her. "You live this entirely different life now. In a fort. With four children. I saw what you're doing for them. The sketches. The books everywhere."

"That part came easily. It's only what you did for me."

"I saw the amazing drawings of the buffalo too." Charlotte waited. "You realize that there is no way I could possibly have been expecting any of this, any of what he is."

"Believe me, neither of us expected any of it either. The first time I saw him, I held the Colt on him. I was scared to death."

"And what did he do?"

"Nothing. He has no fear, not even of an unsteady woman with a revolver. That's just who he is."

"You told him about the Family."

"Yes, I did. Think about what he already knew just from looking at me and where I was, out there all alone. But that's behind us. What's of concern now is Ada's dinner. She wants it to be a celebration. Will you come?"

"I'm afraid I'm not yet ready to celebrate."

"That's fairly harsh."

"Not harsh. Realistic."

Samuel pushed back his chair and stood up. "Come with me, child. I need fresh air. Can we walk somewhere?"

"Only where everyone else does, out to the meadow."

Outside the gates, the sky was filled with lowering clouds and a sharp breeze held the icy chill of the north. Charlotte pulled two shawls close around her, aware that Samuel continually averted his eyes from her form. She put her arm through his and ignored his discomfort.

"The truth is," he continued, "General Bascombe's escorting me this afternoon on the next leg of my journey, to see Tobias in the desert. I hope it's obvious to you that I was stricken with grief over all that happened at home. For that reason, the original purpose of the desert was my own time for reflection."

"But if you're with Tobias, who'll be in charge of the Family?"

"The Council of Elders. Let them govern themselves for a while."

"Why do I feel like this isn't you talking?"

"Maybe it isn't anymore. My other intention was to be with you. And then you didn't get to the desert, or even to the fort for the longest time, taking several years off my life. And then out of nowhere you did get to the fort, but you had four children. And then, poor Tobias, you were having a child of your own with no obvious father or husband in sight, certainly no one from the desert. And now your husband is very much in sight with ideas about all of this that have turned my whole world upside down."

"He feels as strongly about his people as you do about yours."

"I see that and I respect him greatly for it. It only presents yet another challenge for me. He's right about the child being answerable to two different ways of believing."

"Maybe the child will have its own way of believing and not be answerable to anyone."

"Considering how you turned out, that's quite possible. But should I still just sit out in the desert and reflect?"

"I don't know. Should you? I'm very confused."

"I decided there was a rather immediate need for a new plan."

"It seems as if you have one. I'm afraid to ask what it is."

"The more I thought about it, the less frightened I was. I'm still young enough, you know."

Charlotte had stopped dead in her tracks. "Young enough for what, Father?"

"To have another family. If I move quickly perhaps your child and mine wouldn't be that far apart in age."

Charlotte stared at him. "There are so many things wrong with that statement that I can't even begin to count them." She wished she could see Tobias's face. "So you'll be anxious to get home?"

"Maybe I won't have to go home. Maybe there's someone in the desert."

"Good Lord, what kind of someone? It can't just be anybody. You have to have feelings for them, don't you? And don't they have to have feelings for you?" She considered how ridiculous this conversation was, especially as she'd been trying to impress the same point on Ada, who was thirteen.

"There's a purpose to everything, Charlotte. I'm guided by a wisdom much greater than my own. I have faith and so should you."

The image of his music came to her, the voices, his Others, and her heart went out to him.

"No matter what happens, this time promise me that I will see you again," she said.

"You're my daughter," he said.

43

Ada closed the door on Charlotte for the afternoon.

"You're not allowed in the mess hall kitchen either." Charlotte started to open her mouth. "No protests, no arguments." Ada's eyes twinkled. "How does it feel?"

"I was never that bossy," Charlotte said but she was smiling. She took a book and her coat and wandered around the fort until she finally settled at a desk in the schoolroom.

It was only minutes before Chace was there.

"How did you find me?"

"In case you hadn't noticed, there's nowhere else to go."

He sat down on the bench beside her.

"I didn't want them to do anything," she said.

"It's not what you think."

"You know?"

"They wanted my answer first."

"Why?"

"They just did."

"And even though I don't know the question, what was your answer?"

"It was yes."

"All right, I'll give up on that. How did your conversation with my father go?"

"He asked questions, about Grandfather, the old ones, lots of things. He talked to Ellis and Miller about the wagon train. He wanted to know what happened to the parents."

"He did? Then he does care. How would you say he was?"

"I don't know. Quiet."

"He's got a lot on his mind," Charlotte said.

"Like what? Hopefully not you and me."

"No, not right now anyway. He just couldn't see a solution to the problem with the child. Then he found one."

"What is it?"

"He says he's going to have another child of his own."

"He is? When did he decide this?"

"Last night."

"He doesn't give up," Chace said.

"No, he doesn't."

"He would have made a good warrior."

"I hope that thought would be deeply appreciated by him if he'd only stayed to hear it."

Brewster appeared in the doorway.

"Is it time?" Charlotte said.

"It is time. Or Ada might explode."

<>

Charlotte hesitated, then opened the door. In addition to all the other meager but devoted elements in her celebration repertoire, Ada had exceeded herself with curtains of colored ribbons hung from the ceiling and silver streamers that twirled and caught the light.

"Ada, how beautiful!" Charlotte said and hugged her hard.

"Are you ready for the surprise?" Ada said. "Chace already knows."

"So I heard. Why is that?"

"Because sometimes he's easier than you are. Here." She took Charlotte by the hand and walked her to a door in the wall that they'd never had any reason to open or even think about.

"What are you doing?" Charlotte said.

"Where does this go?"

"To whatever's next door. Doesn't it?"

"Guess what. That's not where it goes. Close your eyes."

Charlotte closed her eyes. The door creaked open.

"You can open them now."

Charlotte's hands flew to her face.

"But you have to come in," Ada said, pulling her gently through the door. The room was small, with a window at the front, hooks on the wall, a washbasin and pitcher on a stand. A rag rug covered the wooden floor. A plain iron double bedstead fit narrowly between the walls.

"What is this?" Charlotte gasped. "Why is it here?"

"Mrs. Hutchinson told us about it. It's the servants' room. We stole the bed and everything else from an empty married officers' quarters. Don't tell anyone."

Charlotte's eyes filled as she slowly touched everything, the bed, the hooks, the washbasin, the walls.

"It's just that there's no fireplace," Brewster said. "That's why we brought all your quilts and blankets in." Charlotte belatedly recognized the large stack of bedding.

"It's a good wedding present, don't you think?" Ada said. "Or were you and Chace going to sleep with Grace?"

Charlotte laughed as she wiped away the tears with her sleeve. "No, that wouldn't have worked, would it?" she said, wondering what she'd thought they were going to do and realizing for the first time, with a sudden small rush of warmth, that they were really married. "Thank you. It's the best wedding present ever." She hugged Ada again, and Brewster, who'd gotten used to being hugged, and Jeremy who liked to be hugged and Grace who always hugged her back.

The front door opened and everyone turned. Ellis dropped a saddle and a pile of belonging on the floor and left again.

"Isn't that your saddle?" Charlotte said.

"It is," Chace said, "plus everything else I own."

Ellis returned with a warm beef roast on a platter. Behind him, Miller brought in a pan of steaming vegetables.

Charlotte stared. "You made dinner?" she said to Ellis.

"Despite everyone's opinion to the contrary, I can cook. Ada helped though."

"And I did too," Miller said. "Why does everyone always forget about me?"

"I don't think anyone ever forgets about you for a minute," Ada said, causing Miller to blush and lose track of his thoughts yet again. He hoped that maybe there were cattle in Oregon Territory, or horses, anything that needed rounding up and a lot of range riding, a lot of being somewhere else.

"I made a cake," Ada said, pulling her crowning achievement out from its hidden place in the sideboard. "And it's not even a bad one."

"We tasted it already," Jeremy said.

They sat around the table in the candlelight.

"Grandfather came and talked to us," Brewster said. "He told us he would have come to the party, but there were some very important things he had to do."

"That's an understatement."

"I wish I'd gotten to see the desert. He said he'd write and tell us all about it."

"He did?"

"And he's going to send us more books," Ada said.

"More books? We might have a hundred too many already."

"He said we're missing some that are necessary."

"Wonderful."

"One of them's going to be a book on cows," Jeremy said.

"I didn't even know there was a book on cows."

"Some day he'll be able to take the train over the mountains to come and see us in Oregon Territory," Brewster said.

"And likely you and Ada will both have families of your own by then."

"I won't," Brewster said.

"I will," Ada said, and Miller choked on his roast.

"We've eaten so much," Jeremy said.

"And it was so good, all of it," Charlotte said.

"But could we have cake?"

44

All was quiet. Charlotte lit a candle and closed the door. Her glance took in the small room.

"Do officers always have servants?"

"They're supposed to," Chace said.

"What does a servant do?"

"Cook, wash, clean, chop firewood, take care of the horses."

"What does the officer do?"

"Sometimes you wonder."

"Did Ellis have a servant?"

"For a while he did."

"What was his name?"

"Isaac."

Charlotte studied him for a moment. "The things I don't know."

"Mostly what's not worth knowing anyway." He sat down on the edge of the bed and pulled off his boots.

"There are things you don't know. Or haven't seen yet, at any rate. This'll be one of them." She picked up her voluminous nightgown and lowered the soft material over her head, allowing it to billow to the floor. Then she spent several minutes removing one layer after another from underneath it. He watched, and she knew he was thinking about how there weren't nearly enough hooks for everything she'd just left on the floor.

"Nightclothes," she said.

"Then there's something you haven't seen either." He unbuttoned his shirt and shrugged it off, then undid the buckskin pants.

"Long johns? You? What happened to the icy streams?"

"They're only useful if you're already sleeping in the snow and eating tree bark."

Charlotte let her gaze rest on him. "That's why you're the way you are."

"What way is that?"

"Hard sometimes, but all to the good."

"To you, not to everyone."

"To me then. Who gets in first? My feet are cold."

"I'll take the wall. I could climb over you if I had to but no offense, I don't want you trying to climb over me."

"Insults everywhere. I'll blow out the candle."

"We've been here before," Chace said.

"Will you tell me the Creation story now?"

"It still takes two days."

Charlotte crawled awkwardly into bed beside him and fell back on the pillows.

"This isn't easy," she said.

"No one's likely to think it would be. Do you want to reconsider?"

"Ha," she said and then more softly, "No, actually, I don't."

"I don't either. About anything."

A floorboard creaked in the cold. A shaft of moonlight fell across the bed.

She reached out for him and he held her close, her body warm against him. His hand traveled slowly, tenderly over all of her, her face, her eyes, her mouth, tracing the smooth line of her shoulders under the loosened shift, the stretched expanse of her belly, the curve of her hip, the inside of her wrist. Her breath caught in her throat.

"Everything's different now," she said, her voice gone quiet. "How does it work?"

"I don't know," he said. "We'll figure it out."

Their scents mixed with the smell of candle smoke, raw wood, cold iron. In the moonlight, he kissed her gently, with care and feeling, the wild and beautiful woman who was his wife. When she touched him, gave herself up to him, the small room was the barn, the rain, her bare feet on his, sunlight and shadow, the two of them alone together, hearing no words but their own, finding each other in the dark.

Charlotte saw that when they stood looking out at the new green land, she would only sometimes know what was in his thoughts. Maybe it would be the high empty canyons, the valley with the stream running through it, the white flag, the past. Maybe it would be his voices, the ones that watched over him, took care of him, that saw him safely home. And no matter what, she would never be far from his thoughts. Her heart was sure of that. He would stand beside Ellis and Miller too, that was important, and she would be glad for what they all knew and who they were together.

But for now, when the snows came and the winds howled, when the river froze and game grew scarce, in the moon of the red calf, after a time of long endurance, Ada would, God willing, turn to Chace and hand him their baby, a miracle and a blessing, likely born of the old one's wisdom, a new beginning, life starting all over again.

*****

Dear Chace and Charlotte,

I'm writing today especially because of what day it is, Emma's birthday. How I hold her in my heart and can't wait to see her again. I will never forget that day and night and day. I laugh and cry thinking about it, how cold it was, how I put on the gold ear drops to make myself feel older, how many times I thanked God that Chace and Ellis were there to help me. I hope if my time ever comes, I would be as strong and brave as you were.

We are fine. It has been exciting, as you can imagine. As much as I wish to be there, I would wish even more for you both to be here if that were in any way possible, to see it all. I hold in my hands a first copy of the book and still can't believe that this is all real, that it's actually happening. It's called, it couldn't be called anything else, The People Touched By The River. *The dedication on the second page reads: For Emma White Flower. Every time I look at it, I cry all over again! Kiss her for me.*

Jenkins' book will be published at the same time. They are very clever, almost too much so, these literary people. His is called, it couldn't be anything else either, Mountain Man: A Life. *We are apparently quite the curious couple in the eyes of Easterners who have no acquaintance with the West and frankly don't seem to know what to make of it, or us. But it's my feeling, very strongly, that none of this is for them anyway, it's for the future, so that, as Chace says, no one ever forgets.*

Jenkins has been approached several times on our tour with the idea of publishing a second book, made up of all the beautiful letters he wrote to me in Oregon Territory. I don't know how I feel about it yet, though being very much ahead of things, they already have a name for it too. It would be called: Dear Ada.

I must go. We have so many appearances to make and talks to give. So far, we're told, they've been a great success. As you know, Jenkins loves nothing better than to talk. I want you to know that I wear my wedding presents always, Grandmother's locket and Chace's silver bracelet. The eagle feather is in my luggage no matter where we go. These gifts are my life, who I am, a part of me because they are a part of you.

I'm enclosing a second letter for Grace and Jeremy and yet another for Brewster. I'm told his barn is beautiful and now others want one like it. He's only just beginning and I know will do so much that's amazing and good. It's hard to be apart from him, from all of them. Hold them close for me. Please give my love to Ellis and Isabelle and their daughters—are there four now? And as always, to my first love, Miller, wherever he has got himself to this time.

Write when you can, to the address I gave you from the publishing house. Your letters mean the world to me. The East is fascinating for what it is—yes, the oysters and wine and feather beds and here I am to see them—but I miss Oregon and our house and the fields and horses and goats and geese and our life there more than I can ever say. I've thanked you many times before, but thank you again for believing in me, for seeing the goodness in Jenkins, and even though I was so young, for letting me go. I will come back to you, I promise.

With deepest love and affection,
Your grateful daughter,
Ada McPherson

Made in the USA
Middletown, DE
26 December 2020